BRENT LIBRARIES

Please return/renew this item
by the last date shown.
Books may also be renewed by
phone or online
Tel: 0333 3
On-line www.brent.gov.uk

Also available by Philip Caveney

Sebastian Darke: Prince of Fools
Sebastian Darke: Prince of Pirates
Sebastian Darke: Prince of Explorers
Sebastian Darke: Prince of Spies
A Buffalope's Tale

Eye of the Serpent
Empire of the Skull
Maze of Death

Night on Terror Island
Spy Another Day
Space Blasters

Crow Boy
Watchers
Seventeen Coffins
One For Sorrow

The Calling
The Slithers
The Sins of Allie Lawrence

THE BOOK OF SECRETS

PHILIP CAVENEY

uclanpublishing

The Book of Secrets is a uclanpublishing book

First published in Great Britain in 2020 by
uclanpublishing
University of Central Lancashire
Preston, PR1 2HE, UK

978-1-9129791-4-1

1 3 5 7 9 10 8 6 4 2

Set in 10/17pt Kingfisher by Becky Chilcott

A CIP catalogue record for this book is available from the British Library.

Printed and bound in Great Britain by Clays Ltd, Elcograf S.p.A.

This book is for Ellie Reeves.

THE BOOK OF SECRETS

Chapter One

A QUEST

BOY RODE the black horse to the top of the sand dune and pulled her to a halt. He sat for a moment, gazing down across the vast stretch of desert that lay ahead of him – untold miles leading onwards for as far as the eye could see. The day was very nearly over, the sun close to setting in a tumble of blood-red clouds on the horizon, and Boy still hadn't found anywhere to make camp for the night.

He had ridden hard since first light, stopping only once to snatch a few scraps of food and a mouthful of water. He was well aware that his horse, Belle, was in need of rest, but he was eager to put as many miles behind him and his hometown as he could before the day was out. He was not yet far enough away from Serafin to believe that Master Titus might not come in pursuit. He feared that possibility more than anything else that might lurk in the vast, unknown desert that lay before him. Master Titus was not a man to be slighted easily and was sure to be plotting revenge. Boy realised he could not hope to ride for much longer. His main need was to find somewhere to spend the night if he didn't want Belle to collapse under him.

He was just on the point of giving up and admitting that the top of this dune was as good a place as any, when his keen, blue eyes picked up something in the middle distance – a thin plume of grey smoke rising into the darkening sky. Boy noticed a couple of dark smudges close to the source of the smoke. He stared intently, letting the shapes come into focus. Two men, he decided, and the bigger smudges a short distance behind them ... horses? He couldn't be sure but the thought of possible company tempted him onwards. It was many days since he'd passed conversation with anyone. He clicked his heels gently into Belle's flanks and urged her on, over the crest of the dune and down the slope beyond. Belle whinnied in alarm as her front legs sank into the white sand and for an instant, she was in danger of tumbling over, but she managed to right herself and soon, she had reached the bottom of the slope and was toiling forward across more level ground.

As he rode, Boy thought back to the stables in Serafin, where he had lived and worked for the past six years. After the untimely death of his parents, when he was still a child, he'd found himself alone and thrown onto the tender mercies of the people who ruled Serafin. The town elders had quickly decided that he needed to earn his keep and he had been apprenticed to Master Titus, the town stable master, to be taught a useful trade. Titus was a hard man, who thought nothing of using his horsewhip on anyone who was too slow to follow orders. As a consequence, Boy's back was traced with the lines of old scars that paid testament to this.

Of course, he had once had a proper name – the one his parents had given him at birth – but somehow, over the years, it had fallen into misuse and he had eventually resorted to the thing that every visitor to the stables called him. Boy. As in, 'you Boy, take this horse and feed him,' or, 'Boy! Bring me that shovel and be quick about it!' or, if he was particularly unlucky, 'I am going to beat you, Boy, until you learn better manners.'

From his earliest days at the stables, Boy had nurtured an escape plan – something he'd developed over the years. First, he'd encouraged the people he worked with to think that he was stupid. He had never revealed the fact that his father had taught him to read from an early age or that it was a skill he still practised in secret at every opportunity. Moreover, every single bit of gelt he'd managed to get hold of, he'd put away in a secret place, planning for the day when he was finally ready to make his bid for freedom. Every night, by the light of an oil lamp – when he knew that all the others were fast asleep – he'd read and reread the one thing that his father had left him; the same book that he now carried in a hidden compartment of his saddle. The *Book of Secrets*.

He and Belle were drawing rapidly closer to the campfire now and in the dying light, he could make out two cloaked figures, seated on rocks in front of it. They busied themselves with what must have been their evening meal. They had found themselves a decent spot – a declivity in the sand, ringed by a half circle of large boulders. Boy couldn't see the men's faces and it occurred to him that they were complete strangers who might not appreciate being visited by a traveller. He had been so long without human company that he decided to be bold and approached the fire. He instinctively dropped one hand to rest on the hilt of the sword which he wore in a leather scabbard at his waist. It was carried mostly for show. He was no great shakes as a swordsman, there had never been anybody to teach him the moves, but he knew it wasn't wise to set off across the great plains of Sonalia without some kind of weapon at his side. This one had been "borrowed" from the armoury at the back of the stables. Sure enough, he could see now that there were two horses tethered a short distance behind the men and what looked like a pack mule. The animals were eating from nosebags and seemed oblivious to his approach.

He kept riding and soon, he was too close to think about calling it off, so he let out a polite cough.

The men leapt to their feet and span around to face Boy, reaching for their own swords and staring challengingly towards him. The smaller of them regarded him thoughtfully for a moment and then looked quickly around, as if to assure himself that the newcomer wasn't the leader of a gang of brigands, intent on robbery. He was a thin, wiry fellow, his face clean-shaven with dark eyes peering out from under a wide-brimmed hat. After a few moments he seemed reassured, his lips curving into a welcoming smile. The second man, who was a head-and-shoulders taller than his companion, was less friendly. He had big, impassive features and a neatly trimmed, black beard. He wore no hat and his dark hair was no more than a short stubble on his skull. He glared at Boy as though considering whether he should tell him to clear off or simply run forward and strike him to the ground. Boy lifted his hands where the two men could see them.

'I'm just passing through,' he assured them, trying to sound a lot calmer than he felt. 'I mean you no harm.'

The shorter man's smile turned into a cheerful grin. 'No worries, friend,' he purred. 'You startled us for a moment, that's all. Please, climb down from that splendid mount and rest yourself.'

Boy hesitated. 'I wouldn't want to be any trouble,' he said.

'No trouble at all,' said the man. 'In a place this lonely, we should all be friends.' He glanced at his companion. 'Isn't that right, Kaleb?'

The big man's bearded face didn't change its stony expression. He grunted and took his huge hand away from his sword. He turned back to the fire, kneeling beside a battered, black pan that hissed enticingly over the flames.

'Put on another rasher for our guest,' suggested the small man. 'I'm willing to venture that he's hungry.' He took a couple of steps forward and bowed from the waist. 'I am Gordimo of Ackitara,' he said, 'and I am at your service.'

Boy decided that all was well. He relaxed, dismounted from Belle and stood for a moment, stretching his aching muscles.

'You have ridden a long way,' said Gordimo. It wasn't a question so much as an observation.

Boy nodded. 'From Serafin,' he said.

'Ah, I know it well! A fine desert town. They have very good bazaars if memory serves me correctly. Haven't been there in years though.' He studied Boy for a moment as though taking in every detail. 'And where, I wonder, is a young lad like you heading so far from home?'

'To Ravalan,' said Boy.

Gordimo's bushy eyebrows lifted slightly and briefly disappeared behind the brim of his hat. 'A magnificent city,' he said. 'That's quite a journey for a youngster such as yourself.'

'Not so young,' Boy assured him. 'I'm fifteen, nearly sixteen years.' He turned and reached into his saddlebags to get Belle some oats to eat. He sprinkled a couple of handfuls into a nosebag and hitched it into position around her head.

'A fine age,' said Gordimo. 'I fondly remember those years myself, though as you can no doubt see, it was a *very* long time ago.' He chuckled at his own poor joke, then gestured impatiently. 'Well, come along and settle yourself by the fire, before what little fuel we have is extinguished. We have some fine coffee with us and you are more than welcome to enjoy a cup.'

'You are very kind,' said Boy. He followed Gordimo to the meagre fire and settled himself cross-legged in the sand. He saw that Kaleb had indeed thrown another rasher of tunnel-rat meat into the pan and was giving it an encouraging prod with a fork. 'I . . . I'm afraid I can't pay you for the food,' added Boy, awkwardly. 'I have very little money.'

'My dear fellow, don't give it a second thought.' Gordimo settled himself a short distance away from Boy and arranged his cloak carefully around him. 'You are our honoured guest. Here, Kaleb, pour us two cups of that coffee, will you? Our young friend must be parched.'

Kaleb grunted again, but using a filthy-looking rag, he lifted a metal jug from the flames and poured dark brown liquid into some grubby tin cups. He passed them over. Gordimo handed one to Boy and then seemed to realise something. 'You must think me very rude,' he said. 'I haven't even asked your name.'

'Ah, no, you haven't. It's Boy. People call me Boy.'

Gordimo looked puzzled. 'What sort of a name is that?' he asked.

'The only one I answer to, I'm afraid.' Boy sipped at the coffee. It was very bitter and, he thought, strong enough to halt a stampeding buffalo in its tracks, but after such a long ride, it was exactly what he needed.

Gordimo seemed to consider for a moment and then chuckled.

'What's wrong?' asked Boy.

'Well, I was just thinking. The name suits you *now*, but how will it seem when you're my age? Or even older. Perhaps then you'll simply change it to *Man*.'

Boy smiled. 'I hadn't really thought about that,' he admitted. 'I did have another name when I was little, so I shall perhaps go back to using that.'

Gordimo looked interested but he didn't press Boy and, for some reason he couldn't quite fathom, Boy was reluctant to share the information. He never liked talking about his former life.

'So, what takes you to Ravalan?' asked Gordimo.

Boy pointed to Belle, who was still eating her oats.

'*She* does,' he said.

Gordimo smiled. 'Yes, and as I have already observed, she's a fine-looking mount. Must have cost you more than a few gelts.'

Boy tried not to look guilty. The truth was he'd kind of "borrowed" Belle along with the sword and had left a note for Master Titus, promising to pay him five gold crowns when he returned. He didn't really like thinking about that. Whenever he did, he couldn't help picturing his owner's furious face and it wasn't a pretty picture. Boy was also painfully aware that people who stole horses tended to end up hanging from a length of rope in the market square of Serafin, where the crows could peck at their lifeless bodies.

'That's not really what I meant,' added Gordimo, as though sensing Boy's unease. 'I was asking the reason for going to Ravalan.'

'Oh, I see,' said Boy and felt suddenly evasive. 'No particular reason,' he said. 'I . . . just wanted to see it. I want to be there for the Moon of Elnis.'

'Anything to do with the great competition?' asked Kaleb, speaking for the first time in a deep, gravelly voice.

'Competition?' echoed Gordimo, looking baffled. 'What competition?'

Kaleb gave Gordimo a scornful look. 'You must know about it, unless you've spent the last few months with your head buried in the sand.'

'Apparently I must have,' said Gordimo.

'Everybody's talking about it,' continued Kaleb. 'I can't believe you haven't heard it mentioned. The competition set by Queen Gertrude! They say people from all corners of the known world are making their way there. Inventors, wizards, magicians – all sorts.'

Gordimo still seemed puzzled. He looked at Boy. 'Is your journey anything to do with that?' he asked quietly.

'Umm . . . could be,' said Boy, wishing somebody would change the subject. He had always found it hard to lie to people. 'I mean, while I'm there I might . . . you know, have a quick look and see what's going on.'

'Tell me more about it,' suggested Gordimo.

'Er . . . well, as I understand it, Queen Gertrude decided that she would have a competition,' explained Boy. 'It's open to anyone and everyone. She's looking for new ideas.'

Gordimo frowned. 'How do you mean?' he asked.

'She's offering a prize of ten thousand gold crowns to the person who can come up with the best invention – something that has never been seen before.'

'Ten thousand!' Now, Gordimo was most definitely interested. 'But that's a fortune! What kind of an idea is she after?'

'She only set one rule,' Boy told him. 'That whatever new idea people brought to her, it must be one that would change people's lives for the better.'

Kaleb snorted. 'Hah! She doesn't want much for her money,

does she? Who in the world could possibly think of an idea like that?'

There was a long, uncomfortable silence. Then, Gordimo gave Boy a sly look. 'You must think you're in with a chance,' he said. 'Otherwise, why undertake such a long and arduous journey?'

Boy shrugged. 'Like I said, I just thought I'd go along and see what's what.'

'All that way? On a whim? There must be more to it than that.'

'Well, er . . . maybe I *do* have something,' admitted Boy.

'Something you've invented?' prompted Kaleb.

'Not exactly. Something my father came up with . . . or at least, something he . . . started.'

'Then why didn't he finish it?' asked Gordimo.

Boy frowned. 'He disappeared,' he said. 'When I was a little boy. He and my mother. They just vanished. Nobody seems to know . . .' His voice trailed away. 'They were away from home when it happened. I'd been given into the care of my aunt, while my parents were away, but . . . well, she couldn't afford the expense of looking after a child so I was sent to work for my living. But . . .'

'Yes?' murmured Gordimo.

'My father left me . . . some ideas. It is all I have of him.'

'Ideas?' Gordimo looked disgusted, as though he couldn't think of a more dismal present to leave to a child. 'Something he'd written down?'

'Not exactly.' Boy felt alarmed that Gordimo was already so close to the truth. 'Just things we talked about. You see, my father was a scientist . . .'

'A what?' Gordimo seemed unfamiliar with the word.

'It's a man who knows how the world works,' said Boy. 'A man who tries to uncover its mysteries and find ways of helping other people to understand them.'

'Like a magician?' suggested Kaleb, stirring the food in the pan.

'No, quite the opposite, really. Science isn't magic, even if it sometimes seems as though it must be. My father outlined ideas he'd had for . . . well, for making impossible things happen. There was one particular idea that gripped me. My father hadn't quite got it right when he vanished, but he was close. I worked on it and added some ideas of my own and over the years, I finally finished what he'd started and it works. It really works.'

'Amazing!' cried Gordimo. 'Well done, lad, but er . . . what is it, exactly?'

'Ah well, I can't tell you that,' said Boy. 'Obviously, it has to be kept a secret.'

There was another long silence. Gordimo laughed.

'Is that it?' he cried. 'Is that what you'll say to Queen Gertrude when she asks to see your wonderful invention? That it's a secret? That'll go down well."

'No, of course not. I'll show *her*. Only . . .' He made an apologetic gesture. 'No offence, but I've only just met you two.'

'Ah, I see.' Gordimo shook his head. 'You don't feel we're to be trusted.'

'I didn't say that!' Boy felt awkward now, particularly after they'd been so welcoming to him. 'But you must understand, I . . . I need to keep this to myself. I mean, this could be life-changing.'

'Of course. Absolutely. Say no more.' Gordimo seemed to suddenly lose interest in the subject. 'Well, if that food's ready, we may as well eat,' he said. 'I'm sure our honoured guest must be more than ready to fill his belly at our expense, so . . .'

'Oh, no, please, I hope you're not offended! I mean, of course I'd *like* to be able to show you my invention, but . . .'

'Not a problem. Here, Kaleb, give our guest the biggest rasher, will you? I'd say he looks like he could do with some extra nourishment. He'll need to keep his strength up for his secret competition.'

A slab of sizzling meat was dutifully slapped onto a tin plate and handed to Boy. He took it sheepishly. 'Now look, I really didn't mean to . . .'

'Please, don't give it another thought.' Gordimo waved a hand in dismissal, then leaned over and lifted a leather gourd from beside the fire. 'I dare say you'll take a shot of spiced grog in your coffee?' he ventured. 'It can get very cold out on these plains at night and this will help to keep the old circulation going.'

'Well, perhaps just a little sip. I'm not really used to alcohol.'

'Alcohol?' Now Gordimo looked offended. 'This stuff isn't alcoholic. It's what you'd call medicinal – an old family recipe.' He poured a generous amount into Boy's mug and then added a modest splash to his own. 'Let's have a toast, why don't we? To your upcoming success.'

'Well, I don't want to get ahead of myself,' said Boy. 'They might hate my idea.'

'Hmm. What a shame we don't know what it is. We'd be happy to offer our opinion, wouldn't we Kaleb?'

'We'd be delighted.' Kaleb lifted a rasher to his mouth and took a huge bite.

'Yes, but like I said, I can't . . .'

'Sounds to me like it can't fail,' continued Gordimo. 'You said yourself, it's something that will change the world for the better.'

Yes, I . . . suppose I did.'

'Right then. Kaleb, charge up your own coffee! Now, what shall we drink to? Oh yes . . .' Gordimo lifted his mug. 'To science!' he said. He and Kaleb drained their coffees. They sat there, looking at Boy expectantly.

He raised his own mug, with rather less enthusiasm.

'Cheers,' he said and drank.

Chapter Two

THE MIRACLE

DARKNESS WAS falling fast and Boy was already on his third cup of coffee. For some reason, he didn't feel as secretive as he had before. His belly was full of meat and with each mouthful of coffee he gulped down, he felt more and more content with the world. Its rough edges seemed to blur into an agreeable softness. 'So,' he said, waving his mug at his two companions and inadvertently slopping some of the contents onto his tunic. 'Ask yourself this question, my friends. When you look around . . .' He gestured at the sand dunes on every side of them. '. . . what's the most important thing that a person might need?'

His companions looked blank for a moment.

'Gold?' suggested Kaleb, hopefully.

Boy shook his head. 'No. What would you spend it on?' he asked. 'Gold's all well and good in the right place, but it's no use to you *here*.' He waved a hand at his surroundings, the dunes looking almost spectral in the fading light. 'In a desert, riches would be of no use whatsoever!'

'Say's the lad who's entering a competition to win ten thousand gold crowns,' added Gordimo slyly.

'Well, yes, that's true enough,' agreed Boy. 'Can't argue with that. But obviously, *if* I was lucky enough to win the money, I'd go somewhere else to spend it. Somewhere like Ravalan, for instance. I'm told it's a fine city.'

'Oh, the finest in the known world!' agreed Gordimo. 'I've been there myself, many times. It has huge markets, wonderful buildings and beautiful statues. You should see the Queen's Palace! Extraordinary. Oh yes, I couldn't imagine a better place to be a rich man.' He frowned. 'But you keep saying that gold is of no use *here* . . . you mean on the plains of Sonalia?'

'Exactly. Look around you! There's nothing to spend it on, is there? What would your riches buy you in a place like this? Some sand? The occasional stunted tree? A piece of the night sky?' Boy gestured up to the darkening canopy high above them. 'All things that money cannot buy. So, I'll ask my question again and this time, I want you to think about it before you reply. When you are stranded way out here in the desert, what is the most precious thing a person can ask for?'

'Diamonds?' ventured Kaleb, through a mouthful of meat.

'No!' Boy gave him a scornful look. It was almost as though Kaleb was deliberately failing to get the idea. 'You have to think outside the box! That's what my father always used to tell me. He used to say. "The truly clever man does not look for what is right in front of him, but what is hidden behind the obvious."'

'That's brilliant,' said Kaleb, nodding enthusiastically. 'I haven't the faintest idea what it means, but it does sound clever.'

'I suppose what I'm saying is that diamonds are all well and good, in the right place, but what use would they be to you way out here?' Again, he gestured around, irritated that his companions couldn't see what he was getting at. 'Take a good long look, my friends, and think again. In this wilderness, what's the one thing that stands between you and certain death?'

'A good sword,' said Kaleb, with conviction 'If a pack of hungry wolves attacked us right now, we'd need . . .'

'Wolves?' said Gordimo. 'Not much chance of that. Those things have been hunted to extinction. Nobody's seen one for years.'

'Oh, for goodness sake!' Boy was close to exasperation now. Why couldn't they see what he was getting at? Were they stupid? 'There's something much more important than that. Something that can make the difference between life and death!'

Now, Gordimo was smiling confidently. 'I think I've got it,' he said. 'I believe I know what it is.'

Boy leaned forward. 'Yes?' he prompted. 'Go on.'

'It's water.'

'Yes!' Boy nearly jumped to his feet in his excitement. 'You've hit the nail on the head! Out here on the plains, a man has to carry as much of that stuff as he can and then he has to eke out his supply, bit-by-bit, day-by-day. All the time, he's terrified that he might run out and not make it to the next oasis before thirst makes an end of him.'

Gordimo frowned. 'But in Ravalan, they have all the water they need. They have great big fountains in the city square that spend every hour of every day dispensing the stuff. So why would they . . .?'

'Because everything I have heard of Queen Gertrude tells me that she is not a selfish person,' said Boy. 'Maybe she would be willing to take my gift and share it with those people who are in need of it.'

'And pay you ten thousand gold crowns into the bargain,' added Kaleb bluntly. Boy had to admit, put like that, it did sound faintly damning.

'Well, all right, but . . . look, I think it's only fair for me to seek recompense for all my hard work,' reasoned Boy. 'After all, it took me years to perfect this.'

'Yes, but Kaleb has a point, surely? Why travel all this way? Why not take your invention to the elders of Serafin and offer them the opportunity to . . .' Gordimo broke off mid-sentence. 'Hang on a moment. What are you actually claiming to have invented here? Water? I hate to break it to you, lad, but that stuff already exists.' He reached over to a canteen standing beside the fire and shook it. 'I have some right here, taken from the last oasis we stopped at.'

Boy nodded, smiled. 'Ah yes, but what if I told you that my invention would mean never again having to travel for miles in search of a waterhole? What if I told you that it could produce fresh water right here and now, using the very thing that is most abundant on these plains?'

Once again, the two men looked baffled.

'The thing most abundant?' muttered Kaleb. 'What's that?'

'For goodness sake – sand! I'm talking about sand.'

Gordimo gave Boy a long hard look. 'Maybe you've been out in the sun too long,' he said. 'It's addled your brains.'

'No, I swear to you it hasn't!' Boy lifted his mug and swallowed down the last dregs of his coffee. Suddenly, any last thoughts of caution were flung to the four winds. 'That's my invention in a nutshell. It can turn sand into water.'

There was a long, uncomfortable silence. Gordimo and Kaleb exchanged astonished looks and then the two of them started sniggering. 'So,' said Gordimo, changing the subject, 'tell me, Kaleb, did your friend buy that horse he had his eye on? Or was the price too high?'

'Well, the fellow who was selling the old nag, asked for twenty gelts but . . .'

'You don't believe me!' cried Boy, incredulously, looking from one of them to the other. 'You think I'm making it up.'

Gordimo turned back to look at Boy and there was a new look in his eyes, one of utter contempt. 'I thought you were a nice lad,' he said, 'not somebody who would go around making up such nonsense.'

'Why do you say it's nonsense?' cried Boy.

Gordimo sneered. 'If I told you I could pull a fully-grown buffalo out of my backside, would you believe that?' he asked. Kaleb guffawed loudly and Boy felt his face growing hot. 'No offence, son, but when it comes to tall stories, that one beats the lot.' He mimed the action of picking up a cup. 'Ooh, I'm thirsty,' he said. 'I know, I'll just have a nice cup of cool, refreshing sand!' Kaleb laughed again and the two men pretended to toast each other with imaginary cups.

'Cheers!' cried Gordimo.

'Bottoms up!' added Kaleb.

'Right,' said Boy, clambering unsteadily to his feet. 'I'll prove it. I'll *show* you.'

'Don't embarrass yourself,' Gordimo advised him, but Boy ignored the taunt. He weaved his way over to Belle, reached into one of the saddlebags hitched across her withers and pulled out the muslin sack that housed his apparatus. He swung around and made his way unsteadily back to the fire.

'What have you got in there?' asked Gordimo. 'A fountain?'

'No, not a fountain,' replied Boy. 'Something even better.' He dropped down into the sand again and busied himself, loosening the length of yarn that held the bag shut. He took out the gourd and prised off the lid. He held it out in the palm of one hand. 'Perhaps one of you would be so kind as to fill this for me,' he suggested.

'Fill it with what?' asked Gordimo.

'With sand, of course.'

The two men regarded him in mocking silence for a moment and then Kaleb got reluctantly to his feet. He took the gourd and regarded it suspiciously. 'What's this made of?' he muttered.

'That I cannot tell you,' said Boy, briskly. 'I have to have *some* secrets. Now, if you'd like to fill it for me.'

'What kind of sand do you want?' asked Kaleb.

'Any kind you like,' Boy assured him. 'Just choose whichever bit you fancy.'

'If you say so.' Kaleb stooped over and dredged the open gourd through the soft sand by his feet until it was filled to the brim. He handed it back to Boy. 'Will that do you?' he asked.

'Perfect. Now . . .' Boy reached into the sack and took out the three small bottles of liquid – one pink, one green and one colourless. Holding them close to his chest, he unstoppered each of them in turn, and allowed one drop to fall into the open gourd. He carefully resealed each bottle and put them back into the bag. Finally, he turned his back on the others, reached into his tunic to the metal charm he wore on a leather thong around his neck and undid the clasp. Its hollow interior was stuffed with bright, crimson yaricoola seeds.

He carefully picked one out between thumb and forefinger and pressed it into the sand in the gourd. Before he turned back, he made sure to close the charm again and conceal it from sight, knowing how precious the seeds were and all too aware that this was the finishing touch to the formula. He shuffled back around and replaced the tight-fitting lid onto the circular gourd. He set it carefully down on the ground.

'Now what?' asked Gordimo.

'Now we wait,' said Boy. 'And while we do that, perhaps there's a drop more of that grog in the bottle,' he added, handing his empty cup to Kaleb. The tall man scowled but obligingly poured a generous shot into the cup and handed it back. 'I'm definitely getting a taste for this stuff,' said Boy. 'What's it called again?'

'It's called Mother's Lament,' said Gordimo. 'How long must we wait for this . . . miracle?'

'Oh, not too long,' said Boy, mysteriously, enjoying the fact that he now had their undivided attention.

Kaleb gave a grunt of disbelief. 'You're genuinely trying to tell us that the sand in that gourd is going to turn to water?' he asked.

'I'm not trying to tell you anything,' Boy assured him. 'I'm going to *show* you and when I have, I'll be glad to hear your apologies for doubting me.'

Gordimo pointed at the gourd. 'That little thing,' he said. 'It can hardly hold more than a few cupfuls. That's not going to cure the world of thirst, is it?'

Boy shrugged. 'Certainly not,' he said, confidently. 'But it can be made to any size. It's what it's made *of* that matters.'

'Which is?'

Boy shook his head and Gordimo laughed.

'Of course, I'm forgetting. It's all a great big secret.' He gestured impatiently. 'How much longer?' he asked.

'Not long.' Boy took another gulp of the grog, suddenly aware that it had a powerful kick. He told himself that he really shouldn't have any more, but instantly pushed the thought aside. He was enjoying himself. 'I thought you said this stuff was meddy . . . medi . . . meddyscene-al.' He shook his head, finding it hard to shape his words. He drank the last of the grog and carefully set the empty cup down. 'All right,' he said. He waved a hand at the gourd. 'It should be ready by now but I'm not going to touch it, or you two will accuse me of being some kind of . . . trig . . . some kind of trigste . . . er, trickster.'

Gordimo got onto his knees and shuffled closer to the gourd, his face wearing an expression of boredom. He picked it up and hesitated when he perceived a slopping noise from within. His eyes widened in surprise. He prised the lid off the gourd and gazed into it in mute disbelief. He muttered something under his breath, something terse enough to coax Kaleb back to his feet. The big man scrambled closer and peered at the gourd's contents.

'No way,' he hissed. 'It's not possible.'

'I'm afraid it is,' mumbled Boy and he performed a little bow.

'It has to be some kind of trick,' snarled Gordimo. 'Some sleight of hand.' He stared accusingly at Boy. 'You turned your back on us for a moment,' he snapped. 'It's obvious. You must have another container secreted about your person; a skin bag or something, which you used to fill the gourd . . .'

Boy shook his head. 'No tricks,' he said. 'Like I told you. Science.'

Quite suddenly, all the friendliness left Gordimo's face and was replaced by a cold, hard mask. 'Search him,' he snapped and Kaleb obeyed. He grabbed Boy by the neck of his tunic and yanked him unceremoniously to his feet.

'Hey!' slurred Boy. 'Go easy! You're hurting me!'

Kaleb thrust his big hands under Boy's tunic. His hand brushed briefly against the charm around Boy's neck but the big man seemed to think nothing of it and moved on. 'He has no hidden container,' said Kaleb. He dropped Boy back into the sand and an incredulous expression spread across his features. 'I think . . . I think he's telling the truth.'

Gordimo looked through the muslin sack. He found the three small bottles and examined them with intense curiosity. 'So, I saw him put one drop from each of these into the sand.'

'Hey, take your hands off them,' said Boy, scrambling forward on his hands and knees. 'They're mine.'

'What *are* these liquids?' snarled Gordimo and now, there was no trace of his former cheerfulness. 'Tell me and no harm will come to you.'

'It's no business of yours!' cried Boy. He reeled drunkenly to his feet and reached for the handle of his sword. 'I'll thank you to hand them over!' he roared.

Everything happened very quickly. He was briefly aware of Kaleb's right arm blurring into motion and there was a glimpse of a fist that looked the size of a slab of buffalo meat. It connected with Boy's jaw with an impact that lifted him clean off his feet. He went flying backwards, his arms flailing in a desperate attempt to locate something to stop his fall, but they found only empty air. An instant later, his back slammed hard against sand, the impact driving the breath from his lungs. He lay for an instant gazing up at the night sky as the world see-sawed crazily around him and in the moment before darkness claimed him, he found himself thinking that he had never seen so many stars.

Chapter Three

HANGOVER

BOY CAME slowly and painfully back to consciousness. He opened his eyes briefly and then closed them again when the bright morning sunlight blazed into them. He groaned. His head felt as though several tiny demons were gleefully pounding it with wooden clubs. He waited a moment, hoping the pain would pass, but it didn't. He risked opening his eyes a second time and managed to keep them open until his vision swam into focus. With a major effort, he sat up and had a good, long look around him.

It didn't take long to establish that things were every bit

as bad as they could be. A short distance to his left were the remains of last night's campfire, a few smouldering ashes ringed by a half circle of rocks. There was no sign of Gordimo and Kaleb. The men's horses were gone and so was their mule. Worse still, there was not a trace of Belle.

A jolt of alarm cut through the pain in his head. Belle! They had taken Belle – probably not even aware that the *Book of Secrets* was hidden in a special compartment in her saddle – and of course, they had taken the gourd and the three bottles of liquid. Panic hammered through Boy's chest, but then he remembered something and he slipped a hand under his tunic. His fingers brushed against the metal charm and he took a moment to pull it out, unclip it and look inside. It was still tightly packed with seeds and he felt a momentary sense of relief. Without them, the apparatus simply wouldn't work and Boy was pretty sure he'd managed not to mention them at any point last night, no matter how much grog he'd guzzled down. Of course, if they chanced upon the hidden book, that would be a different matter. His father had definitely mentioned yarricoola seeds in there.

He felt now a powerful sense of shame. What a fool he'd been to trust two strangers with his greatest secret! He couldn't have made himself more of a victim unless he'd walked around with a big sign around his neck saying "please rob me". Despair swept over him and for a moment, he came close to tears, but he reined himself fiercely back from that. Feeling sorry for himself would be of no use whatsoever in his current predicament. No, he had to take stock of the situation and decide what he needed to do to put things right. The first thing was to get himself back on his feet.

That was when he realised why he'd felt a sense of wrongness from the moment he'd woken. One of the first things he'd become aware of was the unfamiliar feeling of sand against his bare heels. He stared down in absolute horror. They'd taken his boots! The rotten, thieving scum had stolen his boots.

Then, the most horrifying thought of all occurred to him. He took a last frantic look around. Surely they must have left him some water? Nobody could be so cruel as to head off without leaving him at least a bottle of the stuff. He looked and looked until his eyes hurt, but he could see nothing.

That was when the tears did overcome him. He sat for a moment, hunched over, his shoulders shaking as he sobbed out his anger and humiliation. Finally, an unfamiliar sensation flooded through him, something he'd never experienced before: cold, hard hatred. He saw the faces of the two men who had robbed him in his mind's eye and thought only of vengeance. He imagined how it would feel to fasten his fingers around Gordimo's throat and to squeeze the breath out of him.

The tears subsided and he managed to get himself upright. It was still early morning, but he knew only too well that as the sun rose, so the sand would get hotter and hotter until it was impossible to walk on. He wondered why Gordimo and Kaleb hadn't killed him. Perhaps, he told himself, neither of them had the stomach for murdering a young lad in cold blood, but in leaving him this way, they had done something infinitely crueller. They had condemned him to a slow and terrible death from thirst. How ironic, that they had taken with them his only means of creating exactly what he needed to keep him alive. He thought again about his reckless boasting of the previous night. Could he have been any more stupid?

He shook his head and spat into the sand. All right, he decided, he was in a terrible fix, but there was no way he was going to give up without a fight. He had a last look around just to be absolutely sure that he hadn't missed anything, but that last faint hope was quickly extinguished. They had taken everything.

He didn't need to navigate. He could see, quite clearly, the tracks of several horses leading off across the dunes and it didn't take a detective to work out where Gordimo and Kaleb must be headed. To Ravalan, of course, to claim the prize they thought could be theirs.

Boy gathered his thoughts, put his head down and began to walk.

★ ★ ★

At first, he made good progress, striding out on his long legs and putting the miles behind him. Despite the awful ache in his skull, he walked hour after hour, hopefully scanning the horizon for signs of life, but there was nobody to be seen. As the day slipped inexorably by, so the heat rose in rippling waves from the sand until the soles of his feet were raw and blistered, and his dry throat ached for a drop of cool water. Somehow, he kept himself moving, but as he trudged onwards, memories began to fill his head, crowding into his mind's eye until he was no longer sure what was real and what was imaginary.

He saw himself as a child, sitting on a stool in front of one of Serafin's market stalls, sipping ice cool sherbet, his insides tingling as the cold liquid spilled down his grateful throat. He stared at a huge glass of yellow liquid, fizzing and popping with its sweet and sour flavours – he could almost taste it.

He saw himself sitting on his mother's lap in the nursery of his old home, as she sang to him, some ancient, half-remembered lullaby that eventually coaxed him into the realms of sleep. Pleasant dreams awaited him and fear, pain and hunger were just ideas – things that you heard about in stories.

Then, he saw himself standing in the doorway of his parents' fabulous, white-painted villa in Serafin, watching as his father and mother climbed into a waiting carriage at the garden gate. He saw how happy they were, the two of them still so much in love – his mother laughing delightedly as her husband helped her into the seat. Boy's father hesitated, as though he'd just remembered something. He left the coach for a moment and hurried back to the doorway. Kneeling in front of his son, so their heads were at the same height, he began to talk urgently, a smile on his lips but a serious look in his eyes.

'My son, as you know, your mother and I have to go away for a few days. Listen carefully: if anything should happen to us while we are away – if for any reason we do not come back – I want you to go to the room at the top of the house; the one where I do all my work. Do you know it? Good. In my desk, there's a little drawer that must be unlocked with this key.' Boy's father pressed a tiny, brass key into his son's hand. 'In the drawer, you will find a little leather-bound book: the *Book of Secrets*. I want you to take it and keep it safe at all times. Do not share it with anyone. It is for your eyes only, do you understand? Good. You won't be able to fully understand it yet, but one day, you will. It is the most important thing that I possess. All my ideas are in there – the secrets to all my inventions.' He smiled. 'Of course, I will be back in a few days' time and you shall hand the key back to me. We will laugh about this but for now, humour me, will you?'

With that his father stood up, strolled back to the waiting carriage and climbed back inside. The driver cracked his whip and the carriage moved away.

It was as if he knew something bad was going to happen, thought Boy, *as though he suspected that he and Mother were going to their doom.*

Nobody knew what had happened to his parents. They had set off for the city of Leetolla – just a few miles south of Serafin – where his father was to talk to a group of elders about his work as a scientist. The carriage never arrived at its destination though, its passengers and driver were never seen again. Boy's parents were suddenly and calamitously torn from his life, but he remembered his father's words and, at his earliest opportunity, he'd gone to the hidden room and secured that little book. He had kept it with him ever since, taking the greatest care to hide it from others. Now, quite suddenly, it was gone – stolen from him by two conniving tricksters.

Boy's hands bunched themselves into fists and he thought about what he would do if he ever caught up with them, how he would teach them the meaning of fear. He saw Gordimo's weasel-like face in front of him, the man's confident smile gone and his eyes wide with panic. 'Please!' he cried, 'spare me! I will give everything back, I promise!'

Boy was not in a forgiving mood. He reached for the sword at his side and pulled it free from its scabbard, but realised that it had changed into a long, spotted serpent that was coiling around his wrist as he tried to shake it free.

The image disappeared and the world came slowly back into focus. Boy was still moving forward but his rate had slowed to a lurching stagger. His throat burned, his face and neck felt as though they were roasting and he barely had the strength to place one blistered foot in front of the other. He looked down and realised, with a dull sense of shock, that the hoof prints he had been following were nowhere to be seen.

'No!' He gazed frantically this way and that, but could discern no sign of them. Perhaps, he thought, the desert winds had scoured them from the surface of the sand or, lost in his thoughts, he had simply wandered off course. He sank to his knees with a sigh. He could still navigate, using the sun as his guide. Ravalan lay to the North. He only needed to keep the sun at his left shoulder and he would be travelling in the right direction, but first, he needed to rest for just a few moments.

He lifted his head and stared at the great stretch of desert ahead of him. He realised that there was simply no point in prolonging this. There was nothing but sand for as far as he could see. All right, so he might manage to stagger onwards for another couple of miles, but then what? He would have to accept that it was all up for him. He was as good as dead.

Then, he saw something in the distance. He gasped, concentrated, trying to focus his failing vision. He quickly realised that this was not his quarry, but a wagon. Maybe even two of them? He didn't know what they were doing way out here but they were now his only hope of survival. He managed to get himself upright again and opened his mouth to shout, but what came out was a feeble moan that didn't have the ghost of a chance of being heard at such a distance. He shook his head.

He stood for a moment, swaying in his tracks as he marshalled what little was left of his strength. He took a deep breath and began to run.

It wasn't a very convincing run – more of a blundering, lurching stagger, but he knew he had only one chance. If he couldn't make the travellers aware of him, he might as well lie down and die. He propelled himself up a sand dune, his leg muscles screaming in protest. Somehow, he made it to the top and started down the other side. Halfway down, he stumbled, twisted around and rolled a short distance. He got himself upright again.

He could see he was following a couple of caravans. He threw back his head and risked a shout, his voice echoing on the empty air. The caravans rumbled onwards, raising dust. Boy shook his head. His skinny frame was soaked in what was left of his sweat and every muscle in his body seemed to be wracked with pain. He made himself keep going, trying to quicken his pace and as he blundered onwards, he was able to make out more details of the nearest caravan, which was brightly painted and had words written across the rear doors.

Another dune rose ahead of him, momentarily blotting the caravan from his sight and he forced himself to climb the steep hill of sand, the effort wringing the last drops of energy from his body. He finally made it to the top and slowed to a halt. He stood, head down, his chest rising and falling as he fought to take in air. He was done, he decided. He could run no further. There was perhaps one last chance . . .

He took in a big breath, tilted back his head to look at the cloudless sky and shouted one word, putting every ounce of strength he had left into it.

'HELP!' he screamed. The word rose on the air. It echoed and then seemed to die away. Nothing happened. The caravans continued on their way, seemingly oblivious to his presence. He had failed.

'Ah well,' he whispered. 'At least I tried.'

Suddenly, the driver of the nearest caravan leaned over and looked back towards him. The caravan drew to a halt. The driver jumped down from the seat. Boy lifted his arms and waved frantically, but the effort took more than he actually had left to give and the desert appeared to lurch abruptly sideways in front of him. It spun crazily around him as a greyness welled up from deep inside. It rushed up his spine and into his head. He just had time to register that the little figure was running towards him. A wall of white sand hit him in the face and a deep blackness spilled through him, blotting out everything else.

★ ★ ★

Boy opened his eyes. He was lying in a shaded place and the floor beneath him was swaying and lurching. For a moment, he thought he was in a boat, but remembered that this was the desert and there didn't tend to be many boats in a place like that. Something hard nudged against his lips and cold liquid filled his mouth, the taste of it so shocking that he almost lifted a hand to push it away. He corrected himself and began to gulp down mouthfuls of the stuff, revelling as he felt fresh vitality flowing into him like nectar.

'Hey, take it easy! We don't have unlimited supplies of this stuff!'

It was a female voice and for the briefest moment, he thought it was his mother speaking to him, but then his vision came into focus and he saw that it was a girl around his own age. She was dressed in boy's clothes, a shapeless felt hat crammed down over her eyes, which were huge and a strange shade of green. She gazed at him intently, and gave him a warm and friendly smile.

He swallowed a last mouthful of water and then allowed her to pull the canteen away from his lips. He sank back onto what felt like a straw mattress and glancing around, realised that he was in the back of one of the caravans he'd been following.

'It's a good job you shouted when you did,' said the girl. 'I was miles away.' She saw the look of confusion in his eyes and added, 'I mean I was daydreaming. I'm afraid I do that a lot.'

'I . . . I . . .' He tried to speak but his voice was little more than a dry croak.

'Take it easy,' she advised him. 'I don't know how long you've been wandering around out here but you're clearly in a bad way.' She glanced down at his bare feet. 'What happened to your boots?' she asked him.

'Stolen.' He managed to get the word out in a form she could recognise.

'Really?' She looked disgusted. 'There are some real charmers out here, aren't there? Honestly, it doesn't pay to trust anybody.' She seemed to realise what she'd just said and smiled disarmingly. 'Obviously, you can trust *me*.' She thought about it for a moment. 'I don't suppose you have any choice, do you? Anyway, don't worry, you're safe now. Why don't you get some rest? We'll talk tonight when we make camp.'

He shook his head and attempted to sit up. 'Got to get . . . to Ravalan!' he gasped.

'Hey, easy now.' She placed a hand on his chest and eased him back down, the power in that arm taking him somewhat by surprise. 'Here, another mouthful of water, I think, just to keep you going.' She held the canteen back to his lips and he gratefully accepted a little more. 'Ravalan, eh?' she murmured. 'Well, you're in luck, my friend. That's exactly where we're headed.'

He stared at her in disbelief.

'But . . . I need to be there for . . . the Moon of . . .'

'Elnis? Yes, us too! Small world, eh?'

'I don't . . . understand . . .'

'Listen, calm down. You need to get some rest. Like I said, we'll talk tonight, when we make camp.' She put the stopper in the canteen and laid it down beside him. 'I'm going to leave this here,' she said, 'but I want you to promise me you'll go easy on it. It's a long way to the next waterhole and—' She broke off in surprise. 'Are you crying?' she murmured.

He nodded, ashamed of himself, but the bitter irony of her words had got to him. Only a few hours earlier, he'd had the means to put an end to such worries.

'Sorry,' he whispered.

'Don't be daft! I guess you must have come pretty close,' said the girl. 'It would make anybody cry. I'm Lexi, by the way.'

He nodded, started to tell her that he was called Boy, but failed before he could shape the words. A voice from outside the wagon broke into their conversation. 'What's going on in there? Is he all right?'

'Yes, he's a bit battered and burnt, but I think he'll survive.'

'Good. Have you asked him yet?'

Lexi looked annoyed. 'No, of course I haven't. He's barely awake.'

'You need to ask him soon.'

'Yes, just not yet, all right?' Lexi gave Boy a smile. 'I'd better get back out there,' she said. 'He's not much good at helming a wagon.'

'I heard that,' said the voice. 'Flipping cheek!'

Boy frowned. He had never heard a voice like it before. It didn't sound human.

Lexi pulled aside the blankets that draped the front of the caravan and climbed out onto the wooden bench seat. Boy caught a glimpse of a figure sitting at the reins. It was a tiny, hairy little marionette, half the size of the girl, its face turned away. Before Boy could properly focus, the blankets swung back into position and the strange voice piped up once again.

'You need to ask him,' it said. 'We don't have a lot of time.'

'Tonight,' said Lexi's voice. 'I'll ask him tonight.'

'He'd better say yes, otherwise I don't know what we'll do.'

Boy heard only the creaking sound of the caravan moving across the desert. He lay on his back, staring up at the wooden ceiling above his head. He wanted to stay awake and figure out exactly what was happening, but for the moment, he knew that he was heading to Ravalan and that was a good thing. The rest he'd have to figure out later. The dark, wooden ceiling seemed to turn to grey clouds and his thoughts drained through his mind like sand in an hourglass.

Chapter Four

SUPPERTIME

I T WAS the thick, appetising aroma of food cooking over an open fire that woke him. His empty stomach gurgled in response and he lay for a moment in semi-darkness, trying to puzzle out where he was, before remembering that he was in a caravan that belonged to a girl called Lexi. A last, lingering trace of dizziness flowed through him, but he managed to brush it aside and he sat there, assessing himself for signs of damage. He realised that his feet felt strange and reaching down a hand, he brushed his fingertips over what felt like tightly strapped bandages. It was evident that somebody had been kind enough to tend to his blistered feet while he slept and, after the rough treatment he'd received from Gordimo and Kaleb, it made him feel strangely emotional.

He rolled off the mattress and struggled onto his knees, wincing as one bandaged foot brushed against the wooden floor. He moved closer to the front of the caravan, aware of sounds of conversation coming from outside. He pulled back a blanket and peered cautiously out into the night. Three people were sitting around a campfire, watching as a black cauldron bubbled and steamed fitfully over the flames. Boy recognised Lexi instantly, even though her back was turned to him. A short distance to her right was an old man; a grey haired, bearded fellow who was staring into the flames. On Lexi's other side sat a middle-aged woman, with a mass of blonde curls cascading onto her shoulders.

'Ah, looks like our guest is finally back in the land of the living,' she observed and her two companions turned to look in Boy's direction.

'How are you feeling?' Lexi asked him.

'Better, thanks to you,' said Boy.

She walked over to him. 'Come and join us if you're able,' she said. 'Here, let me help you.'

She placed a hand in his and once again, he was momentarily surprised by her strength. Boy moved gingerly into the opening, put one foot onto the buckboard and allowed Lexi to ease him down to the ground. He muffled a grunt of pain as one bandaged sole connected with the sand and then followed with the other.

'They're going to be sore for a couple of days,' said the woman. 'I put some of my special balm on them which should speed up the healing process, but they were badly burned.'

Boy nodded and allowed Lexi to help him closer to the fire.

'I am in your debt,' he told the woman.

'Think nothing of it.' She made a dismissive gesture. 'What's the point of life if we can't help each other? I'm Mo, by the way.'

'Pleased to meet you, Mo. I'm Boy.' He waited for them to make the usual noises of surprise but they seemed to accept this without comment. Perhaps, he thought, they had heard stranger names than his. Lexi helped him over to a large rock and he sat down with a gasp of relief.

'What kind of miserable scum would steal a man's boots in a place like this?' asked the old man, looking at Boy. His eyes were two intense, blue spheres in his sunburned face.

'They were just two strangers I met on the trail,' said Boy, forlornly. 'Stupidly, I trusted them. They plied me with drink and then they robbed me. They took everything I owned, including my horse.'

'Then it's lucky we came along,' said the old man. He placed a hand on his chest and bowed slightly. 'I am Orson.' He waved a hand in Lexi's direction. 'I believe you have already met my daughter.'

Boy nodded. 'I have, sir,' he replied. 'She saved my life. If she hadn't looked back when she did, I . . . well, I don't like to think what might have happened to me.'

Lexi had gone back to her own seat a short distance away. 'Then don't ponder it,' she advised him. 'Thinking about what might have been is the most direct route to madness.' She nodded towards the bubbling pot on the fire. 'You're probably starving but I must ask you to be patient. We're expecting a couple of others to dine with us. They are out hunting game for tomorrow's dinner and we make it a rule never to eat until everybody is present. We are all only one meal away from starvation.'

'It's the actor's life,' observed Mo and her companions chuckled.

'Actors?' echoed Boy, puzzled.

'Yes. We are travelling players,' said Mo. 'The Wandering Star Theatre Company. Perhaps you've heard of us.'

Boy shook his head. 'I'm afraid not,' he said.

'Well, that's why we're headed for Ravalan. The Moon of Elnis is always a busy time for us.'

'It's one of the biggest festivals of the year,' agreed Orson. 'One of the few occasions when the populace are happy to part with a few gelts in exchange for some entertainment.'

'I see.' Boy was impressed. He'd never met actors before. 'What kind of things do you do?'

'Oh, wonderful dramas,' said Orson. 'Stories of wild

adventure and high passion. We are, of course, blessed with a wonderful leading lady *and* a great playwright . . .'

Lexi gave him a weary look. 'Dad!' she said, but Orson ignored her and continued.

'. . . and unusually in such circumstances, they are one and the same person!'

Boy struggled to follow this. 'You're saying that . . .?'

'My daughter is both the star of our productions and the author of them. What do you think of that, young man?'

'I, er . . . that's amazing. Are they any good?'

An uncomfortable silence settled around the campfire.

'I mean . . . I'm sure they *must* be,' stammered Boy. 'I wasn't suggesting otherwise. It's just that . . .' He looked at Lexi. 'That's a lot to take on,' he said.

She nodded. 'I won't pretend it isn't,' she said forlornly. 'I accepted the challenge after my mother died. She was a wonderful actor and a brilliant playwright. I have tried my best to do her justice.'

'And you have succeeded admirably,' said Mo. She threw Boy a sharp look as if to warn him not to labour the point. 'Nobody could have done more, isn't that right, Orson?'

'It is,' agreed the old man. 'Ah, Lexi, your mother would be so proud of you.'

Boy sat there uncomfortably, looking from one of his companions to the next, wondering how he had managed to turn a convivial atmosphere into what felt suspiciously like the aftermath of a funeral. 'What show are you taking to Ravalan?' he asked.

Lexi was looking at her feet now. '*The Sorrows of Young Adamis*,' she said. 'It's my latest play. A romance.'

'A romantic drama,' added Orson.

'With sword fights,' said Mo. 'Don't forget the sword fights!'

'It sounds wonderful,' said Boy, trying to be enthusiastic. 'Perhaps I'll get to see a performance of it?'

All three of them looked at him with strange expressions and he had the intense conviction that he'd said the wrong thing again. 'I mean, if that would be all right,' he mumbled. 'I wouldn't want to assume that . . .'

Lexi opened her mouth to say something but was interrupted by the sudden arrival of a huge figure that came looming unexpectedly out of the darkness. It held something out in front of him – something that looked like the carcass of an animal.

'Look what I got,' boomed a deep voice and Boy found himself reaching reflexively for the handle of a sword that was no longer there.

'Oh, brilliant!' cried Mo. 'A nice, fat tunnel-rat. Well done, Grud! That'll see us through another couple of days.'

Boy realised that this was just another member of the company and reminded himself to sit down again. He examined the newcomer in awe as he strode forward into the light of the campfire. He was enormous – maybe seven or eight feet tall. He was a great, gangling fellow with tousled, black, shoulder-length hair and a ragged beard. He beamed as he came closer. He saw Boy sitting by the fire and turned towards him. 'You're awake!' he cried delightedly. 'How are you feeling?'

'I'm er . . . d–doing very well, thank you.'

'Look at this,' said Grud, swinging the hanging carcass up into both hands and displaying it proudly a few inches from Boy's face. 'I chanced upon its burrow unexpectedly. I waited and waited and when he popped his head out, I grabbed him and beat him to death with my bare hands!'

Boy gulped. 'Th–That's l–lovely,' he stammered. He didn't know what else to say, but he knew he wasn't enjoying being quite so close to what was essentially a mangled corpse. 'I'm rather fond of a bit of tunnel-rat myself.'

'Are you really? There's not much else to eat around these parts.' Grud leaned closer and lowered his voice. 'If you like, you can have the eyeballs. I won't tell the others.'

Boy sensed his features turning pale, but hoped nobody else had noticed. 'Oh no,' he said, 'I wouldn't presume to . . .'

'But you're our *guest*!' cried Grud, sounding somehow like an excited, young child. 'We don't get many of those. The eyeballs are the best bits. Everyone knows that. If you like, you can take one now and I won't tell anybody! Go on, pop one in your mouth!'

'Grud, maybe you should hang the meat up,' suggested Lexi. 'We'll butcher it later.'

Grud looked disappointed, but seemed to accept the order. 'All right,' he said. 'But you will offer our guest the eyeballs, won't you?'

'Yes, of course,' said Lexi and she gave Boy an apologetic smile.

'Good.' Grud leaned close to Boy again. 'Glad you're feeling a bit better,' he murmured. 'To be honest, I took one look at you and reckoned you were a goner.'

'Grud!' hissed Lexi.

'No, I mean it. You looked as though you didn't have a hope.' He turned aside and Boy remembered to breathe.

'I don't suppose you saw what happened to Pompio?' asked Mo, as the giant turned and strode across the clearing.

'I think he was after birds,' said Grud. 'Said he was tired of eating tunnel-rat and fancied a bit of poultry. I told him, you won't find many birds in the desert, mate, but he reckoned he knew better than me.'

'I *did* know better!' announced a voice dramatically and everyone turned to appraise another figure walking towards the fire.

Boy's eyes nearly popped out of his head. The voice was the one he'd heard earlier that day and the tiny, hairy shape was the same as he'd glimpsed sitting at the reins of the caravan. Pompio was no more than two or three feet in height. As the firelight illuminated his grinning features, Boy understood what he was looking at. Pompio was a boobo; one of the hairy, long-armed, long-tailed creatures that inhabited the Southern jungles of the known world. Boy had occasionally seen them sitting on the shoulders of travellers or bashing tambourines at travelling shows. He knew that such creatures were thought to be highly intelligent, but he had never before seen one dressed in clothes and chatting away as confidently as any human. Pompio was carrying the carcasses of a couple of flightless birds over one shoulder and a little bow across the other.

'These lads thought they were out of range, so they didn't run quite as fast as they should have,' he explained. 'You should have seen the surprise on their faces when two arrows came zooming out of the darkness and—' He broke off in surprise as he noticed Boy sitting there. 'Oi, oi' he said. 'Somebody's perked up a bit since the last time I saw him.' Pompio looked at Lexi. 'Have you asked him?' he said.

Lexi looked really irritated. 'Give me a chance,' she hissed. 'He's only just opened his eyes.'

'You don't want to let the grass grow,' Pompio warned her. 'Strike while the iron's hot, that's my motto. I'm going to hang these beauties up and when I come back to eat, I'll expect you to have popped the question.'

With that, he scampered after Grud, the pair qualifying as one of the oddest-looking couples in history.

Boy sat there baffled, looking from Lexi to Mo to Orson and back again. 'Ask me what?' he demanded.

Lexi was studying her feet again. 'Well, I didn't want to rush into this,' she said. 'But you see, when we found you in the desert, we were in a bit of a fix . . .'

'More than a bit,' Mo corrected her. 'I'd describe it as a disaster.'

'That's putting too strong a word on it,' insisted Orson. 'A major inconvenience is what it is, but there are ways and means around these things.'

'I hardly think it's that easy,' said Mo. 'The point is, we're—'

'Please!' Lexi looked from one to the other. 'If you could just give me a moment to explain myself?'

They nodded, fell silent and Lexi turned her attention back to Boy. 'You see, up until a couple of days ago, there was another member of our cast. Ninian.'

'Nincompoop would have suited him better,' growled Mo.

'Well, that's probably fair.' Lexi frowned. 'Ninian was our leading man. Our main actor. He was a good-looking fellow—'

'That's a matter of opinion,' said Mo, grumpily.

'Mostly *his* opinion,' added Orson.

'I couldn't help noticing that a certain person was rather enamoured of his looks,' continued Mo, giving Lexi a sly grin.

'Yes, all right, you've made your point! He auditioned for us and he seemed . . . well, I thought he seemed very accomplished.

So, we took him on and I gave him the role of Young Adamis.'

'As in *The Sorrows of Young Adamis*,' said Mo.

'Your new play,' said Boy, trying to be helpful.

'Yes, exactly. Well remembered! But unfortunately, when we agreed to take him on, there was something that we didn't know about him.'

Boy frowned. 'Which was?'

'He suffered from stage fright.'

'What's stage fright?' asked Boy.

'Literally what it sounds like,' said Orson. 'He was fine in rehearsals, but the minute there was an audience waiting to see him, he would freeze.'

'Freeze?'

'Yes. He couldn't speak. He couldn't move. He just stood there with a look on his face like he'd been bitten by a swamp serpent.'

'Oh dear,' said Boy.

'Oh dear is right,' sighed Mo. 'The first show was a total disaster. We were booed off the stage and we had to refund every ticket we'd sold.'

'Ninian assured us it wouldn't happen again,' continued Lexi. 'He said he had a solution to the problem and he would be just fine for the next performance.'

'Of course, we had no option but to trust him,' said Orson, shaking his head.

'What was his solution?' asked Boy, intrigued.

There was a long silence. 'He got drunk,' said Lexi, mournfully.

'Stinking drunk,' added Mo.

'He came out on stage like a runaway buffalo,' said Orson.

'But he *could* speak his lines?' asked Boy.

'Oh yes, he could speak his lines,' agreed Lexi. 'But not necessarily in the right order.'

'And mostly when other actors were trying to speak *their* lines,' said Mo.

'In fact, some of the lines he spoke *were* theirs,' added Lexi. 'It was a total disaster.'

'We were left with no alternative,' said Orson. 'We had to give him his marching orders. We felt terrible about it and he wasn't best pleased either, but I explained the situation and he finally accepted that this really wasn't working.'

'We left him in Caderrat,' said Mo. 'In a tavern, drowning his sorrows.'

'So now,' said Lexi, 'we're on tour with *The Sorrows of Young Adamis* and we don't actually have anybody who is capable of playing the title role.'

Just then, Pompio and Grud came back to the fire. Pompio looked at Lexi.

'Have you asked him?' he said.

'I was just about to,' snapped Lexi.

'Go on then.' Pompio stood there with his hands on his tiny hips, glowering. 'Do it now.' Lexi took a deep breath.

'We were wondering . . .' she began.

Boy stared at her. 'Yes?' he murmured.

'We were wondering if maybe *you'd* like to do it,' she said.

'Do it?' Boy stared at her. 'Do what? You don't – you can't mean . . .?'

She nodded. 'We wondered if you would be willing to star in our show,' said Lexi. 'If it's not too much trouble.'

Chapter Five

THE DECISION

THERE WAS a very long silence. Boy laughed. It probably wasn't the reaction they had hoped for but to be fair, they took it well. Maybe he laughed a little too loudly. It echoed around the clearing. When he noticed that everyone else still had sombre expressions on their faces, he stopped laughing.

'You cannot be serious,' he said.

'You wanna bet?' asked Pompio.

'But I'm not an actor!' protested Boy.

'Oh, are you not?' asked Pompio, affecting a look of surprise. 'Well that's a blow! I just naturally assumed you would be. Let's face it, who else is stupid enough to be robbed of everything they own and left for dead in the desert?'

Lexi gave the boobo a sharp look. 'That really isn't helping,' she said.

'I know, but honestly . . .' Pompio scampered closer to Boy and fixed him with an exasperated look. 'Of course you're not a flipping actor! It would be a pretty big coincidence if you were. Let me just explain something. I wasn't an actor either and now, I'm in the show.'

'Yes, but to be fair,' said Boy, 'I'm sure you're not called upon to *act*. I expect you just leap about and make noises, don't you?'

There was a sudden hiss as everybody else around the campfire drew in a sharp breath.

'Oh, I see,' said Pompio. 'I get it. Because I'm a boobo, you don't take me seriously. You think I'm only capable of playing the fool, is that it?'

'Oh, no, of course not. You don't actually act in the play, do you?'

Pompio drew himself up to his full height. 'Well, if you really must know, I play Bartrum – Adamis's closest friend and confidante. It may not be the lead role, but it's more than just a supporting player.' He glanced at Lexi. 'Isn't that so?' he asked.

'Absolutely,' said Lexi. 'Look, Pompio, maybe I should take it from here.'

'I don't like being patronised,' said Pompio. He pointed an accusing finger at Boy. 'I suppose you'd have me turning somersaults and bashing a tambourine, wouldn't you?' He glared across the fire at Orson. 'What did that pamphlet say about my performance last year? Oh, yes. "In the role of Galymeade, Pompio gives a performance that would wring tears from the eyes of a stone idol." *They* certainly didn't suggest I should be capering about bashing a tambourine!'

'Look, I'm sorry,' said Boy. 'I didn't mean to upset you. I'm sure you're very good. All I'm saying is, I don't think I'm the sort of person who's cut out to stand on a stage. What if I turn out to be like that Ninny?'

'Ninian,' Lexi corrected him.

'Yes. What if *I* suffer from stage fright? What happens then?'

'Hopefully you won't,' said Orson soothingly. 'Actually, you come across to me as a very confident, young fellow.'

'Yeah, so did Ninian,' Mo reminded him.

Everyone chose to ignore that comment.

'Let me just say something,' suggested Lexi. 'In two days' time, the Wandering Star Theatre Company are due to appear in the town square of Gallibab, where we are expected to give the good citizens a performance of *The Sorrows of Young Adamis*. If we show up there without an Adamis, we'll probably be lynched. To be honest, we were pretty lucky to get out of Caderrat alive.'

Boy frowned. 'Caderrat?' He murmured.

'The town that witnessed *The Sorrows of Drunken Adamis*,' said Mo helpfully.

'Ah, right.'

'But,' continued Lexi, 'having had to return all the money for our last two shows means that this company is perilously close to going bankrupt. If we don't turn up and perform, we are as good as finished.' She looked at Boy from under her lashes. 'And well, not to put too fine a point on it, we *did* save your life.'

'No pressure,' added Orson.

Boy's mouth hung open. He looked at Lexi in disbelief. 'But you can't say that!' he cried. 'That – that's blackmail!'

'No, it's not,' said Mo. 'It's just well, she's desperate, isn't she? *We're* desperate. We'd like to feel that having given you a bit of a helping hand, you might be willing to return the favour. Look, you don't have to decide anything right now. Why don't we all have something to eat? I bet you're hungry, aren't you?'

Boy nodded. He was more than hungry. His stomach thought his throat had been cut. He asked himself, would the act of sharing their food make him even more indebted to them? After all, he had shared food with Gordimo and Kaleb and look how that had turned out.

'If I eat with you,' he said cautiously, 'I'm not agreeing to anything. I want to make that clear.'

'Of course.' Mo stood up and started giving directions. 'Grud, get an extra bowl for our guest. Pompio, see if you can find him a spoon. Lexi, you can dish up. Oh, and Orson, surely there must be a bottle of wine somewhere in one of the caravans?'

'I'm not having any of that!' shouted Boy, anxiously. He noted their startled looks and softened his tone. 'Water is fine, thank you,' he said. 'I'm on the wagon.'

'Suit yourself,' said Orson.

Everybody busied themselves with their appointed tasks and soon after, Boy was tucking into a bowl of earthy tunnel-rat stew. The hot chunks of food hit his empty belly like a warm hug and he had to make an effort not to moan with the pleasure of it. Glancing sideways, he noted that Lexi had somehow contrived to get the seat right next to him.

'Listen,' he said. 'I hope I haven't come across as difficult, but—'

She looked at him and he saw a terrible sadness in her eyes.

'No, I understand,' she assured him. 'It's a lot to take on and I hope you realise that we wouldn't even dream of asking you if we weren't desperate.' She realised how that sounded and her face flushed a little. 'Oh, I'm sorry, that came out wrong,' she said. 'What I meant was—'

'It's all right,' he assured her. 'I realise I'm nobody's idea of a leading man.'

'Not at all,' she assured him. 'I reckon you look quite presentable.'

'Yes, but that Ninny, you mentioned—'

n. From what you were saying, he was a handsome fellow.'

'Lexi certainly thought so,' said Mo, under her breath. Lexi threw her a scowl.

'Well, he had a certain look,' she admitted. 'The look you associate with a part like that. A hero. Of course, my interest in him was purely professional.'

'Oh, definitely,' said Mo and Lexi shot her another look, before gazing imploringly at Boy.

'You know, you're not so bad yourself.'

Boy might have taken that better if Pompio hadn't sniggered quite so loudly.

'You don't have to flatter me,' he said. 'I know I'm just ordinary.'

'Oh, but you have lovely eyes,' said Mo, gazing across the fire at him. 'And a nice slim build.'

'And a winning smile,' added Orson. 'That always helps.'

'I don't suppose . . .' said Lexi awkwardly. 'I don't suppose you can read at all?'

Boy looked at her indignantly. 'Of course I can read!' he retorted. 'I'm a very good reader. I learned from an early age.'

'Oh, that's definitely an advantage. You'd certainly have no problem learning the script then.'

Boy put down his spoon. 'I thought I made it clear,' he said. 'I haven't agreed to anything yet. I did say that.'

'Yes, of course, but I was only speaking theoretically. As in, *if* you decided you wanted to do the script, you'd have no problem reading it.' She smiled. 'It's actually refreshing to meet somebody who can read. Some people have to learn their lines differently.' She threw a casual glance at Pompio, which didn't go unnoticed.

'You can't expect *me* to read!' he protested. 'I'm a boobo. Most of my lot can't even put two words together, so you should be flipping grateful for what you've got.'

'So how *do* you learn your lines?' Boy asked him, genuinely interested.

'Orson reads them aloud to me and I memorise them,' said Pompio.

'It's an unusual approach,' said Orson, 'but it seems to work.'

Boy picked up his spoon again and took another mouthful of stew. He chewed thoughtfully. 'All right,' he said. 'Tell me about the story,' he suggested.

Lexi studied him for a moment. 'Story?' she muttered.

'The story of your play.'

'Oh, right. Well, obviously it's about young Adamis.'

'And his friend and *confidante*, Bartrum,' chipped in Pompio.

'Yes. Let me tell him, all right?' Lexi gathered her thoughts and continued. 'Adamis is a handsome prince, shortly to become the king of Mycelium. His father – old Adamis – is doomed to an early death by a curse placed on him by the wicked witch, Grimelda.'

'That's me in one of several roles I play,' announced Mo with a wink. 'Mistress of disguise me. I also play—'

'Later!' snapped Lexi, cutting her off in mid flow. 'One day, a magician comes into the royal court – a man called Simister.'

'I play him,' said Grud. 'I have to look evil. It isn't easy.'

'Simister appears to be an honourable man and he promises to lift the curse from old Adamis if, in exchange, he can be allowed to live at the court. Adamis believes him and gives him a fine villa in the palace grounds, but it turns out that Simister is a con artist. He has no magical powers whatsoever. Instead, he steals the crown jewels.'

'Which are priceless,' rumbled Grud. 'Diamonds, emeralds, rubies – a fortune! We've got some prop jewels in the caravan. Would you like to see them?'

'Not right now, Grud,' warned Lexi. She took another moment to gather her thoughts. 'Simister takes Adamis's best horse and flees the palace and when old Adamis learns of this treachery, he collapses and dies.'

'My daughter wrote me a wonderful death scene,' said Orson. 'Seriously, I don't like to boast but—'

'Dad!' Lexi shot him a vexed look.

''Scuse me,' he said, and went back to eating.

'Ahem! Now, where was I? Oh, yes. Adamis vows revenge on the man who deceived him. He and Bartrum saddle some horses and go in pursuit.'

'How will you do that?' asked Boy, mystified.

'I beg your pardon?'

'How will you put two horses on a stage?'

'Oh, we don't, obviously. Adamis and Bartrum mime being on horseback.'

'What's mime?'

'It . . . it's just a technique.'

'I can teach you,' offered Pompio. 'It's dead easy. Honestly, I had it down in five minutes. You just have to *think* you're riding a horse.'

'It's a bit like my story,' murmured Boy.

'Hmm?' Lexi looked at him in surprise. 'How do you mean?'

'Well, you know. I met with some confidence tricksters last night, didn't I? They seemed friendly enough and they took my horse—'

'And your jewels?' asked Grud.

'Er, no, not exactly. I mean, I didn't have any jewels but they took something else that was as good as treasure to me. Something irreplaceable.'

'Really? What was that?' asked Pompio.

'Just something my father gave me.' Boy gestured impatiently to Lexi. 'Please carry on,' he said.

'Right. Well, on his travels,' continued Lexi, 'Adamis meets a mysterious and beautiful young woman called Neve.'

'No prizes for guessing who plays *her*,' muttered Mo.

Lexi flushed a little. 'She is searching for her parents, who were lost in a storm at sea. When she and Adamis meet, it is love at first sight.'

'It's *always* love at first flipping sight,' said Pompio grumpily. 'One day it would be a real novelty if you'd write a play that didn't have such an occurrence.'

'Audiences *like* love at first sight,' argued Lexi. 'It's their favourite thing.'

'Well, we'll never know because it's in every play we do!'

'I can't help it if I have a romantic streak!'

'It's not so much a streak as a flipping background colour.'

'Quiet, Pompio,' snapped Orson. 'Let her finish.'

Pompio went sulkily back to his bowl of food and Lexi pressed on. 'As I was saying, the two of them fall deeply and hopelessly in love. Adamis considers abandoning his quest and taking her back to the palace to be his Queen, but Neve persuades him to carry on with his pursuit of Simister. She tells him that he must avenge his father at all costs and the two of them carry on their pursuit.'

'The *three* of them,' Pompio reminded her. 'Bartrum goes along as well.'

'Yes, the three of them. Finally they meet up with Simister in the city of Bylum . . .'

'And?' prompted Boy.

Lexi gave him a sly look from under her lashes. 'And, what?' she murmured.

'Does Adamis have his revenge? Does he recover his jewels? Do he and Neve become man and wife?'

Lexi took a crust of bread and ran it slowly around the bottom of her empty bowl. She put the bread into her mouth and chewed slowly until she had swallowed it. 'That would be telling,' she said. 'I wouldn't want to spoil it for you.'

Boy stared at her. 'That's not fair,' he protested.

'Perhaps I'll give you a copy of the script tonight,' she suggested, 'and you can read it yourself.'

Boy looked slowly around the campfire, realising that everyone was watching him intently, waiting for his reaction. Finally, he chuckled. 'Very clever,' he said. 'I can see what you're trying to do. But like I said . . .'

'You haven't made your mind up yet,' said Lexi. 'Of course. I get it.' She sighed, put her bowl down beside her, lifted her arms and yawned. You know, I think I'll stretch my legs,' she announced. 'The muscles get cramped from riding around in that caravan all day.'

Boy nodded and set down his empty bowl. 'I feel full of aches myself,' he said. 'I wonder if I might accompany you?'

She looked at him doubtfully. 'Are you sure you're up to it? Your feet . . .'

'If I don't start using them, it'll be harder in the long run,' he said. 'Besides,' he whispered, glancing around the campfire, 'I feel like everyone's sitting there waiting for my decision.'

'I understand.' She stood and put an arm around him to help him upright. He managed it with a grunt of pain.

'Going somewhere?' asked Mo with a smile.

'Just for a walk,' Lexi told her. She led Boy slowly away from the fire as he placed one foot gingerly in front of the other.

'Don't go too far,' Orson warned them. 'This is wolf territory.'

'There are no wolves anymore,' insisted Pompio.

'I'm sure I heard one howling a little while back. You don't want to be caught out in the open when those things are on the hunt.'

'Point taken.' Lexi paused to snatch up a sword from a collection of weapons stacked against her caravan and quickly buckled it around her waist. She looked enquiringly at Boy. 'Want one?' she asked. 'I've got a spare.'

Boy shook his head. 'I wouldn't be much use with it in my condition,' he said. 'If wolves come, I'm afraid you'll have to handle them.'

'Fair enough,' she said. She slipped an arm around him again and they headed into the night.

Chapter Six

AN INTERRUPTION

THE FULL moon hung in the sky, throwing a strange silvery light across the dunes. Boy and Lexi could see for miles in every direction and everywhere they looked appeared to be completely deserted. Boy's feet hurt badly, but he found that with each step he took, the pain grew a little more bearable. Lexi was finally able to withdraw her arm and he could manage something approaching a normal, walking pace. He glanced at her and saw that she appeared to be deep in thought, head bowed and eyes on the ground in front of her.

'So,' said Boy, 'how long have you been doing this?'

She glanced up at him as though surprised to hear his voice.
'Hmm? What, you mean Wandering Star?'

He nodded.

'Pretty much as long as I can remember.' She smiled fondly.
'Some of my earliest memories are of travelling with my parents.
We visited towns and cities all over the known world. I wasn't
acting or writing then, of course, just helping out wherever I
could; fetching, carrying, making props – whatever they needed
from me.'

'Sounds exciting.'

'It was! Of course, the company was a much bigger affair
in those days. We owned a whole string of caravans and there
were twenty actors in the cast. We were acclaimed. My father
was the director and my mother – well, she was the star. Her
performances were famous across the known world. She played
to packed houses everywhere we went. Perhaps you've heard of
her? Velina Cline?'

Boy looked at her in surprise. The name *did* ring a bell from
somewhere. He thought perhaps he had heard Master Titus
mentioning it back in the day. 'Did your mother ever perform
in Serafin?' he asked.

'Oh, yes, many times! The grand theatre there was one of her
favourite venues. I can still remember the dressing room. It was
always filled with orchids whenever she appeared. She had a lot
of admirers. Father used to get so jealous!'

'I'm sure I've heard her name,' said Boy, 'though of course, I would never have been allowed out to see something like that.'

Lexi frowned. 'Why not?' she asked.

'Well, for one thing, I worked in the town stables. There wasn't any free time. They worked us like dogs.' Boy walked on a few more steps, pondering the situation. 'Theatre just wasn't something that figured in my life.' There was an uncomfortable question that needed to be asked. 'So, what happened to your mother?' he asked.

Lexi looked distraught. 'A fever,' she said, and there was a slight tremor in her voice. 'It always starts that way, doesn't it? A fever, that becomes ague, that becomes full-blown plague. We had the finest doctors to attend her but they could do nothing. She wasted away in front of our eyes and was dead within the week.'

Boy swallowed. 'I'm sorry,' he said. 'How long ago was that?'

'Three years,' she said. 'I was thirteen years old when it happened. I had thought she would be with me forever and then she was gone, like a leaf blown on a breeze.' She shook her head. 'My father was devastated by the loss. He had always taken care of the day-to-day running of Wandering Star, but my mother was the driving force, the name that drew in the crowds. At first, he spent his time in the taverns drinking himself to death, but somehow, I managed to persuade him to keep going. I eventually took over my mother's duties. The acting first and later, when we couldn't afford to pay professionals, the writing. Of course, I can never be the star that she was, but I like to think I do a decent enough job of both tasks.'

'I'm sure you do. Your father said—'

'Fathers tend to say good things about daughters, don't they? I don't know if he's not just being kind.'

'Oh, I'm sure you're good.'

'Well, perhaps soon you'll be able to judge for yourself.' She waved a hand to change the subject. 'Naturally, with my mother gone, our fortunes soon began to fade. We found ourselves booked into smaller and smaller theatres. People that had wanted us back every year when my mother was the star, were not so loyal. The rich merchants and royalty who had patronised us, started looking elsewhere.' She shook her head. 'In just three years, we have come to our present sorry state. Now, all we have is what you saw around that campfire. Two dilapidated caravans and the strangest bunch of actors the world has ever seen. Sometimes, I think we are fighting against the inevitable, that we should just pack it in and find something else to occupy us.'

'Oh, I don't know,' said Boy, trying to sound cheerful. 'The world would be a sorry place without travelling players to perk it up, wouldn't it?'

She gave him a thin smile. 'That's good coming from somebody who seems to be in no great hurry to team up with us!'

Boy smiled, nodded. 'I take your point, but you must understand. This is unfamiliar to me. You've been in the world of theatre since you were a child. I only know horses. Ask me the best way to saddle one, to feed it, exercise it and I'll give you an answer straight away. But ask me who played what part in which production and I wouldn't have an idea where to start.'

'That doesn't matter,' she assured him. 'I'm asking you to try being an actor, not to compose a history of it.'

'Even so, I feel out of my depth.'

'You can't always have been a stable boy,' she reasoned.

'No, of course not. I came from a prosperous family but like you, I lost them. They died when I still a little boy – my father and mother both.'

She looked mortified. 'I'm sorry,' she said. 'Sometimes we're so busy wallowing in our own troubles, we don't think that others might have had it rough too. What happened to them?'

'They disappeared.'

She raised her eyebrows and was about to comment further, but he cut her short. 'I don't really like to talk about it,' he said. 'Suffice to say that I was orphaned as a child and sent off to an apprenticeship to earn a living. End of story. At least you still have your father.'

'I have what's left of him,' admitted Lexi. 'Ah, but you should have seen him back in the day, Boy! He was young, handsome and dynamic. Poor Orson. He seemed to age twenty years the

day my mother died. It is as though a light within him went out.'
She shook her head as though trying to cast off her mood. 'It
would seem we have much in common, you and I,' she observed.
'You know what? I actually think we'd make a good team.'

He looked at her doubtfully. 'What's that supposed to mean?'

'That we'd be good together on stage. We're around the
same age, aren't we? Neither of us is exactly hideous to look at
and . . . well, you did say you want to go to Ravalan, right?'

'Yes.'

'Well, that's exactly where we're headed! I daresay you'd
rather ride in comfort in one of the caravans than walk all that
way, especially with your feet in such a state. We'll be stopping
off at a couple of towns en route to do performances, but we will
be there for the Moon of Elnis.'

'Yes, but—'

'That's when we're booked to do the big show. I'm sure you'll
want to earn your keep, won't you?'

'There are other ways I could do that,' he told her. 'I could
help with the buffalo and the hunting – stuff like that.'

'The buffalo can look after themselves and Pompio and Grud
take care of the hunting. I bet we'd even find a pair of boots to
fit you amongst the costumes. All I'm asking is that you give
the idea proper consideration. I mean, what are you afraid of?'

'Who said I'm afraid?' he cried.

'Well you're certainly acting like you are!'

Boy opened his mouth to give her a piece of his mind but she suddenly reached out a hand to still him. 'Shush!' she hissed. 'Did you just hear something?'

He frowned, listened for a moment and shook his head.

'Don't think so,' he said. 'What sort of—'

'Quiet. Listen!'

He did as she asked him. There *was* something, he decided; a strange muted rumbling sound that seemed to be coming from somewhere deep beneath them.

'What *is* that?' he murmured. 'It sounds like—' He broke off mid-sentence. He could sense a vibration against the soles of his blistered feet, gentle at first but rapidly growing more agitated. He opened his mouth to speak again but in that instant, the ground in front of him erupted in a great explosion of sand. Something huge emerged from the earth and reared up in front of them – a long, scaly shape with a bulbous head and two, glowing red eyes that seemed to glitter malevolently in the moonlight. A massive pair of jaws opened and the head came thrusting towards Boy in a mesmerising blaze of speed. He had the briefest glimpse of a pulsing red throat fringed by rows of glittering teeth. He stood there, frozen in position, unable to move a single muscle as certain death came racing towards him.

A hand grabbed him by his collar and he was thrown down hard onto the sand. Lexi's body crashed on top of him and rolled to one side. As he lay there, watching in mute terror, she twisted onto her knees. One hand flew to the hilt of the sword at her side and pulled it effortlessly from its scabbard. In one sinuous move, she drove the blade of the sword upwards into the creature's massive body as it continued its lunge. The sharp point slid deep into scaly flesh and as the beast lurched onwards, the blade cleaved a deep furrow along the length of its body.

From somewhere up above, there was a deafening bellow of pain and the sword was wrenched from Lexi's hand. The creature coiled and twisted spasmodically on the sand, green blood spraying from the wound. Lexi grabbed Boy's arm and pulled him to his feet. She led him in a breathless run across the sand. They looked back, trying to catch their breath. Only now could Boy see the full size of their attacker.

It was a sand serpent, some fifteen or twenty feet in length – a great silvery whip of a beast. Boy had seen them before, of course, but only ever at a distance, plunging in and out of the dunes. This one was still too close for comfort, writhing and shuddering in agony as its blood spilled out onto the sand. Boy turned to look at Lexi in amazement. She was watching the creature's death throes in silence, her face expressionless. There was a smear of green down one cheek.

'I hate those things,' she said, quietly.

Three figures came running from the direction of the campfire, weapons at the ready. There wasn't much that needed to be done now, but Pompio lifted his bow and sent an arrow deep into one of the serpent's eyes, stilling its frantic struggles. Its head fell abruptly sideways, jaws gaping as it dribbled saliva.

'You all right?' asked Orson.

Lexi nodded. 'Those things are always solitary,' she told him. 'Panic over.' She walked slowly back to the carcass, took the hilt of her sword in one hand and with an effort, pulled the blade free. She wiped it clean of gore in the sand and returned it to its scabbard.

Grud came over to Boy. 'What about you?' he asked.

Boy was still trying to find words. He pointed at Lexi in astonishment. 'She . . . handled it,' he said. 'I didn't even know what was happening.'

Grud chuckled. 'She's good with a sword is Lexi,' he agreed. 'Very fast. Saved my neck a few times.'

Pompio stood looking at the serpent's still carcass, his hands on his hips.

'Just our luck,' he complained. 'It's huge but totally inedible.'

'Next time, I'll try and kill something tastier,' said Lexi, matter-of-factly. She strolled back over to Boy. 'Are you all right?'

He nodded. 'Now I can't say no, can I?' he murmured.

She looked puzzled for a moment but then she grinned. 'You mean you'll do the play?' she asked him.

He nodded. 'You've saved my neck twice,' he said. 'How can I refuse? I'll give it my best shot.'

'Yes!' She stepped closer and impulsively kissed him on the

cheek. 'Thank you so much!' she cried. 'This means a lot.' She ran after Orson who was already heading back to the caravans, shouting for him to wait. He stopped for a moment and then the two of them walked on, chatting animatedly. Boy stood there, slightly stunned by what had just happened. He lifted a hand to touch his fingers to his cheek.

Grud chuckled. 'Welcome to the company,' he said.

Chapter Seven

READ THROUGH

THE CARAVAN rumbled slowly onwards along the straight, desert road. Lexi sat at the reins, seemingly lost in thought and Boy was slumped at the other end of the buckboard, doing his level best to read a handwritten script she'd presented him with at breakfast. It was, he realised, too late to reconsider last night's decision. He knew he really ought to be spending his time drawing up plans to get back the *Book of Secrets*, but told himself that, for now, he'd just have to put it out of his mind for a while. It was difficult to concentrate on the script because Pompio sat between him and Lexi, staring intently at Boy as he read.

'What do you think?' he muttered. It was about the eighth time he'd asked the question and Boy was starting to get irritated. 'Good, isn't it?'

'It seems to be,' said Boy shortly.

'What do you mean, "seems to be"? Either it is or it isn't.'

'If I could just have a few moments' peace and quiet, I might be able to come up with a stronger opinion,' said Boy grumpily.

'Ooh, touchy,' muttered Pompio. 'I'm only trying to help.'

'I'm sure you are,' said Boy, 'but . . .'

'Listen, if you want me to read through one of the scenes with you, you only have to ask.' Pompio lifted a hand and examined the nails on it. 'Of course, I already know the script word-for-word.'

'This is the first time I've seen it,' Boy reminded him.

'I know that! All I'm saying is some people are quick learners and others take longer. So, you know, if you're a bit slow at that sort of thing, I can always—'

'Pompio, maybe you should go and chat to Grud in the other caravan,' suggested Lexi.

'Oh no, I'm fine,' Pompio assured her.

She turned her head and fixed him with a certain look.

'Ah, right,' said Pompio. 'I get the picture. Don't worry, I know when I'm not wanted.' He jumped to his feet, clambered across Lexi's lap and swung himself nimbly down to the road.

'Catch you later,' he called and promptly disappeared. Boy offered Lexi a grateful smile.

'Thanks,' he said. 'I appreciate it.'

'No worries. Pompio is great in small doses, but he never can tell when he's starting to grate on people's nerves.'

'How did you come by him?' asked Boy, setting the script aside for a moment.

She looked doubtful. 'You really want to know?'

'Yes, I'm interested.'

'We did a show in Gullamir a few years back. Big fishing port. There was a travelling carnival visiting at the same time and I went along to have a look.'

'Sizing up the competition?' asked Boy.

'Pretty much. They had Pompio dressed in a red waistcoat and a fez, dancing for coins at the entrance to their tent. There was a leash around his neck and whenever the owner didn't feel he was dancing energetically enough, he would come over with a whip to offer some encouragement.' She shook her head and Boy could see the anger in her eyes at the memory of it. 'When he was struck, Pompio didn't just yelp, like a normal beast. He protested, very loudly. In words. I was fascinated. I'd seen boobos before, of course, but I didn't know they could learn to speak like humans.'

'Me neither,' admitted Boy. 'First I've ever seen.'

'It's pretty rare. Apparently, pirates keep them as pets and a few can pick up the odd phrase but Pompio's skills were already way beyond that. Anyway, I asked his owner why he wasn't putting Pompio's talents to better use, maybe encouraging him to sing or recite poems in the main tent. The man told me to mind my own damned business, unless I fancied a taste of the whip myself.'

'Sounds like a charmer.' said Boy.

'A real treasure. He also said he didn't care for my sort and if he had his way, we'd be banned from visiting places like his.'

Boy was baffled. 'What did he mean . . . your sort?' he asked.

Realisation dawned in her green eyes. 'Oh, of course, you probably don't know,' she exclaimed. She reached up a hand and removed the shapeless cap from her head. Her long hair tumbled free, framing her face and hanging to her shoulders. The hair was dyed a vibrant shade of purple, but that wasn't the biggest surprise; just before it fell into place, Boy caught a glimpse of the ear that was closest to him. He couldn't help but notice that it was long and slightly pointed at the top.

'You're elvish!' he cried.

'Yes.' She looked at him apprehensively. 'Is it a problem?'

'Of course not. Why would it be?'

She shrugged. 'A lot of people don't like us,' she said. 'Oh, they don't always say anything, but you can see it in their eyes. A look of superiority.'

'I'm no bloodliner,' he assured her. 'I was just surprised, that's all. You never mentioned it to me.'

'No, but then you never told me you were human, did you?'

He smiled. 'Fair point,' he said. He thought for a moment. 'Orson looks entirely human, so I'm guessing it must have come from your mother's side of the family?'

She smiled. 'Yes, didn't I say that she was a pureblood elf? I usually do, I'm quite proud of it. A lot of creative people are elvish, you know. It's supposed to be in our blood.'

Boy nodded, and then remembered what they'd been talking about earlier. 'So what did you say to Pompio's owner?'

'I didn't *say* anything. I knocked him flat on his back.'

Boy stared at her. 'You didn't!' he cried.

'Oh, yes I did and when he came to, I told him I'd give him a gold crown in exchange for Pompio. At first, he said that wasn't enough, so I told him if he didn't make the deal, I'd spread the word that the owner of the carnival had been knocked off his feet by a fifteen-year-old girl. He said, maybe he should get up and give me a taste of my own medicine. I said he was welcome to try, which is when he backed down and agreed to the deal. I gave him a crown, I took Pompio away with me and he's been in the company ever since.'

Boy laughed. 'Remind me never to get on the wrong side of you,' he told her.

'Well, I hate to see cruelty of any kind,' said Lexi. 'And Pompio just seemed a natural fit for us. Once you get used to the way he looks, you have to admit he *can* act. Besides, to tell you the truth, we still make use of his original skills.'

'Do you?'

'Yes. Whenever we approach a new town we dress him up in a red waistcoat and send him in ahead of us to announce our arrival. He's very good at drawing a crowd.'

'I bet he is.' Boy chuckled. He picked up the script again and continued reading for a moment, but then another thought occurred to him. 'What about Grud?' he asked.

She grinned. 'I thought you wanted to read?' she reminded him.

'I do, but . . . I'm interested. Where did you meet up with him?'

'We found him begging on a street in Yamclatz. Of course, he's originally from the island of Faravelia. Have you heard of it?'

Boy shook his head.

'They're all giants there. Would you believe me if I told you that Grud was always considered the runt of his family?'

'Seriously?'

'Yup. He got a lot of stick about his short stature back home.'

'But he must be seven feet tall!'

'That's true, but that didn't stop everyone in Faravelia referring to him as "titch". Faravelians are also known for their fierce natures and as I'm sure you've noticed, Grud is as soft as a brush. He fell out with his father and his siblings and ran away from home. Of course, here on the mainland, people were just terrified of him. Whenever he approached them – asking for food, looking for work, begging for help – they'd run away screaming. He ended up starving on the streets.'

Boy studied her for a moment. 'But you saw the other side of him?'

Lexi shook her head. 'Oh, that was Dad, more than me. He found Grud begging outside of a tavern one evening and gave him a couple of gelts. The two of them got chatting. Dad was surprised to find that Grud was so gentle and naive. It occurred to him that he'd make a useful addition to the company. He makes a really convincing villain as long as he keeps his mouth shut and he's great whenever we need somebody to do some heavy lifting.' She grinned. 'He can be very useful when somebody is slow to pay what they owe us. We always send him around to collect the money. They take one look at Grud and suddenly, they remember that they've got coins stashed away somewhere.'

'Looks can be deceptive,' admitted Boy. 'I was terrified the first time he spoke to me.' He smiled. The more he talked to Lexi, the more he found to like about her.

'What about Mo?' he wondered.

'Never mind Mo. What about this script?' She reached over and tapped the pages of parchment with an index finger. 'You need to have that memorised by tonight.'

'Oh, go on, she's the only one I still don't know anything about. Tell me her story and I promise I'll go on reading.'

Lexi sighed. 'Well, all right. Mo has been with us since the early days. She was my mother's wardrobe assistant, back when we actually had a budget for that kind of thing. She was devoted to my parents. Travelled the world with them. She was there when I was born and she was heartbroken when Mum died. She stayed with the company even as its fortunes dwindled. Over the years, her role changed. She took on acting parts whenever we needed her. Turned out she had hidden talents, though even now she's still the first person to go to if you tear your costume or lose a button. She's still hopelessly devoted to Dad.' She gave Boy a knowing look.

'What? Oh, you mean . . .'

She nodded. 'He doesn't see it. Mum was so glamorous; she enchanted everyone she came into contact with. It's as though she blinded Dad to anyone else.'

'Does he even suspect?' asked Boy.

Lexi snorted. 'No. He's totally self-centred. Can't see what's right under his nose. Mo wouldn't dream of saying anything to him. She's far too respectful of my mother's memory.'

'What do *you* think?' asked Boy.

'Me? I just want Dad to be happy but somehow, I suspect he never will be.'

'That's a shame,' admitted Boy. 'He seems a nice fellow.'

'He is, really.' She seemed to consider for a moment. 'What about *your* parents?' she asked him. 'Were *they* happy?'

'I believe they were. The last memory I have of them, is that they were laughing and looked as though they were very much in love.' He felt his cheeks colour and looked away from her. 'That probably sounds dreadfully slushy,' he said.

'Not at all. It's nice that you remember them that way.' She tapped the script again. 'And don't forget, it *is* a romance you're reading.'

'Yes, I wanted to ask you about that,' he said.

'Oh really?' She sat a little taller in her seat and fluttered her eyelashes. 'You wanted to ask me how I can possibly write such a brilliant script at such a tender age?'

'Umm. No, not exactly.'

She frowned. 'That was a joke, by the way,' she assured him. 'I'm not *that* conceited.'

'I hope not. I mean, I'm sure you're not.' He waved a hand at the page. 'I was just reading this scene between Adamis and Neve.'

'Me and you,' offered Lexi, helpfully.

'Er, absolutely. Us. It occurred to me that some of this talking—'

'Dialogue.'

'I'm sorry?'

'We call it dialogue.'

'Ah, right. Well, it occurred to me that some of it is . . .'

'Yes?'

'Kind of hard to say.'

She glared at him. 'How do you mean?' She sounded annoyed.

'Well, no offence, but . . .' He pointed at the page in front of him. 'here – where I'm supposed to say this, "how now, me proud, tempestuous beauty! Would's't thou not look upon me more favourably? For I am smitten and would'st—"'

'"Follow thee to the ends of eternity,"' she finished proudly. 'Yeah, what's wrong with that?'

He had the impression he was venturing out onto thin ice but decided to press on regardless. 'I don't really understand what he's saying.'

'That's because it's in theatre-speak,' explained Lexi.

'Is it?'

'Yes. That's how you're supposed to talk on stage. That's written in the style of Boldimo, that is.'

'Boldimo?'

'Yes, the great playwright, Boldimo! Boldimo of Seduticon.' She looked at his blank expression as though he had somehow disappointed her. 'Don't tell me you've never heard of him. He's famous!'

'Not in the stables of Serafin, he isn't.'

She scowled. 'Well, maybe not, but trust me, he's the most acclaimed playwright that ever lived. They say he'll be taught in schools in years to come.'

'That may be so but I can't really make head nor tail of this. Do your audiences understand it?'

'Well, most of them. That's just the way theatre's done.'

'But what does this bit actually *mean*?'

'Isn't it obvious?'

'Not really.'

'I suppose what he's saying is something like, "Hey, Neve! What's happening with you? My, but you are looking good today. I just wish you'd turn those eyes in my direction, once in a while, because you know what? I would go to the ends of the earth for you!" See? Simple.'

'Oh, right.' He looked at her. 'Then why not just say that in the first place?'

She was staring at him now, as though horrified. 'Nobody has *ever* talked like that on the stage!' she cried. 'It's just not done.'

'I see,' he said. He thought for a moment. 'Why not?'

'Because – because of tradition. Centuries of tradition. Theatre isn't supposed to resemble real life, you know.'

'I don't get it. We're pretending to be real people, aren't we?'

'Well, yes, in a way . . .'

'So, wouldn't it make sense for us to speak *like* real people?'

She seemed to ponder his suggestion. 'It's . . . radical,' she said. 'Is it?'

'It would be. I don't know what Boldimo would have to say about it.'

'Maybe we could ask him?'

She looked at him scornfully. 'He's been dead for decades,' she told him.

'Oh, so he couldn't really object then?'

'It's not so much that he would object. He'd be outraged by the daring of it,' she said. 'I mean to say, actors talking like real people! What would that be like?'

'Helpful?' suggested Boy. 'For your audiences.'

She gave him a look. 'Let me think about it for a moment,' she said. 'I mean, of course I *could* simplify Adamis's lines to make it easier for you to understand them, but we couldn't have just one character talking like that. That would look absolutely ridiculous. No, we'd have to encourage *everyone* to do it.'

'Look, I don't want to be any trouble,' said Boy. 'It was just a silly thought off the top of my head and you know, I have my own problems to worry about – like finding those two men who robbed me and getting my stuff back.'

'No, wait a minute – just let me think about this.' She was staring straight ahead with a misty-eyed expression. 'You know, when you put it that way, it *does* sound ridiculously simple. It's never been done, to my knowledge, but . . . maybe that's a good thing.'

'Really? Why do you—?'

'Maybe it would give us an edge over the competition.' She pondered for a moment longer. 'Let me think now. What's my next line? Ah yes, "oh bold Adamis, methinks you hath stepped outside the boundaries of acceptable taste. I am a noble woman of renown." So that would be something like . . .' She took a deep breath and readied herself. "". . . hey Adamis, I reckon you've gone a bit too far this time. I'm a princess, me, I don't take that kind of guff from a chancer like you!"' Her eyes widened and she laughed at her own words. 'You know what?' she gasped, 'I think you might have something! It's certainly closer to real life and when you think about the kind of audiences we're playing to these days – people in market squares, builders, traders – maybe it would speak more directly to them.'

'Look, this is beginning to sound like a lot of work,' reasoned Boy. 'I've got my own stuff to worry about.'

Lexi was warming to the idea. 'We could go over the script tonight when we make camp. There wouldn't be time for a proper rewrite but I suppose we could tell everyone . . .' She pulled a face.

'Tell them what?' he prompted her.

'To write their own lines,' she said and looked as though she couldn't quite believe what she was saying. 'It might just work.' She waved a hand at him. 'What's next in the script?' she asked him. 'We'll run a few more lines.'

He looked at the pages. 'Oh,' he said quietly.

'What's wrong?'

He pointed to the page. 'It just says, "they kiss,"' he murmured.

Neither of them spoke for a long time after that.

Chapter Eight

CONTROVERSY

'**H**ANG ON a minute!' cried Pompio. 'Are you telling us that you want to change the entire flipping script? By tomorrow? Just because *he* suggested it?' He pointed a finger accusingly at Boy, who was sitting on a boulder and doing his level best to blend into the scenery.

It was night-time again and the company was sitting around the campfire, waiting for the stew to be ready. On the long, slow journey there, Lexi and Boy had worked their way methodically through the entire script, making suggestions for how the lines might be improved. As Boy had feared, the moment Lexi casually announced their idea to the assembled company, things began to kick off and, predictably, it was Pompio who was doing most of the kicking.

'I know that script by heart,' he continued. 'It took me *ages* to memorise it.'

'I appreciate that,' said Lexi. 'And nobody knows better than me how hard you worked on it. Look, Boy and I were chatting and he just came up with this suggestion. I'll admit it sounded ridiculous at first, but the more I thought about it, the more it seemed to make perfect sense.'

'So let me get this straight,' said Mo, furrowing her brow. She was sitting on the far side of the fire, stitching a tear in the sleeve of a tunic. 'The main idea is to just rip up the script?'

'Well, not literally,' said Boy.

'Less than twenty-four hours before we're due to perform it?'

'I know it sounds like a tall order,' admitted Lexi. 'I'm not pretending it isn't, but the story won't change. The only real difference is that we'll say exactly the same things but in everyday speech. For instance, Pompio, you have the opening lines of the play, do you not? Remind us of them.'

Pompio made a face. 'What's the point if you're going to change them?' he protested.

'Just humour me,' suggested Lexi.

'If you insist.' He clambered up onto the nearest boulder, took a moment to gather his thoughts and then looked proudly around at his companions. 'Good citizens of the fair town of . . .' He paused. 'Where are we playing tomorrow?' he asked.

'Gallibab,' said Mo.

'Ah yes. Good citizens of the fair town of Gallibab, I pray you listen with the greatest concentration. I bring you a story of high adventure and tempestuous romance! An epic saga of mystery and derring-do. My mellifluous saga concerns the tumultuous fortunes of handsome Prince Adamis, who lived in the distant and fabled city of Mycelium. I know him intimately for I was his closest friend and confidante . . .'

Lexi lifted a hand to still him. 'All right,' she said. 'Thank you, Pompio, very nicely done. Now, Boy will show you how it might be performed.'

'He'll *what*?'

'Trust me. Boy?'

'Look, I really don't want to cause any—'

Lexi waved a hand in dismissal. 'Show him what we mean.'

'Oh, very well.' Boy got up from the boulder. He was suddenly aware that everyone was staring at him with apparent resentment. 'We're suggesting that we do it more like this,' he said. He took a deep breath. 'People of Gallibab. Listen up! I have for you a tale of adventure and romance – of mystery and wonder. It's about my best mate Adamis, Prince of Mycelium. He trusts me with all his secrets . . .' Boy waved a hand. 'And so on,' he said.

Pompio glared at him. 'And so on?' he cried. 'Great galloping custard!'

Lexi sighed. 'You have a problem?'

'I'll say I have a problem! He's cut most of my flipping lines and he's got me talking like . . . like some oik in the street.'

'That's exactly the point,' said Lexi. 'Why not make it more realistic?'

'It's not meant to be realistic,' retorted Pompio. 'It's *theatre*.'

'Yes, but don't you think that lately we've been losing the audience a bit?'

Pompio gave her a withering look. 'Well, let me see. Could that be because we had somebody in the lead role who couldn't put two flipping words together?' he snapped. 'A great, big lunk who you were convinced was destined to be the next big star of the stage, but who turned out to be as useful as a mallet made of jelly?' He nodded at Boy. 'As for Sonny Jim there, he's an unknown quantity. We don't even know if he can act! He's only been here ten flipping minutes and you're asking us to put our faith in him?'

'To be fair, she isn't asking anything of the kind,' said Boy. 'Look, this has got out of hand. I just made a suggestion. I honestly didn't think she'd take it as seriously as she—'

'Do we still get to use the fake treasure?' asked Grud, looking concerned.

'Of course we do,' said Lexi. 'That'll be just the same.'

'Yes!' said Grud, a big smile on his face. 'I like the fake treasure.'

'Nothing else would change,' Lexi assured them. 'Only the dialogue.'

'Only the dialogue,' snarled Pompio. 'The most important bit!'

'Yes,' said Lexi, 'but think about it for a moment. We used to perform for royalty, didn't we? For rich merchants and those of noble birth. These days, who makes up our audiences? Ordinary people. People for whom fancy language is simply an obstacle.' Lexi looked across the fire at her father. 'Dad, you haven't said anything yet. What do *you* think?'

Orson frowned and looked down at his feet. 'As I understand it,' he said. 'You're suggesting that we simply dispense with centuries of tradition. That we just bundle it up and throw it away like an unwanted mitten.'

'Well, I—'

'You're saying that all those pioneers of theatre who have gone before us were wrong; that they were selling audiences a lot of high-minded drivel.'

'I wasn't exactly—'

'You are telling me that everything your Mother did in the finest theatres of the known world is now meaningless.'

'Oh Dad, I really don't mean that. I just—'

'Well, Lexi, I'll tell you exactly what I think of this idea.' He stared at her for several moments. 'I love it.'

There was a moment of shocked silence.

'You do?' whispered Lexi. The expression on her face suggested she thought she'd misheard him. 'You actually like the idea?'

'It's brilliant,' said Orson, getting to his feet and for the first time since he'd met him, Boy saw something approaching excitement on his grizzled face. 'For too long now the Wandering Star Theatre Company has been struggling desperately to recapture past glories, striving for the impossible. Times are changing and by gosh, if we are to survive, then we need to change with it. So I say, yes, yes and yes again! Let's take that tired, old script by the scruff of its neck and shake it until it cries for mercy!'

'Hear, hear!' said Mo, clapping her hands. She was gazing up at the old man with adoration in her eyes and Boy asked himself how Orson could remain oblivious to her love.

Pompio glared at her. 'You too?' he cried. 'You approve of them taking lines away from me? This is a conspiracy.'

'Oh, Pompio, you nitwit, nobody is taking anything from you!'

'They're not?'

'No. When you think about it, they are only giving you a chance to shine.'

'They are?' Pompio looked bewildered. 'How do you make that out?'

'Just think about it for a moment! Think what a wonderful improviser you are. Never short of a witty remark. Always the first to speak your mind. A reworked script will be giving you the ultimate freedom. You'll finally be able to be yourself.'

Pompio looked as though he'd just had a revelation. 'I hadn't thought of it like that,' he admitted. 'You're saying I get to write my own lines?'

'Yes,' said Lexi. 'We all do. You know, I'm very excited about this. I wouldn't be surprised if in years to come, this style of theatre starts a whole new movement. We should probably think of a name for it.'

Boy had an idea. 'Well, since we have everyone acting more naturally,' he said. 'Maybe we could call it "naturalism".'

Everyone looked at him for a moment. They all shook their heads.

'That'd never catch on,' said Lexi.

'And we still get to use the fake treasure?' asked Grud, just wanting to be sure.

Lexi laughed. 'Yes, Grud,' she assured him. 'That stays exactly the same. Now, everyone, you all have a copy of the script. I want you to study it and think about how you might alter your lines to suit this new approach. Tomorrow will be our chance to try it out and we need to be the best we've ever been. Pompio, why don't you go and get that bottle of wine we've been saving for a special occasion? I think we should all drink to our new direction.' She glanced warily at Boy. 'That's if you're not still on the wagon,' she murmured.

'I suppose one drink can't hurt,' he said, cautiously. Pompio scampered away to get the bottle and some goblets. 'I hope we're doing the right thing,' said Boy, awkwardly. 'When I made that suggestion, I never dreamed it would go as far as this.'

'But that's the way us theatre people are,' Lexi assured him. 'Seize the day! Isn't that what people tell you all the time?'

'I don't think anyone's ever said that to me,' muttered Boy.

Orson came around from the far side of the fire and gave his daughter a fierce hug. 'We'll have our work cut out getting this ready,' he admitted, 'but I believe we can do it and you know what? For the first time in ages I feel genuinely challenged.' He released her and turned to look at Boy. 'It seems as though we have our newest member to thank for this!'

Boy looked at him in surprise. He hadn't thought of himself as a member of the company, just somebody looking for a ride to Ravalan – somebody who had his own pressing reasons for getting there.

'What about it, lad?' asked Orson. 'Are you ready for your first foray into the world of the theatre?'

Boy grimaced. 'Ready as I'll ever be,' he said, and decided to leave it at that.

Chapter Nine

GALLIBAB

LEXI PULLED the caravan to a halt on top of a hill and gestured to the town that lay below them on the banks of a winding river. It was still early and the water glittered enticingly in the morning sunlight.

'There's Gallibab,' announced Lexi. Boy lifted his head from the script and stared apprehensively down. It looked like a perfectly ordinary town. Situated on the very edge of the desert, it comprised a few imposing, stone buildings, arranged around a cobbled square where a collection of canvas-covered, market stalls were already doing a bustling trade. Further back from the centre, rows of more modest dwellings clustered tightly together in a half circle, as though keeping each other company. Even at this distance, Boy could see that workmen were putting the finishing touches to something in the very middle of the square – a roughly constructed, wooden stage. He pointed.

'Is that for us?' he asked, trying, but totally failing, to keep the trepidation out of his voice.

'It is,' said Lexi. 'Don't worry, it's not a scaffold.' She chuckled but when he didn't join in, she added, 'you're not nervous, are you?'

'No,' said Boy, quietly and wished he felt more confident than he actually did.

'Good. Just promise me you won't do a Ninian on me.'

'I'll try not to.'

'Excellent. Pompio? Are you ready?'

'I was *born* ready,' said Pompio, clambering out of the caravan, where he had been changing his clothes. He was dressed in a bright, red waistcoat and fez and carried a large tambourine. Boy felt a smile twitching at the corners of his mouth and Pompio gave him a warning look. 'Don't say anything. I know how ridiculous this looks.'

Boy shook his head. 'I was just going to say how smart it is,' he lied. 'I was thinking maybe you should dress like that more often.'

'Ignore him,' Lexi advised the boobo. 'We've about an hour before we perform, so maybe you should start working the crowd.'

'Leave it to me,' said Pompio, confidently. 'I'll get 'em all riled up.' He leapt nimbly from the caravan and scampered away along the trail. Boy watched him go, wishing he could feel as fearless. Still, he told himself, he'd made no secret of the fact that he wasn't an actor, so the other members of the company could hardly complain if his efforts didn't amount to very much. Could they?

Footsteps came from behind and Orson appeared beside the caravan. He stared thoughtfully down at Gallibab.

'A decent town this one,' he told Boy. 'I seem to remember we went down fairly well the last time we visited. We even managed to make a small profit.' He studied Boy for a few moments. 'Now, lad, I can see you're nervous, so I'm going to share a little trick that we actors use to make ourselves feel more confident.'

'All right,' said Boy. 'I'm listening.'

'When we get down there and you clamber up onto that stage . . .'

'Yes?'

'. . . and the audience is all gathered around watching you intently, just waiting for you to make a mistake . . .'

Boy swallowed and nodded. If this was meant to be making him more confident, it really wasn't working.

'. . . at that precise moment, I want you to picture everyone in the audience naked.'

★ 98 ★

Boy stared at him. 'Naked?' he croaked.

'Absolutely.'

'And that helps, does it?'

'Always works for me,' said Orson and with that, he headed back towards the other caravan. 'I reckon there's time for a cup of coffee before we head into town,' he shouted over his shoulder.

Boy looked questioningly at Lexi. 'Naked?' he muttered again.

Lexi shrugged. 'Dad went to drama school,' she said, as though that explained everything. 'It doesn't work for everyone. I tried it one time and ended up forgetting half of my lines!' She began to clamber down from the wagon. 'I'll see what bits of firewood we've got left,' she said. 'I don't expect anybody fancies their coffee cold, but we're very low on fuel. We'll need to stock up before we head off to Ninsago.'

'Ninsago?' he echoed.

'Next stop on the way. We've a few gigs booked before we get to Ravalan.'

'But we *will* be there for the Moon of Elnis?' he reminded her.

'Yes, of course. Like I told you, that's the big one.' She gave him a questioning look. 'What's the deal with Ravalan?' she asked him. 'You keep mentioning it.'

'I think the men who robbed me might be heading there.'

'I see. And, er, what exactly did they take from you? You've never said.'

'Oh, just something that belonged to my father.'

'Something valuable?'

'Not exactly. But it means a lot to me.'

She seemed satisfied with that and went around to the back of the caravan. Boy returned his attention to Gallibab. He could see a tiny speck of bright red scampering along the road into town and the sunlight glinted on the metal cymbals of Pompio's tambourine. 'It'll be fine,' he told himself but already, he found himself wishing that his debut performance was over.

★ ★ ★

They rode slowly down the hill and into the town square. Boy had to admit that Pompio had done a pretty good job of pulling in a crowd. There was a noisy cluster of people arranged around the front of the low stage, all jostling each other for the best view. Street traders moved through their ranks, carrying trays of hot snacks and mugs of ale. The caravans pulled to a halt behind the stage. Mo and Orson hurried up into the wings. Pompio climbed the wooden steps at the front and turned to face the audience.

'Come closer, good citizens of Gallibab!' he cried, his voice echoing around the square. 'The Wandering Star Theatre Company has travelled many miles to be with you today. Just allow us a few moments to ready ourselves and our play will begin!'

A ragged cheer went up from the crowd. Pompio moved

quickly into the wings where Mo was waiting with his costume – an embroidered, silk frock coat and a wide-brimmed hat with a colourful feather sticking out of it. Once dressed, he moved to the rear of the stage and shouted down to the caravans where Boy and Lexi were getting ready. 'Come along,' he cried. 'My, but you two are tardy! I've got this lot all worked up and ready for action.'

Boy had been preparing himself in the first caravan, changing into his ill-fitting costume. This comprised a metal breast plate, arm and leg guards and a helmet with a hinged visor. The latter had an unfortunate habit of closing itself whenever he moved his head too vigorously. There was also a huge and rather unwieldy sword hanging in a scabbard at his waist. He managed to clamber clumsily out of the caravan and made his way towards the steps at the back of the stage. Lexi climbed down from the other caravan, dressed in her costume and Boy actually stopped in his tracks and gaped at her. He couldn't help it. He had already known about the long, purple hair, of course, but dressed in a tightly corseted, yellow gown that fitted her slender frame perfectly, she looked like a different person entirely. She had also applied makeup to her face, ringing her eyes with black kohl and painting her lips a deep crimson.

'I don't look that bad, do I?' she asked him.

'You look . . . like a woman,' he said.

'Well, that's something,' she said, and then seemed puzzled. 'What did I look like before? A fish?'

'No, of course not! But now you look...' He struggled to find an appropriate word. 'Now you look... *more!*'

'More what?' she hissed.

'Just ... more.' He made a valiant attempt to change the subject. 'What about me? Do I look all right? This costume is a bit on the generous side.'

'You look very heroic. Are you ready? Pompio is waiting for you onstage.' She lifted a hand and waved to Pompio, presumably the signal for the play to start. 'Listen out for your cue!' she reminded Boy and she moved away into the wings. Boy walked closer to the rear steps, listening intently for the sound of Pompio's voice. The occasional line of dialogue drifted in his direction.

'... his best friend, the one who knows all his secrets...'

Ah yes, that was familiar enough, one of the lines they'd rehearsed the previous night. Any minute now, he'd be expected to walk out onto the stage.

Boy placed a foot on the bottom step and started to climb, horribly aware that his costume was rattling loudly with every move he made. He continued to listen as he went. Pompio's voice was now a little clearer.

'... but where is he? He said he'd meet me here at two o'clock.'

That still wasn't his cue, Boy decided, but it would be coming at any moment. He took another tentative step upwards.

'. . . here he comes now.'

Boy twisted his head around. Was that the cue or simply a few lines before it?

'I said, HERE HE COMES NOW!'

Registering the urgency in Pompio's voice, Boy attempted to hurry up the last few steps, but caught one foot, tripped and went flying onto the stage. He crashed headfirst onto the bare floorboards, making an ear-splitting racket and slid a short distance on his belly. The audience erupted into gales of laughter. Pompio, panicking, slipped back into his next line as originally written.

'Ah, look how trippingly he approaches!' he cried.

Another blast of laughter came from the crowd. Boy attempted to get upright, but the weight of the armour made that a difficult task. He flailed helplessly around for a moment.

'Allow me to help you, my Lord,' improvised Pompio, stepping forward to give him a hand and, as he staggered to his feet, Boy attempted to deliver his first line.

'Ah, Bartrum, how handsome you look today!' he spluttered; at which point, his metal visor swung shut with an almighty clang. The ensuing laughter sounded muffled to his ears, and it didn't feel encouraging. Boy lifted a hand to try and prise the helmet open again but it was momentarily stuck.

'My Lord, where have you been these past few days?' asked Pompio.

Boy obligingly gave him the next couple of lines, but from behind the helmet, all that emerged was a series of unintelligible noises.

'You've been in Mercadia? Studying the local wildlife? That sounds . . . fascinating,' said Pompio and now, the laughter threatened to engulf anything else that was said. 'Here, let me help you with your visor!' improvised Pompio, but because Boy was now standing and Pompio was only a couple of feet in height, the boobo was obliged to leap up onto Boy's shoulders, where he swung his legs around Boy's neck and attempted to open the visor from there, putting all his strength into the task. Boy staggered helplessly around the stage for a few moments, raising his voice in a vain attempt to be heard, until finally, Pompio got the visor open just in time for Boy's next line of dialogue to emerge as a bellow.

'Finally, I can see the dazzling future that lies ahead of me!'

Boy gazed out at his audience in dismay. They were, virtually helpless with laughter, some of them actually having to hold each other up. He tried imagining them naked, but that didn't help one little bit. He just saw a lot of naked people laughing hysterically. He looked towards the side of the stage where Mo and Orson were watching him, open-mouthed in horror. Realising that he had to rescue this somehow, Boy spun quickly around to face the audience, but the suddenness of his movement caused Pompio to slide sideways until his backside was facing the crowd. Worse still, his trousers slipped down at the waist revealing his bare bottom. Boy's next line was spoken into Pompio's belly and once again, the result was little more than a muffled grunt, quickly swamped by another barrage of laughter. Pompio managed to scramble free and drop down to the stage, pulling his trousers up as he did so. He turned back to the audience, clearly confused and shouted the next line he could remember.

'Ah, but here comes your true love, the Lady Neve,' he cried. 'I must go now and stroom my greed – er, groom my steed!' He scampered gratefully off into the wings.

Lexi strode on, clearly determined to rescue the proceedings. 'Ah, my love, how handsome you look today!' she cried.

Boy spun around in surprise and his visor clanged shut again once again making his reply completely unintelligible. Lexi dutifully reached up to try and help him. She managed to prise it back into the open position.

'How I have missed you,' she said. 'What news have you of the stolen treasure?'

At this point, Grud, who had been waiting patiently in the wings, heard his favourite word and – doubtless unsettled by what had already happened onstage – decided it must be a cue. He lumbered out onto the stage, holding an open, wooden chest, stuffed with fake jewels.

'Here it is!' he cried. He stood there grinning down at them.

There was a long moment of indecision while they stood there staring back at him in surprise.

'Er, yes . . .' said Lexi. 'That's . . . exactly like the treasure that the wicked magician, Simister, stole from you. I had this copy made so you could show it to people – so they'd know what it looked like. This helpful giant offered to carry it for me as it's so heavy.'

'I'm good like that!' added Grud.

Boy nodded, then realised his mistake as the visor started to swing down again. He managed to get his fingers in the way just in time and yelped as the tips of them were trapped between those metal jaws. 'Oh, for goodness sake.' He reached up, pulled the helmet forcibly off his head and flung it over his shoulder. 'Sweet Neve, that was very helpful,' he cried. A loud clunk registered behind him, followed by a groan and a thud. He turned in dread to look into the wings and saw Orson, lying flat on his back, the helmet rolling away from him. Mo was looking down at him in surprise.

'Er, sorry!' shouted Boy.

'Never mind that!' said Lexi, trying once again to wrest control of this mess. 'Look at me, Adamis. I said look at me!'

Boy swung back to face Lexi and carried on talking. 'Sorry that you had to go to . . . so much trouble,' he said. 'It's not easy making fake treasure . . .' His voice trailed away and he stared at her in dismay. Somehow, as he'd turned, the long blade of his sword had managed to get hooked into the fabric of her dress and was lifting it up to reveal a pair of bright, red bloomers.

She carried gamely on. 'There is something in the air tonight,' she cried. 'Something that feels magical!'

Once again, the crowds were bellowing with laughter. Boy did his best to disentangle the sword, but in so doing, he managed to snag the delicate fabric of her dress on the jewelled scabbard and ripped it right up the middle. She instinctively grabbed the two halves and pulled them closed around her. 'Alas, I fear I am undone,' she said. It was her next line but it somehow fit perfectly

'Oh, I'm sorry, Princess,' he jabbered, floundering desperately to remember his next line. 'You look like a rose in full bloomers – er, in full bloom. I shall always picture you this way!'

That did it. Anything else they might have said would have been lost in the tidal wave of laughter that spilled out of the crowd and washed over the stage. Boy stood there, looking helplessly out at them, thinking to himself that he clearly wasn't cut out for the theatrical life and in the midst of confusion, something familiar registered with him. A bearded man was leading a black horse across the square by its halter, moving in and out of the crowds. Boy registered instantly why the horse was so familiar to him. It was Belle and the man leading her was Kaleb.

There was an instant of pure shock. Then, Boy acted without thinking.

'Hey, you!' he roared, pointing an accusing finger and the crowd fell suddenly silent. Kaleb turned his head in surprise and looked at the stage. For a moment, his expression remained blank. Then, he recognised Boy and his eyes widened in alarm. He turned back to Belle and began to scramble up into the saddle. Boy acted without thinking. A short distance from the stage he spotted a wooden cart from which somebody was attempting to sell nuts. Boy ran forward and took a flying leap, slammed one foot onto the wooden boards of the cart and pushed down hard, propelling himself through the air. He sailed over the heads of the nearest onlookers and crashed into Kaleb, knocking him clean out of the saddle. The two men tumbled over Belle's flanks and hit the ground hard, the impact momentarily slamming the breath out of Boy.

Kaleb was up first and he started to make a run for it, but Boy hurled himself desperately forward, threw his arms around Kaleb's lower legs and brought him to the ground. Kaleb twisted around and aimed a punch at Boy's face, catching him with a powerful blow on his left temple. Boy momentarily saw a flurry of stars whirling in all directions and collapsed onto his back. Kaleb got to his feet and advanced, his hands bunched into fists, a grim smile on his face. 'You should have died in the desert,' he snarled. His smile dissolved in an instant when a huge hand came out of nowhere, grabbed him by his collar and lifted him clean off his feet. Boy looked up in surprise and realised that Grud had followed him off the stage and had come to his assistance. Kaleb hung there, kicking and thrashing strenuously, but Grud held him in a powerful grip and would not let him go.

'You bad man,' he growled. 'You hit my friend.'

Boy got himself upright and moved unsteadily closer, shaking his head to dispel the fog inside it. 'You stole my horse!' he snapped. 'You stole my boots. You stole everything I had.' There was a loud gasp then and for a moment, Boy was puzzled. Then, he realised it had come from the audience, who were still watching intently, as though they thought this was all part of the show. 'Where is my apparatus?' cried Boy.

'Yes,' yelled a voice in the crowd. 'Where is his apparatus?'

'Gordimo took that!' snapped Kaleb, still struggling to free himself. 'The two-faced serpent double-crossed me. He got me drunk and ran out on me last night. Took all the money we got from you. It's a wonder he left me a horse and a canteen of water.'

'You fell for the same trick as me?' cried Boy.

'You fell for the same trick as him?' shouted several voices and Kaleb looked around in surprise, but Boy carried on regardless.

'That was careless, wasn't it? Right, I'm taking back my horse.' He looked at Kaleb's feet. 'And my boots,' he said.

'I'll get them,' said a voice beside him, and Boy saw that Lexi had also come down from the stage. She hurried forward to pull the boots off Kaleb's feet. She managed to remove them and threw them to the ground. Boy turned back to Belle and gave her a reassuring pat on the neck. 'Good girl,' he said. 'You're safe with me now.' He noticed that there were fresh scars across her withers and he turned back to glare at Kaleb. 'You've used a whip on her!' he cried.

'I had to. She was disobedient.' Kaleb struggled again. 'You need to teach a horse who is the master.'

'No you don't,' snarled Boy. He turned back to Belle and now his gaze moved from her scarred flanks to the saddle, where another shock awaited him. It was one he'd never seen before. He span back to look at Kaleb. 'Where's my saddle?' he bellowed.

'Yes, where's his saddle?' cried a score of voices from the audience.

'Gordimo took that,' said Kaleb. 'His was nearly worn through. He preferred the styling of yours. Here, tell this monster to let me go!'

'I'll do nothing of the kind,' snapped Boy. 'Not until you've told me what I need to know. Where is Gordimo now?'

'Yes, where is Gordimo now?' shouted a legion of voices.

'How should I know?' snapped Kaleb. 'Making for Ravalan, I suppose. He thinks he has a chance of claiming that prize, though we tried to reproduce your trick the very next day and we couldn't get it to work. I told him there was something we'd missed, that we should turn back and find you, but he wouldn't listen.'

This gave Boy a feeling of hope. He told himself that perhaps Gordimo still hadn't found the compartment where the *Book of Secrets* was hidden. He took hold of Belle's halter and turning away, he started to lead her around the side of the stage. 'Come on girl,' he said. 'Let's get some ointment on those scars.'

'Hey!' yelled Kaleb. 'What about me?'

'What about you?' muttered Boy. 'As far as I'm concerned, you can fly away.'

Grud listened to the advice and then nodded. 'Bye bye, bad man,' he said. He promptly swung Kaleb up into his arms, lifted him above his head and with a slight grunt of effort, flung the man over the heads of the crowd. Kaleb went speeding over them like a discarded doll, his arms and legs flailing madly. He finally crashed headlong into a bunch of drunken revellers, knocking them down like skittles. There was a big commotion and then Kaleb disappeared under a flurry of vengeful fists. Boy looked at Grud in dismay. He'd forgotten how literal the Faravelian could be.

Boy was halfway to the stage when the next sound hit him, stopping him in his tracks. It was the last thing he'd expected to hear – the sound of thunderous applause. He turned back to look in absolute wonder. The entire audience was standing and clapping their hands, holding their arms high above their heads. They were whooping and roaring as though they'd just watched the best day's entertainment of their lives.

Something pinged off Boy's breastplate and fell to the ground at his feet. He looked down at it in astonishment. It was a five gelt piece. He stooped and picked it up, looking at it in surprise. More coins began to rain down around him. Lexi came running towards him, an excited grin on her face. She was holding his boots in one hand and the torn strips of her dress with the other.

'They're throwing money!' she yelled. 'They are actually throwing money. That's never happened before.'

Boy was aware of a slow grin spreading across his own face. 'That's great,' he said. He heard a voice behind him and turned to look at the stage. Orson was staggering out from the wings, reciting his opening lines. 'Ah hah, bold Adamis, I see you have—' He broke off and stood there swaying slightly, looking around in complete bafflement. Then, he registered that three cast members were standing on the ground below him, one of them leading a horse.

'Did I miss something?' he asked. A gold crown hit him square on the forehead and knocked him flat on his back again.

Chapter Ten

PLANS

THAT EVENING, the company abandoned their campfire in favour of a tavern off the town square. The Dancing Mutt was a noisy, but friendly establishment, frequented by eager townsfolk. The landlord gleefully told them he had enjoyed their performance so much, he wanted to give them their meal "on the house", something they were more than happy to accept. He clearly knew what he was doing. Once word got around that the "bunch of maniacs" who'd performed on the stage earlier that day were in the tavern, it brought in a huge crowd of people, all eager to meet the travelling players. They wanted to buy them drinks and in some cases, even ask for their autographs – a complicated arrangement which meant they had to approach their heroes carrying quill pens, bottles of ink and parchment.

Eventually, it all became too much and the cast were obliged to adjourn to a private room at the back of the inn, where they sat around a long wooden table. The landlord brought fresh drinks and hearty bowls of stew, assuring them he would only allow the occasional visitor in to speak to them – those he deemed to be of special importance.

Boy sat with the others, nursing a tankard of ale and picking half-heartedly at his stew. He was still slightly stunned by what had happened earlier that day. What had felt to him at the time like a humiliating disaster seemed to have somehow turned itself into a triumph, which was fine, but he wasn't entirely sure how it had happened.

Despite the fact that he was now sporting a huge, coin-shaped bruise on his forehead, Orson was in particularly good spirits. 'I am happy to report that after carefully counting up all the money, I can confirm that our company has enjoyed its best day's business in years,' he announced brightly.

'That's wonderful!' cried Mo. 'Hurrah for Gallibab!'

'If we go on like this,' added Orson, 'we might actually be able to pay off some debts!' He raised a foaming tankard of ale to toast his companions. 'Cheers!' he said. 'To a brighter future!'

Lexi frowned. 'Yes, but hang on a moment, Dad. We

shouldn't lose sight of something. The reason it went down so well is because—'

'It was *funny*!' finished Orson. 'Absolutely. I never realised this company was so good at making people laugh. Today's events made me realise that this is the direction we should be going in. Comedy!'

Pompio stared at Orson in evident disbelief. 'Comedy?' he cried. 'Is that what you call it?' It was clear he wasn't as cheerful as his companions. He sat cross-legged on a high stool, a glum expression on his little face. 'I looked a right Charlie up there,' he complained. 'They were laughing at me!'

'They were laughing at all of us,' Lexi reminded him.

'Yes, it might be all right for some of you, but I'm a serious actor. I didn't join up to fall around like a clown.'

'None of us did,' reasoned Mo, 'but you can't knock success, Pompio.'

'Success? Ha! We looked like a bunch of idiots.' He pointed at Boy. 'Thanks to Sonny Jim, there.'

'You can't blame me,' Boy told him. 'That stupid costume—'

'We've been using it for years,' said Pompio. 'It's never been a problem before. Even Ninian managed to wear it without mishap.'

'Oh, he *looked* fine in the costume,' agreed Lexi, 'but that's about the only positive thing you can say about him. At least Boy didn't stand there in silence like a great lump. At least he *tried*.'

'He made us a laughing stock!' insisted Pompio. 'When

he came crashing onto the stage, I didn't know where to put myself. I've never been so humiliated.'

'I got my cue wrong,' announced Grud mournfully. Even on the lowest stool they could find for him, he still loomed over the others. A large tankard of ale looked like an egg cup in his mighty hand. 'I heard somebody say "treasure" and I thought that was my cue.' He scowled. 'Do you think anybody noticed?'

'Not at all,' said Lexi, 'and if they did, it just added to the merriment.'

'Merriment!' sneered Pompio. 'So that's what we're all about now, is it?' He gazed down into his half-empty tankard as though completely unfamiliar with the word. 'There was me thinking I was a thespian!'

Grud looked at him in surprise. 'I thought you came from Gullamir,' he said.

Pompio looked at him. 'That is a theatrical term, you nitwit,' he growled. 'Of course, I wouldn't expect you to understand. I don't mean to be cruel, Grud, but if brains were gunpowder, you wouldn't have enough to blow your hat off!'

'I'm not wearing a hat,' said Grud, looking puzzled.

'I was the only one up there who actually remembered his lines,' persisted Pompio.

Mo chuckled. 'Oh yes. I particularly liked the bit where you told everyone you were off to "stroom your greed",' she reminded him. 'That was a classic.'

'Yes, go on, make fun of me!' suggested Pompio. 'Why not? Everybody else does!'

'Oh, lighten up,' said Orson. 'As usual, Pompio, you're missing the potential in this situation. Don't you see? This could be the start of a whole new career for you.'

'A career?' cried Pompio unhappily. 'You call that a career? Making people laugh is no way to earn a living.'

'Don't knock it,' said Orson. 'Some of the greatest and most successful acts in history have been comedians.'

Lexi leaned forward over her plate. 'I think we need to get this in perspective,' she told her father. 'The reason it went so well today was because of a whole series of accidents.'

Orson shrugged. 'True enough, but—'

'Well, we can't expect things to go wrong like that every night, can we?'

'We certainly can't set about some poor unsuspecting fool in the crowd,' reasoned Mo. 'Boy just chanced to see the man who stole his horse and the audience thought it was all part of the act, but that isn't going to happen again, is it?'

Orson looked thoughtful. 'Perhaps it could,' he reasoned.

Boy stared at him. 'What are you suggesting?' he asked.

'We could hire a stooge.'

'A stooge?' Pompio looked horrified. 'A flipping stooge?'

'Why not? We'd pay some local a couple of gelts to do it. You have to admit, it *did* go down a storm.'

'But that would be downright dishonest!' protested Pompio.

Grud frowned. 'Wouldn't the stooge mind me throwing him into the crowd?' he asked. 'I mean, I reckon that must have hurt.'

'Obviously we'd have a different person in each town,' Orson assured him. 'So each of them would only have to do it once. Perhaps we wouldn't mention the bit about you throwing them.'

'But the one I threw was a bad man,' persisted Grud. 'He punched Boy. It wouldn't be fair to just throw an ordinary person, would it?'

'Well, it's tricky, I'll grant you that,' admitted Orson, 'but look at us – living the high life for once! When was the last time we were able to afford to eat and drink like this?'

'This was a freebie,' Lexi reminded him.

'Well, yes, fair point, but nevertheless . . .' He gestured around at the food-laden table. 'Shall I tell you what we'd normally be doing, right now?' Orson looked slowly around the table. 'We'd be sitting by a campfire, eating scraps and trying to reassure each other that it didn't go quite as badly as it seemed.'

'Perhaps,' admitted Lexi. 'But—'

'No, hear me out! We did this same event last year. You know how much we came away with, once everything was paid off? Thirty-four gelts! That was our sum profit. Thirty-four miserable gelts. This year, we've made eight gold crowns. Think about that for a moment.'

The room fell silent as they did as he suggested. It was Lexi who spoke first.

'That *is* a lot of money,' she admitted.

'It's more than we've seen in a very long time and think about Ravalan! The richest city in the known world. There are merchants there who wouldn't think twice about giving that much as a tip to a waiter. If we can perfect a brilliant comedy show before we get there, we could come away with a small fortune – enough to get this company back on its feet.'

Pompio shook his head. 'Yes, but—'

'I'm not even saying it has to be a permanent thing,' continued Orson. 'Not at all. Once the Moon of Elnis has come and gone, we could easily return to our established genre.'

'Which is?' muttered Boy.

'Serious drama, of course!'

'Oh, right. Yes. Serious drama. Obviously.'

'Here's the point. This company has always performed every show to the very best of its ability. Just because we'd be playing for laughs, doesn't mean that there'd be anything slapdash or half-hearted about it. Oh no. On the contrary, we'd make it the funniest, most accomplished comedy show that's ever been seen. I wouldn't dream of doing anything that doesn't measure up to the high standards we've already achieved.' He looked around the table. 'So, what do you think?' he asked.

Boy shrugged. 'Well, as somebody who's only been in the

company a day or so, I think the decision should be down to everybody else,' he said. 'I'll sit this one out.'

'Quite right,' said Pompio. 'I'd say you've caused enough trouble.'

'It's not exactly trouble, is it?' Mo reminded him. 'All right, so he may be a talentless idiot—'

'Thanks for that,' muttered Boy.

'He has unwittingly shown us a way out of our problems. If Orson believes this is the right thing to do, then I support him wholeheartedly.'

'No surprises there,' muttered Pompio sarcastically. Mo gave him a dagger-like glare. Pompio ignored it and turned to look at Grud. 'What about you?' he asked. 'What do you think?'

'I'll just do what I'm told,' added Grud.

'All right,' said Pompio. 'I'm telling you to say that you don't want to do this.'

'But I *like* the idea of making people laugh!'

'So you're not doing what you're told then, are you?'

Grud thought for a moment. 'I'll do what *Orson* tells me to do,' he decided.

Pompio lifted a hand to his forehead and muttered something under his breath. He turned to Lexi.

'That leaves you,' he said, 'arguably the most important person in the company.'

Lexi raised her eyebrows. 'I wouldn't say that,' she murmured.

'Oh, come on! The person who writes the plays. Let's not forget all the effort you put into those original scripts, only to have Sonny Jim here—'

'I wish you'd stop calling me that,' snapped Boy.

'He comes marching along and insists you change everything.'

'To be fair,' said Lexi, 'that really isn't what happened. Boy made a chance remark and after some consideration, I decided to act on it. It's not like he made me do anything.' She looked across the table at her father. 'Dad, this has always been your company. If you genuinely think this is the right way to go, then I'll support you.'

Pompio slammed his tankard down on the tabletop. 'So, it's only me who objects!' he snarled. 'Typical! Once again, I'm the one true voice of reason. I just want to go on record here and say when all this goes wrong, when you lot fall down and break your legs, don't come running to me!'

There was a short silence as everybody considered his words and then, as one, they all burst out laughing.

'It's not funny!' protested Pompio. 'Shut up! Stop laughing!'

The door opened and the landlord stuck his head into the room. 'I've got somebody out here wants to talk to you lot,' he said.

Orson made a dismissive gesture. 'I think we've spoken to enough drunken autograph hunters for one evening,' he said.

'No,' the landlord corrected him. 'This is different. It's somebody from the press. He wants to interview you.'

The members of the company exchanged puzzled looks for a moment.

'What's the press?' asked Mo.

'What's an interview? asked Pompio.

Orson shrugged. 'I haven't the foggiest,' he admitted. He sighed. 'I suppose you'd better send him in.'

The landlord nodded, opened the door wider and ushered a young man into the room. He was a tall, skinny fellow wearing a red jerkin, green tights and brown leather boots. His long face was accentuated by a neatly trimmed goatee beard, and Boy noticed that he carried a large, leather satchel over one shoulder and some kind of stringed instrument across his back. He strode imperiously up to the table and performed an elaborate bow. 'Greetings, friends,' he said. 'Archimaldo, at your service!'

Orson examined the youth suspiciously. 'The landlord said something about an interview?' he murmured.

'That is correct,' said Archimaldo. He pointed a finger towards an empty stool. 'May I?' he asked.

'Yes, of course,' said Orson.

Archimaldo took a seat and cleared a space. He produced a pot of ink, a quill pen and some parchment from his bag. He set them on the table. 'I represent Troubadours Unlimited,' he said, grandly. He paused for a moment as if expecting a reaction, but when he didn't get one, he continued. 'I was fortunate enough to catch your performance earlier today and I must say, I was thoroughly entertained; so much so, I deemed it worthy of inclusion in this year's Moon of Elnis Festival Roundup.'

'Er, that's nice,' said Orson. 'I'm sorry, I don't understand. How exactly does this work?'

'Oh, forgive me. You're not familiar with our service?' Archimaldo glanced around as though surprised and received blank looks from everyone at the table. 'Ah well,' he said, 'I suppose we *are* fairly new.'

'We?' echoed Lexi.

'Yes, there are three of us in the company – all based in different areas. Whenever a festival approaches, we gradually converge upon it and, as we travel, we stop off in each town along the way and sing the praises of the most promising shows we've seen. Think of it as advance publicity.'

Pompio fixed him with a look. 'So, what, you write something about us?'

'Well, more about the show itself, really – its plot and so forth. Then, I use my special talents to turn your words into a jingle.'

Boy was completely bewildered now. 'A what?'

'A jingle. Oh, come now, you must have heard of the term? It's a short song, extolling your virtues. I travel a day ahead of you, stopping in all the locations you will appear in and I, quite literally, sing your praises. This tips off the local customers to your imminent visit and raises their expectations.' He registered everyone's puzzled expressions and swung the lute on his back around to his front. 'Perhaps you'd like to hear a recent example of my work?' he suggested.

'Ooh, yes please,' said Grud. 'I like a singsong.'

'Excellent. Well, here's one I've recently written for Master Elgin's Travelling Pies. I'm sure you're familiar with their products?' Again, Archimaldo received blank looks, but he continued undeterred. 'They are also heading for Ravalan, with the same stops along the way as most of the other shows. The idea is to get people in each new town salivating at the thought of those pies and for customers to ensure they only buy from Master Elgin. This should give you an idea of how we work.'

He cleared his throat, put his hands to the strings of the lute and started to play a whimsical tune, whilst singing in a clear and quite pleasant voice.

'Oh, gather round people and hark to my song,
It's short and it's merry and won't keep you long.
If you're looking for flavour to thrill and surprise,
You need to try Elgin's most wonderful pies!
They come in all flavours from savoury to sweet;
The softest ripe fruit, the most succulent meat,
And with prices this low, they're the keenest of buys.
Make sure you try Elgin's most wonderful pies!
And here's a great offer, I'm sure you'll agree:
Buy one tasty pie and the other one's FREE!

You'll taste them and praise them right up to the skies,
It's Elgin's, yes Elgin's, most wonderful pies!'

He finished with a flourish and lowered his head. Boy realised he was waiting for applause, so he started clapping politely and the others joined in. Archimaldo smiled serenely and swung the lute out of the way. 'So, there we are,' he said. 'Those who have used our services have reported a dramatic increase in their fortunes. So . . .' He indicated the writing implements on the table. 'I have a contract here. May I add you to our growing roster of clients?'

'Hold on a moment,' said Pompio. 'How do we know you'll say good things about us? You could write any old nonsense about our show, couldn't you? You could go around singing that we're terrible and we smell bad, that people shouldn't bother wasting any time on us and we wouldn't even be there to hear it.'

Archimaldo shook his head. 'Obviously, I wouldn't dream of singing a word without your approval. No, no, I will compose the jingle right here and now,' he said. 'We offer a "while you wait" service. We wouldn't proceed until you're one hundred percent happy with my words. That's our guarantee.'

Mo gave the troubadour a suspicious look. 'What's in this for you?' she asked him. 'I mean, you're not doing this out of the goodness of your heart, are you? I take it there's a cost for the service?'

'My dear lady, of course there is,' said Archimaldo, looking slightly wounded. 'You wouldn't expect me to work for nothing, would you? I mean, do you people work for nothing?'

'No. We work for next to nothing,' muttered Pompio.

'I beg your pardon?'

'Ignore him,' said Orson. 'How much do you charge?'

'One gold crown,' said Archimoldo. 'Paid up front, but fully inclusive. That entitles you to five performances of your jingle in every town you are planning to visit. Extra performances are of course, negotiable.'

Orson seemed impressed and it looked as though he might be ready to accept the offer, but Mo got there ahead of him. 'We'll give you fifty gelts,' she said. She crossed her arms. 'Take it or leave it.'

For a moment, Archimaldo looked as though he might be about to argue the case, but he sighed and reached across the table to shake hands with Orson. 'Times are hard,' he said. 'As you're a new customer, we can offer an introductory deal, but if you decide to use us again, I'll expect the full rate.' He glanced quickly around the table. 'Right,' he said. 'Let's get a few basic facts down on parchment, shall we? Who would like to tell me something about the show?'

Orson smiled. 'Well, I think you should start with our leading lady,' he began, looking towards his daughter but Lexi, sensing an opportunity, quickly cut in and placed a hand on Pompio's tiny shoulder.

'No, you should talk to the world's most talented boobo!' she said. 'I'm sure Pompio here will be happy to tell you all about his incredible plans to take this company in an exciting new direction.'

Pompio brightened up immediately. He leaned closer to Achimaldo. 'Well,' he said. 'I don't like to boast but when it comes to touring the stages of the known world, I have picked up a few tips along the way. First of all, let's make sure you spell my name correctly. It's P-O-M-P . . .'

Boy leaned closer to Lexi and clinked his tankard gently against hers. 'Nicely done,' he said under his breath. 'Never mind acting and playwriting, you should consider a career in politics.' He looked at her and sighed. 'I won't pretend I'm not worried, though,' he added.

'Worried? What about?'

He frowned. 'The others are expecting me to be funny,' he said, 'but I don't have the first idea how that works.'

She grinned. 'Oh, I don't know. You did a pretty good job today. When you tripped over that step, oh boy. That certainly made *me* laugh!'

'Yeah, thanks for that,' he murmured. 'I still say it was the fault of the costume. We can get rid of that, right?'

She shook her head. 'Are you kidding? That was one of the funniest bits. I'm thinking we might add to it, put on a few more things to trip you up.' She gave him a curious look. 'By the way,

I didn't get a chance to ask you before. What was all that about your saddle?'

He feigned a wide-eyed look. 'What saddle?' he asked.

'Oh, don't try to play innocent with me. You know what I'm talking about. You mentioned it when you were arguing with the guy who stole your horse. You seemed really concerned. What's so special about the saddle?'

'I told you before,' he said. 'It belonged to my father. It means a lot to me, that's all. A comfortable saddle is a hard thing to find.'

She nodded but was clearly far from convinced. 'He said something about an invention? That he and the other fellow hadn't managed to get it to work properly?

'I don't know what he was raving about,' said Boy, dismissively. He was uncomfortably aware of her eyes on him as he turned back to listen to Pompio, who had now hit his stride and was seeing recent events in an entirely different light.

'Then it occurred to me,' he announced, a little too loudly. 'It came to me like a bolt out of the blue. "What about comedy?" I thought. "Maybe *that's* where this company is destined to make its mark! Why not make 'em laugh?"'

Grud looked around the table in bewilderment. 'The comedy was Pompio's idea?' he cried.

'Apparently,' said Orson. Everybody laughed.

Chapter Eleven

CLOSE

THE HARSH desert landscape had finally given way to rolling hills and areas of lush green forest, while the fierce heat that had plagued them for so long had now subsided into something decidedly gentler. The caravan rumbled along a country road, en route to its next destination, the town of Drumreedy – the final call before Ravalan. Boy sat beside Lexi on the buckboard of the first caravan, opting to leave Belle hitched to a rail at the back of it, trailing sedately along behind them. He was finding that as the days went by he was enjoying spending time in Lexi's company. She was warm and funny, and sometimes when she looked at him with those bright, green, Elvish eyes, he felt something inside his chest flutter like a caged bird. It was almost enough to make him forget about his most pressing worry – the need to get to Ravalan and claim what Gordimo had stolen from him, that precious book that his father had left him.

It had been an arduous few days. Boy's body ached from the various bumps and bruises he had incurred at the two performances they had enacted since Gallibab. Nobody could complain of the warm reception they'd received in the towns of Ninsago and Sumac. Archimaldo's jingle had clearly worked a treat, pulling in eager crowds and Boy had to admit that it *was* annoyingly catchy. He'd even found himself whistling the melody from time to time.

> '*Hey there people, don't be down,*
> *There's something heading to this town*
> *And it's a cure for every frown –*
> *A comedy for you!*
> *There's Bertram, who's a super wit,*
> *Adamis who's a total twit,*
> *And Neve, who blunders quite a bit –*
> *A comedy for you!*
> *Our tale concerns a handsome lad,*
> *A crime that drives the boy quite mad,*
> *A dark magician who is bad –*

A comedy for you!
So call your friends and head this way,
Dismiss your woes, come out to play,
I swear you won't forget this day.
A comedy for you!
A comedy – a comedy – a great rip-roaring comedy
They've travelled miles to bring you smiles –
A comedy for you!
A comedy! A comedy! A great rip-roaring comedy!
No need to frown, just come on down! A comedy for you!'

Before the performance in Ninsago, the cast had added a few modifications to the show. Boy's costume had been augmented with a whole collection of heavy items – swords, daggers, water bottles, a telescope – all designed to trip him up and cause him problems at every step. The visor of his helmet had been treated with lamp oil to make sure it fell down at every opportunity and the point where Boy flung it away in desperation, had been rehearsed and rehearsed to ensure that it always hit Orson square on the head. He consequently had a collection of livid-looking bruises on his baldpate, but the money that was thrown at the stage at the end of each performance was more than enough to compensate for his discomfort.

Lexi's costume had been lightly sewn back together, so it would tear open at the slightest touch from Boy's sword and Grud had been encouraged to do more in the show. He invariably got things wrong and challenged the rest of the cast to incorporate his unwitting disasters into the storyline.

Pompio, of course, had insisted that Lexi provide him with his fair share of funny lines and despite his initial reluctance to embrace this new direction, he'd proved to be an extremely accomplished comedian, rattling out a series of witty-one liners as though born to the art.

As well as singing the company's praises, Archimaldo had been called upon to carry out an additional assignment. He was to secretly recruit somebody in each town he visited, paying them a few gelts to attend the following night's show and, when a certain cue line was said, to approach the stage and start loudly heckling the performers. It had been decided that the stolen horse idea could not be successfully duplicated, so the stooge was simply encouraged to be as loud and obnoxious as possible. The members of the cast had equipped themselves with a series of specially prepared put-downs, designed to make him look a complete fool. At the conclusion, instead of flinging him into the crowd, Grud would simply pick the heckler up, carry him onto the stage and hang him by the lapel of his jacket from a convenient high point, where he was safe from the vengeance of the crowd but looked suitably ridiculous. After the show, the stooge was lifted down and given a little extra pay-off to make him feel less annoyed about being treated so roughly.

At any rate, it was all working brilliantly. The audiences had loved the shows and the takings had been substantial. In Ninsago, they'd come away with a profit of seven gold crowns. In Sumac, a town known for its wealthy inhabitants, it had been closer to eleven.

Boy reminded himself that there were just a few days to go before the final performance for the Moon of Elnis and the great competition that was to be held on that same evening. He wasn't sure what would happen when he got to Ravalan but he knew that whatever else came or went, he had to be there when the judging took place. If Gordimo turned up and tried to pass off the sand-into-water apparatus as his own, then Boy would be ready to challenge him.

'A gelt for them,' said Lexi.

Boy turned and looked at her. 'I'm sorry?' he said.

'A gelt for your thoughts,' she elaborated. 'You're miles away.'

'Oh, I was just thinking how unexpectedly your life can change,' he said.

'How so?'

'Until a week ago, I'd never thought of pursuing the life of a travelling player. Now look at me! A member of a successful comedy troupe. I don't know what my parents would have said about such a thing. It's certainly not what they wanted for me.'

She looked at him with interest. 'You don't talk about them much,' she said.

'No, I don't suppose I do.'

'You said something about them once – that they disappeared.'

'Yes, that's right.'

'Would you like to tell me more about it?'

'Well . . .' Boy had been about to say that he didn't want to dwell on it, but then he remembered how readily he had told Gordimo and Kaleb about his parents, after his tongue had been loosened by wine and he felt a twinge of guilt. Why was he so reluctant to tell Lexi about them? It wasn't as if she wanted to steal anything from him. 'It's a long story,' he said.

'That's all right,' she assured him. 'We've still quite a way to go before we make camp for the night.'

'Well, all right. I—'

'Woah!' Lexi pulled the buffalo to a sudden halt, rocking Boy forward on his seat. He saw several riders coming along the winding road towards them, the hooves of their horses raising dust. Boy's hand dropped instinctively to the handle of his sword. Most of the mounted men were soldiers, dressed in gold-crested helmets and dark, red cloaks. They were all armed. In their midst, mounted on a white horse, rode a wiry old man, dressed in expensive-looking, embroidered clothes. He had a white goatee beard and when he raised a hand to halt his companions, the fingers of the hand flashed with jewelled rings. He rode his horse a little closer and stopped a short distance from the caravan, a friendly smile on his face. 'Good afternoon,' he said. 'I wonder, do I have the pleasure of addressing members of the Wandering Star Theatre Company?'

Lexi and Boy exchanged puzzled looks, before Lexi turned back and said, 'Yes sir, that is correct. How do you know of us?'

The man bowed slightly from the waist. 'Allow me to introduce myself. My name is Tristan, and I am the personal envoy of—'

'Hey, what's the flipping hold up?' snapped a voice and Pompio appeared from the back of the caravan, where he'd been enjoying a nap. He clambered up beside Boy and inspected the newcomers suspiciously. 'Hello, hello,' he said. 'What's all this then?'

The old man stared at Pompio for a moment, as though he couldn't quite believe his eyes and then he laughed delightedly. 'Well, bless my soul!' he cried. 'I was told you had a talented boobo, but I had no idea it could actually *talk*! Who are you, sir, if I may be so bold?'

'I'm the brilliant comic actor, Pompio. Who might you be, if it's not too much to ask?'

The old man bowed again. 'I am Tristan, special envoy to Queen Gertrude of Ravalan,' he said.

'Blimey!' said Pompio. 'Hold everything!' He scampered quickly down from the caravan and ran back to the others, waving his arms and shouting loudly for them to come and meet an unexpected visitor. 'He's flipping royalty!' Boy heard him yell. 'Come on, move yourselves! You don't see something like this every day!'

Tristan waited patiently until the rest of the company had gathered. He studied their faces, amused by their astonished expressions. 'Now then,' he said. 'If everyone is present, may I enquire which one of you is in charge of the company?'

'That would be my father,' said Lexi, pointing to Orson.

He made an awkward bow and stepped a little closer. 'I am the official leader,' he said. 'These days we are more of a collective – maybe even a cooperative.' Everyone looked at him. This was clearly the first they'd heard of it.

Tristan made a dismissive gesture. 'Whatever you like to call yourselves is of no concern to me,' he said. 'I am here to tell you that advance news of your performances has reached us in the great city of Ravalan.'

'Have they really?' cried Pompio. 'How's that? Archimaldo shouldn't even be there yet. Our next stop is Drumreedy.'

'I know nothing of this Archimaldo character,' admitted Tristan, 'but I did hear about a performance you did in Gallibab a little while ago.'

'Oh yes?' said Pompio. 'I'm afraid we don't do refunds!'

Tristan chuckled. 'Very amusing,' he said. 'No, a friend of mine was there on business and he claims it was the funniest thing he has seen in his entire life.'

'Did he really say that?' asked Grud. 'About us?'

'He did indeed.' Tristan looked suddenly uncertain. 'Are you saying it wasn't your company that did the performance? *The Sorrows of Young Adamis?*'

'Oh, yes,' said Orson. 'That was definitely us.'

'My friend had gone along expecting something more serious—'

'He wasn't the only one,' muttered Pompio.

'He was astonished to find it was actually a comedy.'

Orson smiled. 'Yes. It was the first presentation we did of our . . . new style. Prior to this, we have concentrated on drama.'

'We fancied a change,' added Lexi.

'Yes,' said Mo. 'You know what they say: a change is as good as a rest.'

'Well, according to my friend, this was the best laugh he'd had in a very long time and let me assure you, he is not the sort of person who laughs a lot.'

'Oh?' said Pompio. 'Why's that? What does he do for a living?'

'He's a funeral director,' said Tristan and there was a short silence. Tristan cleared his throat. 'Now, we have noted that you are already booked to perform a mid-morning show in the city square in four days' time.'

'Yes?' said Orson, cautiously. 'Is that going to be a problem?'

'Not at all, not at all! A delight for the populace by the sound of it, but Her Majesty was wondering . . .'

'Her Majesty?' shrieked Pompio. 'You mean, the flipping Queen?'

One of the soldiers waiting behind Tristan reached for his sword, but Tristan made a dismissive gesture and the soldier let the weapon slip back into its scabbard.

'Yes indeed,' said Tristan, calmly. 'Queen Gertrude of Ravalan was wondering if you good people could find time in your busy schedule to perform an extra show on the same day? In the evening. At the palace.'

'The palace?' croaked Orson.

'Yes. As I'm sure you're aware, the Queen has recently emerged from a long period of official mourning.'

'Morning?' murmured Grud, misunderstanding. 'Do the mornings last longer in Ravalan? Ours only go on till midday.'

'You turnip,' snapped Pompio. 'He doesn't mean *that* kind of morning! He's talking about somebody snuffing it.'

'Er, quite.' Tristan looked pained by the remark but carried on regardless. 'The Queen's husband, King Clitus, died just over a year ago, and as I'm sure you're aware, a royal widow is required to dress in black and refrain from any kind of frivolity for a full year.'

'Oh yes, of course,' said Mo. 'I *did* hear about that. How very sad for her.'

'Now the mourning period is over, her Majesty is determined to preside over a happier, more creative kingdom. To this end, she has put forward some new initiatives. So, of course, there is the great competition she devised for the Moon of Elnis.'

'Yes,' said Boy. 'We know all about that.'

'No we don't.' Lexi corrected him and Boy felt his cheeks flushing.

'Oh, sorry, I thought it was common knowledge,' he muttered, and was uncomfortably aware of Lexi's curious look.

'Actually, that reminds me.' Tristan snapped his fingers and one of the soldiers urged his horse forward and pulled from a leather shoulder bag, a roll of parchment which he handed to Lexi, before turning back to join his companions. 'Here are some posters advertising the event,' continued Tristan. 'I appreciate the time is short, but if you would be kind enough to hand those out in any town you visit along the way, we'd be most obliged. Her Majesty is concerned that we haven't had quite the level of response she might have hoped for.'

Lexi unrolled one of the posters and read the elegant words aloud. 'Attention all inventors! Ten thousand gold crowns will be paid to the person who can devise an invention that will benefit mankind. The winning design will be unveiled at a special ceremony at the Moon of Elnis festival. Open to all.'

'Ten thousand gold crowns,' murmured Pompio, dreamily. 'Imagine winning that! What kind of an invention might be deemed worthy of such a fortune?'

Boy shrugged. 'Search me,' he said, but he could tell that Lexi wasn't fooled for a moment.

'Anyway, I digress,' said Tristan. 'When my friend spoke of your performance, Her Majesty overheard and remarked that it was a very long time since the sounds of laughter had echoed around the corridors of the royal palace. So, she suggested that we might book you for a special performance to which we would invite all members of the royal household, their friends and guests. I told her that I would set out immediately to arrange it.' He looked slowly around the group. 'Or perhaps you have already accepted another booking for that evening?'

It was Orson who found his voice first. 'Oh no . . . nothing like that!' he said.

'We've had enquiries, of course,' Mo reminded him.

'Oh yes, naturally we have. Many, many enquiries!'

'We're in big demand,' added Pompio. 'After our recent successes, we've been reluctantly turning away bookings, left, right and centre.'

'Have we?' muttered Grud. 'I don't remember—'

'But,' said Orson, hastily, 'obviously, if it's for Queen Gruntwood—'

'*Gertrude!*' hissed Lexi.

'Yes, for Queen Gertrude, we'd be ready to turn away those other er, commitments, in order to—'

'What commitments?' muttered Grud.

'To make ourselves available to play.'

'At the palace,' finished Pompio, dreamily. 'The *royal* palace.'

'Excellent.' Tristan looked puzzled. 'Of course, we haven't yet discussed a fee.'

'A fee?' shrieked Pompio, as though unfamiliar with the term. 'A flipping *fee*?'

'Well, usually,' said Orson, 'it's only—'

'What people throw at us,' finished Grud and everyone looked daggers at him. 'Did I say something wrong?' he asked, looking helplessly around.

Lexi made a valiant attempt to take control of the situation. 'The fee we usually charge for such occasions is—'

'Her Majesty has instructed me to offer you the sum of—'

'Five—'

'One hundred gold crowns—'

There was a long silence while this information sank in. Everyone stared at Tristan, open-mouthed in disbelief.

'I hope you will find that agreeable,' he said quietly. He looked at Lexi. 'Or were you going to ask for more?' he asked her.

'Er, no,' she whispered. 'No, one hundred seems perfectly fair.'

'Agreeable to us,' added Mo. She looked at Orson. 'Don't you think?'

Orson's eyes had filled with involuntary tears. He opened his mouth but no words came out, so he just nodded vigorously.

'I think everyone's fairly happy with that,' said Boy.

'Imagine if they threw that much at us,' said Grud. 'That would *hurt*.'

'Umm, excellent,' said Tristan. 'Right then.' He reached into his embroidered tunic and pulled out a leather pouch. 'Here you go,' he said and threw it to Lexi.

She caught it in one hand. 'What's this?' she asked.

'Half your fee,' he told her. 'You'll have the other half after your performance. Report to the main gates of the palace at six of the evening and you shall be taken to the royal theatre, where you can prepare for your show at seven.'

'What about the grand competition?' asked Boy. 'When's that happening?'

'That will be judged directly after your performance,' said Tristan. 'Why do you ask?' He studied Boy for a moment. 'Don't tell me you have something up your sleeve, young man.'

'Me? No, of course not! I was just interested, that's all.'

'Well then, I shall bid you farewell until the evening of the Moon of Elnis.' Tristan leaned a little closer. 'I'm sure I don't need to remind you how important this will be to her Majesty, so I would ask you all to be on your very best form.'

'What happens if she doesn't like our show?' asked Pompio and there was a long and rather uncomfortable silence.

'We're all depending on you,' said Tristan and with that, he pulled his horse around and rode back to the soldiers, who all turned as one and rode away. The cast of Wandering Star sat there watching until they had dwindled into the distance.

Lexi looked at the cloth bag she was holding. 'Fifty gold crowns,' she murmured. 'Right here in my hand.'

'Amazing,' murmured Boy.

'I wonder what ten thousand would feel like?' she added and once again, he felt his cheeks flush.

'Who can say?' he muttered.

'Incredible!' cried Orson. 'Money up front. It's like the good old days.' He performed a jig where he stood. Impulsively, he grabbed Mo in his arms and whirled her around for a few impromptu dance steps. 'We're back!' he told the world. 'The Wandering Star Theatre Company is back!'

Chapter Twelve

COMING CLEAN

THE ATMOSPHERE around the campfire was one of great elation. Orson was in unusually high spirits and insisted that a couple of bottles of wine should be opened and doled out. When all the mugs were charged with drink, he raised his in a toast. 'Here's to the Wandering Star Theatre Company!' he roared. 'Now by royal appointment!' Everybody drank.

As Boy ate his stew, however, he was aware of Lexi's eyes on him the whole time and he was not particularly surprised when, after the meal was finished, she wandered over to him. 'We need to talk,' she told him, quietly. He nodded and got up obediently from his seat. The two of them headed towards a grove of miccoona trees on a nearby hilltop.

They walked away from the fire until they were safely out of earshot. It was a clear night and a full moon sailed serenely above them, minting the rolling countryside with a clean, silver light. Soft winds stirred the foliage of the trees ahead of them, making a restless, rustling sound.

'What's on your mind?' asked Boy.

'I think you know,' she told him. 'What's going on?'

He affected an innocent look. 'I don't know what you mean.'

'Of course you do. Look, I'm not stupid.'

'I never said you were!'

'Yes, well stop acting like you think I am! I thought from the very beginning that something about you didn't make sense. You were so intent on getting to Ravalan in time for the Moon of Elnis. It was the first thing you asked about when you woke. Earlier today, when Tristan mentioned the big competition, well, surprise, surprise, you knew all about it.'

Boy spread his hands. 'So? It's not exactly a secret, is it? You saw the posters. It's a big event.'

She clearly wasn't convinced. 'When Tristan asked if you had something "up your sleeve", you looked so guilty, and it got me thinking. That saddle you keep going on about. You got your horse back. You'd have thought that would have made you happy but it wasn't enough, was it? You told me the saddle was your father's, but that doesn't really add up. What's so special about it?'

Boy sighed. He had no other option but to come clean.

'It's not the saddle so much as what's hidden *in* it,' he said.

'Now we're getting somewhere. What's that?'

'A book. My father's book. The *Book of Secrets*.'

She looked intrigued. 'Go on,'

'My father was an inventor,' explained Boy. 'I think I told you, my parents disappeared when I was only little. The book is something my father left me. All his inventions are written down in it. There was one, in particular, that always fascinated me; something he started and I completed over the years. The truth is, Lexi, I *was* going to Ravalan to enter the great competition.'

'You think this thing, whatever it is, has a chance of winning the big prize?'

He nodded. 'A very strong chance,' he said.

She laughed at his apparent bravado. 'Well, there's nothing like confidence!' she observed. 'And yet you've never struck me as the confident sort. So, what is it, this invention? What does it do that's worth so much money?'

He stopped walking and turned to look at her. 'It turns sand into water,' he said.

There was a long silence while she stood there looking at him. 'Go and take a running jump!' she said. 'Like that's even a thing!'

'Oh, it is,' he assured her. 'I promise you. I know it sounds a little unlikely.'

'Unlikely? Impossible, is what it sounds. Like a magic trick! The kind of thing you might see somebody do in the marketplace.'

'Yes, I've seen those acts. They're impressive, sure enough, but just tricks. My invention actually works.'

She shook her hand. 'You can't expect me to believe that,' she protested. 'You really can't! Sand into water? My family lived in the desert when I was little. We struggled every day to find enough water to keep us alive. An invention like that, well, it really *would* change the world. You're asking me to accept that you're some kind of Boy Wonder!'

'Why do you think I was so reluctant to tell you about it? I knew you wouldn't believe me.'

'This magic process you use . . .'

'It's not magic! It's science. I had this same conversation with Gordimo.'

'Gordimo?'

'One of the men who robbed me. The other was called Kaleb – the one who had Belle. Well, at least he's out of the picture now, but the more I think about him, the more I realise he was just a big, thick lug who went along with the idea. It was his companion, Gordimo, who was the mastermind.'

Lexi seemed to consider for a moment. 'This Gordimo character? Did *he* believe in your invention?'

'Of course he did.' Boy shook his head. 'Why wouldn't he? Look, Lexi, I was an idiot. He gave me something to drink and I ended up telling him way too much. I even demonstrated it to him. That's how stupid I was. Not so much a Boy Wonder as a Boy Blunder! I turned sand into water right in front of his eyes.'

Lexi turned away for a moment, as though she needed a moment to think. Then, she turned back to him. 'All right,' she said. 'Here's the thing. I want you to swear to me.'

'Look, I don't—'

'Hear me out. I want you to swear on the lives of your missing parents; swear to me that you're not making this up and then I'll believe you.'

'I swear,' he said.

'That's not enough. I want you to *say* it!'

He sighed. 'All right.' He thought for a moment, trying to find the words that would convince her. 'I swear on the lives of my missing parents that I really have invented a device that can turn sand into water. It's not a trick. It actually works. If I'm lying, let the great god Mungus strike me down dead, right now.' There was a silence while the two of them waited, but no bolt of lightning was forthcoming. 'There,' said Boy. 'Will that do?'

'I suppose it will have to,' she said. She took a deep breath. 'Very well. I believe you. It's the most ridiculous story I've ever heard, I'd be embarrassed to tell anybody else about it but yes, I think you're telling the truth.' She gazed around at the silvery landscape for a moment as though seeking inspiration. 'So, this Gordimo, he could go to Ravalan and claim the prize?'

'Well, possibly.'

'Possibly?'

Boy turned and continued walking. Lexi fell into step with him.

'He has my apparatus, yes, and he has most of the things he needs to achieve the transformation, but he is missing one vital ingredient.' He reached under his singlet and pulled out the charm. He opened it and showed her what was inside. 'Yaricoola seeds,' he said. 'It can't work without them.'

'They grow just about everywhere,' she reasoned. 'They're as common as weeds.'

'Oh yes, but Gordimo didn't realise he needed them. I had the presence of mind to conceal that from his sight. It was about the only thing I got right.' He closed the locket and slipped it back into place.

'You said that he already has the book. Are the seeds not mentioned in there?'

'They are, I'm afraid. I added notes myself when I discovered their properties, but he may not know that he *has* the book.'

'I don't understand.'

'It's hidden in a secret compartment in the saddle. Of course, if Gordimo has already chanced upon it well, then I rather think the game's up.'

Lexi seemed to ponder for a moment. 'Well, what's to stop you from building some new apparatus or whatever you call it? I mean, it's only stuff like yaricoola seeds, right? You can buy them at any marketplace.'

'It's not as simple as it sounds. The ingredients are easy enough to find but they must be mixed in a container made from Gendlesnarp, so—'

'Gendlesnarp?' she said incredulously. 'Now you're just making words up!'

'No, I swear, it's a real thing. It's a rare substance that can only be found in the mines of Samilan, way up in the frozen North. It's not impossible to get more but it would mean mounting an expedition up there that would take months to carry out.'

'All right then. Here's what you should do. When we get to Ravalan, you need to contact Tristan and tell him what's happened. Tell him to have Gordimo arrested. Then, you can go to the palace and explain the situation.'

Boy shook his head. 'You think they'd take any notice of me? It would be my word against his. He's older than me and looks respectable.'

'*You're* respectable!'

'No offence but I'm a travelling actor. We're not exactly the most trusted profession in the world, are we?'

Lexi frowned. 'People do seem to have a dim view of us,'

she admitted. 'I've never understood why.' She looked at him. 'So, what *are* you going to do?'

'Well, this royal command performance may have handed me a huge opportunity. It will put me right in the place where the competition is to be judged. If Gordimo turns up there, I'm sure to see him and I'll be able to challenge him in front of witnesses.'

'And if he doesn't turn up?'

Boy looked at her. He didn't have an answer for that.

Lexi continued. 'You know, there's one thing about all this that still puzzles me.'

'What's that?' asked Boy.

'Why haven't you told me any of this before? I knew you were hiding something, but every time I asked you about the robbery, you changed the subject.'

Boy shrugged. 'I guess I was nervous of being too open about it. I told those two strangers about my invention and look what happened to me.'

Her eyes widened. 'Did you really think so little of me?' she gasped. 'That I couldn't be trusted with the truth?'

'It's not that,' he reasoned. 'When you've been tricked once, it's hard to trust *anyone*. Surely you can see that?'

She frowned. 'If it does work out for you in the end – if you *do* end up winning that big prize – what happens then?'

'I don't understand what you mean.'

'What will you do with yourself? You'll be a rich man. You'll be able to have whatever your heart desires. Everything will change.'

'I suppose so.'

'What will the Wandering Star Theatre Company mean to you then?'

'I . . . I'm not sure.'

She looked at him searchingly 'Maybe I was hoping for a different answer; that you would tell me you really liked being with Wandering Star; that you'd discovered you were good at acting and that you wanted to continue. Or perhaps I got it all wrong. Perhaps it was just something you were doing to pass the time.'

'Lexi, that's not fair! I told you when you first asked me to join the company, being an actor wasn't something I'd always dreamed of. I'm an inventor! But you were stuck and I felt I owed you something. After all, you *did* save my life."

She stopped walking. 'That's it then?' she murmured. 'It was just something you did because you felt obliged? Because you needed a lift to Ravalan?'

'Oh no, that sounds a bit—'

'Too close to the truth?' She turned suddenly on her heel. 'You know what, I believe I'll head back now,' she said. 'It's beginning to feel a little chilly out here.' She started walking towards the distant light of the campfire.

'Hey, hang on a minute,' he said. 'I'll come with you.'

'Oh, no,' she said flatly. 'Don't bother. You stay here and continue making plans for your brilliant future.'

She strode onwards and in a few moments was lost in the shadows.

Boy stared after her in complete bafflement.

'What did I say?' he asked the surrounding darkness.

Chapter Thirteen

DRUMREEDY

WHEN THEY pulled in to Drumreedy the following day, the town square was rammed with hundreds of eager people.

'Looks like Archimaldo's jingles really are spreading the word,' observed Boy brightly, but Lexi just grunted. She'd hardly spoken a word to him all day, despite his increasingly desperate attempts to start conversations with her. 'Listen,' he said. 'You'll have to talk to me soon won't you? We'll be on that stage together.' He indicated the big, wooden platform in the middle of the square, where Pompio was already in position, waving his tambourine and cajoling the crowds to step closer.

Again, Lexi said nothing, but she urged the buffalo towards the rear of the stage and pulled the caravan to a halt. Mo manoeuvred the second caravan in alongside it and the usual scramble to get ready for the show began. Orson climbed down from the buckboard and grinned up at Boy and Lexi. 'Remind me to buy that Archimaldo a drink the next time I see him!' he bellowed. 'This is the biggest crowd yet! There must be a thousand people out there.'

Lexi climbed down from the buckboard without a word and stalked across to Orson's caravan to get changed, leaving Boy where he sat.

'What's wrong with her?' asked Orson, puzzled by her silence.

'I think it must have been something I said,' muttered Boy.

Orson frowned. 'I hope you two haven't fallen out,' he said. 'That could make for a poor performance.'

'I'm sure it will be all right,' Boy assured him and wished he felt as confident as he sounded. He clambered into the back of the caravan and started getting himself into costume. Finally dressed, he opened the rear door of the caravan and clattered down the steps, his helmet tucked under one arm. As he approached the rear of the stage, he saw Lexi coming towards him and as always, experienced that strange thrill of seeing her unlikely transformation. He purposefully barred her path for a moment.

'You *are* going to talk to me out there, aren't you?' he implored her. 'We'll look a right pair of idiots if you don't.'

She gave him a simmering look. 'I'll consider it,' she growled.

'I still don't understand what I said wrong,' he reasoned. 'If I *did* win the competition – and it's looking increasingly unlikely that I will – but if I did, I haven't the first idea what I'd do with the money. I certainly wouldn't—'

'Hey, you two,' shouted Mo, from the wings of the stage. 'Chat later. You need to get yourselves in position. Pompio has already started!'

'We'll discuss this after the show,' said Boy. He lifted the helmet and lowered it onto his head. He started his clanking, rattling ascent of the steps, listening out as best he could for his cue. Soon enough, it came.

'Ah, here comes young Adamis now!'

Boy dutifully pretended to trip on the last step and threw himself face down onto the stage, wincing as he struck the wooden boards. *Another couple of bruises to add to my collection*, he thought, but it got the required laugh.

'Ah, look how trippingly he approaches!'

The line got a bigger laugh this time as Boy struggled to his feet. Now, he and Pompio went into their rewritten routine, reciting the lines with well-practised ease. Every time they performed this, it felt tighter and more assured. The oiled visor kept snapping down right on cue, prompted by the slightest nod of Boy's head. By the time they got to the end of their exchange, they had the audience right where they wanted them and then it was time for Pompio to go and "stroom his greed". He scampered off to enthusiastic applause and on came Lexi, ready to deliver her first line which thankfully, she did.

'Ah, my Lord, how handsome you look today!'

Clank! Down swung the visor and up rose the laughter from the crowd. *This is going brilliantly*, thought Boy. He was beginning to believe that he really was rather good at this acting lark and then, suddenly, shockingly, a loud voice from the midst of the crowd yelled, 'Get off! You're rubbish!'

It threw Boy for a moment and he turned to look down into the crowd, peering through the slit of the visor. Of course, he'd been expecting a heckler to shout *something* at them, but not yet. This was way too early in the proceedings. There was a whole lot of script to get through first. Maybe Archimaldo hadn't been clear about the man's cue. Boy lifted a hand and raised the visor. He saw now that a man was pushing his way through the crowd, rudely shoving other spectators out of his way. He was a great, big, muscular fellow, wearing a horned helmet and sporting a ginger beard that had been plaited into pig-tails. His bare chest sported a selection of tattoos and he was armed, Boy noted, a huge sword hanging in a leather scabbard at his waist.

'Too soon,' hissed Boy urgently, but the big man took no notice of him. He came to a halt a short distance from the stage and glared aggressively up at Boy. 'Who are you looking at?' he snarled. 'Would you like a painting?'

'Yes, please,' said Boy, slipping automatically into one of his rehearsed put-downs. 'I'll put it on the mantelpiece. It'll keep the kids away from the fire!'

That got a big laugh from the crowd, but Boy was wondering what they were supposed to do about the big chunk of script they had been forced to skip. Ah well, he decided, there was no option now but to go with it.

'What did you say?' snapped the heckler, his eyes bulging as though he couldn't quite believe what he had just heard.

'What's the problem?' asked Lexi, getting in on the act. 'Too many syllables? Allow me to help. You. Have. A. Face. Like. A. Buff-a-lo's. Bum!'

Again, the crowd laughed delightedly, but the big man didn't seem to find it in the least bit funny. He fixed his attention on Lexi. 'That's good coming from an ugly, Elvish mare,' he said and there was an audible gasp of astonishment from the crowd.

Boy was horrified. 'You can't say that!' he cried. 'At least keep your insults polite.' He realised this made no sense but didn't know what else to say.

'People like her should go back to where they came from,' added the heckler.

'Well I would,' retorted Lexi, 'but it took me two days to get here. Mind you, I'm glad I made the trip. Somebody told me that Drumreedy had the biggest idiot in the known world and I didn't believe them. Now I can see they were right.'

More laughter.

'You should know better than to take work from local people,' insisted the big man.

'Well, if there's any work for idiots, you've cornered the market,' retorted Lexi.

This earned a round of applause from the crowd.

'At least I'm a pure blood,' argued the heckler.

'You clearly don't do *anything* by half,' snapped Lexi. 'You're a pure bigot. Congratulations.'

'Yeah,' added Boy, determined to support her. 'You're so nasty, if you went into a haunted house, you'd come out with an application form!'

'You're so stupid,' added Lexi, 'if somebody ordered you to kill a fish you'd try and drown it.'

'Think you're funny, don't you?' yelled the heckler.

'We *know* we're funny,' said Boy, 'but here's the thing: we're being paid to make fools of ourselves. You're doing it for free.'

A long 'ooh' came from the crowd. The big man studied Boy contemptuously for a moment as though examining some dirt under his fingernails. He reached to his belt and pulled the huge sword slowly from its scabbard. It made a nasty hissing sound as it came out. 'Got any more funny lines?' he asked. 'Why don't we see if you can still make jokes without a head?'

Boy felt a sudden cold chill run through him. This wasn't anything like the hecklers they'd had previously.

'Look, didn't Archimaldo tell you how far you could go?' he asked quietly.

'Never heard of him,' said the heckler, shaking his head. He started to climb the stairs that led up to the stage.

'He's the man that hired you,' insisted Boy.

'Nobody hired me,' said the heckler. 'I'm a free agent.'

Lexi took a step forward to intervene. 'Hey, now just a minute, sunshine,' she said. 'I think you're taking this too far. Why don't you—'

She didn't see the punch coming. The man swung his left hand suddenly upwards and struck her hard on the chin. She went down in an ungainly sprawl on the stage. Her eyes fluttered for a moment and closed.

'Lexi!' gasped Boy. He tried to help her but stopped in his tracks as the heckler's sword slashed a deadly, silver arc inches from his throat, forcing him to jump back out of harm's way.

'What do you think you're doing, you maniac?' he cried.

The man's eyes blazed with deadly intent. 'I'm preparing to kill a clown,' he said. He stepped closer still, raising the sword. Boy instinctively pulled his own sword free of its belt and lifted it in a desperate attempt to block the blow, but he'd momentarily forgotten it was only a prop, made of balsa wood. The heckler's blade sliced clean through it, leaving

Boy standing there with just the handle.

'You've gone too far!' protested Boy. 'You're only supposed to—'

He broke off as the heckler's left hand thrust forward hitting him right in the middle of his breastplate. He hit the stage with a loud crash and skidded a short distance on his back until his head was brushing against the curtain. Behind it, he knew, Grud was hiding, waiting patiently for his cue. Boy tried to fight the panic rising within him.

'Look, can we talk about this?' he pleaded.

The big man shook his head. 'You've already talked way too much,' he said. 'Let's see if you find *this* funny.' He raised his sword high and ran forward.

Boy froze momentarily but at the last instant, a desperate idea occurred to him. 'TREASURE!' he roared and right on cue, Grud jumped out from behind the curtain holding the open wooden chest of prop jewels in front of him.

'Here it is!' he yelled and then grunted in surprise as the big man's sword struck the chest, embedding the blade deep in the wood, flinging glittering, multi-coloured jewels in all directions.

'Hey!' roared Grud. 'You've ruined our treasure!' He dropped the heavy chest onto the heckler's feet. The man gave a squawk of pain as the weight of it crushed his toes and then Grud struck him in the face with a fist the size of a joint of ham. The heckler flailed backwards off the edge of the stage, scattering people in all directions.

Boy rolled over with a gasp of relief, intending to get up and go to Lexi's assistance. As he turned, his gaze registered movement at the back of the stage.

Orson's caravan was in motion, heading away from its parking place. At the reins, sat a wiry, thin-faced fellow that Boy had never seen before. As Boy watched, bewildered, the man cracked a whip and urged the two buffalo into a run, steering the caravan away from the square and along a busy side street, obliging people to scramble out of its way. It dawned on Boy exactly what was happening here. Orson's caravan held the padlocked, metal chest in which all the company's money was kept – every gelt they'd earned for their performances so far. The heckler wasn't the stooge that Archimaldo had hired. He was merely a distraction for a robbery.

Boy clambered frantically upright and ran towards the steps at the rear of the stage, pushing past Orson and Mo who, transfixed by what had just happened on stage, were unaware of what was occurring behind them. Boy lifted the helmet from his head and threw it aside. He half-ran, half fell down the stairs to the town square and stumbled towards Lexi's caravan, casting off bits of his costume as he went. Belle was thankfully still hitched behind it, so he untied her and took a few moments to remove his arm and leg guards. The breastplate had too many straps holding it in place, so after struggling with it for a few moments, he gave up, vaulted into the saddle and urged Belle around the side of the caravan.

'Hiyah!' he yelled and she took off at speed, doubtless glad to have the first proper gallop she'd had in ages. As Boy steered her towards the side street where the caravan had gone, he was aware that a large part of the audience was breaking away from the front of the stage and following him at a run, though of course, Belle soon left them behind.

The street ahead was lined with busy market stalls and Boy yelled a warning for people to get out of his way if they knew what was good for them. He kicked his heels into Belle's flanks, urging her to go faster. Pretty soon, he saw Orson's caravan a short distance ahead of him, juddering and rattling as it bounced over the rough dirt surface of the street. Belle quickly began to shorten the distance between them. Suddenly, the caravan's rear door flew open and Boy saw a man framed in the opening, aiming what looked like a crossbow. There was a blur of motion and Boy simply didn't have time to react. The crossbow bolt whizzed across the intervening space and he felt the impact of it slamming into his chest.

For a horrible moment, he thought he was dead. Then, he looked down in amazement and saw that the bolt was protruding from the metal breastplate that he had tried so hard to remove. The thought of what would have happened if he hadn't been wearing it filled him with a hot surge of anger. Undeterred, he urged Belle onward until they were only a few feet behind the caravan, running at full stretch.

The man was still in the doorway, rocking from side to side as he attempted to reload the crossbow and Boy knew that he couldn't allow him to do that. A bolt fired at such close range would undoubtedly go straight though his tin armour so he unhooked his feet from the stirrups and clambered precariously up onto Belle's back, a trick he had mastered when he was a child. They were approaching a bend in the road and the caravan made the turn, its wheels shrieking in protest. Boy kept Belle galloping at full speed as though to overtake the caravan, but at the last moment, he flung himself off her back towards the open door. His outstretched hands caught the edge of its frame and he hung there for a moment, desperately clinging on.

The man, who was hooded and had a silk scarf pulled across the lower half of his face, gave up trying to load the crossbow and used it like a club, attempting to swat Boy away from the door. Boy released one hand and caught the string of the weapon as it swung towards his face. He gritted his teeth and pulled as hard as he could, yanking the man out through the doorway. He yelled something behind his mask and released his hold on the crossbow. It whirled away but as he fell, the man grabbed at Boy, desperately trying to hold onto him. His fingers closed on the edge of the breastplate and for an instant, Boy was aware of an irresistible force dragging him backwards towards the street. The straps of the breastplate tore free, and the man fell and hit the road hard.

With a supreme effort Boy managed to swing his lower body forward, until he had managed to place one foot on the lowest step of the caravan. He hung at an angle and for a moment, debated what to do next. At that instant, the caravan went over a bump in the road. The open door swung back and Boy was able to quickly transfer his grip to the edge of the door frame itself. He pulled himself inside with a gasp of relief and dropped onto his knees. He took a moment to catch his breath. The interior of the caravan was jolting and swaying madly around him and glancing about, he made sure that the padlocked money chest was still where it ought to be. It was. The thieves must have been planning to break it open at their leisure.

Boy took a deep breath and dropped forward onto his hands and knees. He edged slowly closer to the opening at the front of the caravan. The thief was still hunched behind the reins, cracking his whip, seemingly oblivious to what was happening behind him. Boy inched closer. Looking out past the driver, he could see that the caravan was now heading out of the town's outskirts into more open country. Boy kept moving and got himself up into the opening, until he was right behind the driver. He leaned forward and shouted into the man's ear.

'BOO!' he yelled.

The man leapt up from the seat as though he'd just been stung by a hornet. He overbalanced, performed an ungainly somersault and crashed down onto the buffalo's haunches, startling them. They started kicking their back legs and, with a yell of alarm, the man flailed sideways and tumbled onto the road. The caravan raced on past him. Boy emerged from the opening and sat himself down on the buckboard. He took hold of the reins and pulled back hard. 'Whoah!' he cried. 'Easy now. Easy!'

The buffalo gradually slowed to a halt and after giving them a few moments to settle themselves, Boy managed to get them turned around and started back towards Drumreedy. After a short distance, he encountered the thief sitting in the road, holding his head in his hands and looking rather the worse for wear. He staggered upright and started to reach for his sword, but a shout from further up the road alerted him to the fact that some of the people following the caravan were already drawing near.

'It's up to you,' Boy told him. 'In your place, I wouldn't wait around for that lot to catch up with me.'

The man looked apprehensively at the approaching people for a moment, swore under his breath, turned and began to run away.

'Wise move,' Boy shouted after him and urged the buffalo onwards.

Pretty soon, the first of the townspeople ran towards him, cheering gleefully as they saw who was sitting at the reins.

People reached up to shake his hand as they went by and some of the younger men carried on after the fleeing villain. 'We have the other two,' one man shouted to him, as he raced past. 'They've been taken to the mayor for punishment. We don't tolerate their sort in Drumreedy.'

Another man came along leading Belle by her reins and at Boy's instructions, tied her up behind the caravan.

Boy smiled and nodded his thanks. As he drove back, the road became increasingly blocked by crowds of people, all cheering and waving at him. Most of them turned around and escorted him back towards the town.

'Best show ever!' a young woman shouted up to him. 'Amazing. How do you make it look so real?'

'It's a gift,' Boy assured her.

A short distance further on, he spotted a familiar figure in the crowd, a great, bearded fellow towering over all the others.

'Boy!' cried Grud, sounding relieved. 'I came to look for you.' He clambered awkwardly up to sit beside his friend. 'Are you all right? Did the bad men hurt you?'

'I'm a bit bruised,' admitted Boy. 'They didn't get our money. What about Lexi? She took a real punch from that heckler.'

'She's all right but she's as mad as anything. They took the bad man away. He was unconscious, otherwise I think she'd have made him very sorry for himself.' Grud looked distraught. 'He ruined our treasure chest. It's split right down the middle.'

'We'll get another one,' Boy assured him. 'Don't worry about it.'

By now the road was so crowded that progress was painfully slow, but they finally got back to the town square, accompanied by throngs of cheering people. As Boy pulled the caravan in alongside the other one, the crowd swept around the sides of the stage to fill up the area in front of it. Boy and Grud climbed down and Boy saw that the rest of the cast were all standing up on the stage, looking down at the audience, so he and Grud climbed the steps to join them.

'Everybody all right?' asked Boy, and Lexi turned to look at him. Her green eyes blazed and she had a dark purple bruise on the left side of her jaw. She didn't say anything, but simply stepped forward and put her arms around him, hugging him close. A huge cheer went up from the crowd and then the coins started flying towards them, a veritable blizzard of copper, silver and gold. Lexi and Boy barely noticed.

'Blimey,' said Pompio, staring around in utter amazement. He looked up at Orson. 'How are we going to improve on this?' he asked.

Chapter Fourteen

GETTING CLOSE

TOWARDS LATE afternoon of the following day, after a long and uneventful journey, Boy noticed something on the far horizon – a tall, slender spire that seemed to reach the clouds. He pointed and turned to Lexi, who was riding on the buckboard beside him. 'What on earth is that?' he asked.

She followed the direction he was indicating and smiled. 'Oh, that's just the steeple of the Queen's palace in Ravalan. It's visible for miles. Have you never seen it before?'

He shook his head. 'I've never been anywhere near Ravalan,' he reminded her.

'Surely you must have heard of the steeple? It's famous.

That's the highest, man-made structure in the known world. Somebody told me that once.'

'So, the city is close now?' reasoned Boy.

'Pretty much. We'll camp by the River Geela tonight and be there by midday tomorrow – just in time for the next performance. Don't worry,' she assured him. 'We'll be in time for the Moon of Elnis.' She looked at Boy sheepishly. 'I haven't really thanked you, have I?'

He looked at her in surprise. 'For what?' he asked.

'For going after Dad's caravan.'

Boy shrugged. 'There's no need for thanks,' he assured her.

'Of course there is. You put your life at risk. You could have been injured – even killed. I saw the state of that breastplate.' She shook her head. 'I want you to know, I'm extremely grateful. We all are. We'd have been in deep trouble if they'd got away with all that money.'

'I'll say!' said a voice from just behind them. Boy saw that Pompio had roused himself from his regular nap in the back of the caravan and come out to do what he did best – shoehorn himself into other people's conversations. 'What I don't understand is this: how did those thieves know which caravan to take? I mean, they could have grabbed this one and all they'd have got for their trouble is some spare costumes and Lexi's old scripts. Let's face it, nobody wants them.'

Lexi gave him a look. 'Thanks very much.'

'Oh, you know what I mean! Words are all well and good, but they aren't actually worth anything, are they?'

'That's a matter of opinion,' said Lexi.

'Yes, all right. I take your point but what I'm saying is, it's like those brigands knew which caravan had the money in it.'

'I spoke to the town sheriff about that,' said Lexi. 'He reckoned those villains had followed us all the way from Sumac. They probably had us under observation the whole time we were there and worked out exactly where we stashed our takings.'

'The cunning rogues,' snarled Pompio. 'It's lucky for them I was distracted or I'd have given them a pasting.'

'It's funny they didn't try to jump us out in the open,' said Boy.

'Not really,' said Lexi. 'There were only three of them and six of us.' She raised her eyebrows. 'They'd probably heard about my fearsome reputation with a sword.' She waved an imaginary weapon and mimed the act of running Boy through. 'It made sense for them to cause a distraction and make off while our attention was elsewhere.' Once again, she looked at Boy. 'It's just lucky you spotted them when you did.'

'What will happen to them?' asked Boy.

'Well, two of them were already in the town dungeon when I spoke to the Sheriff. His men were still looking for the driver. I reckon they'll all be for the chop.'

'The chop?' echoed Boy.

Lexi held out one hand, palm up and brought the edge of her other hand down onto it, miming the action of an axe. 'That's how they deal with thieves in Drumreedy,' she said. 'Not nice, but I guess they knew the risks.'

'I'd be happier if they'd just imprison them for a while,' said Boy. 'Until they've learned their lesson.'

'Some people never learn,' said Pompio. 'At least this way, they won't be doing it again, will they?'

'True, but it seems a bit . . . barbaric.'

'Maybe,' admitted Pompio, 'but I reckon it's a timely warning to us, especially after all the money we took at Drumreedy. Another eighteen gold crowns – not to mention the fifty that Tristan gave us! We'll doubtless take a lot more in Ravalan. We'll have to keep somebody watching over that chest around the clock.'

'How can we?' asked Boy. 'We need everyone on stage.'

'Maybe we could put it all into bags and ask Mo to sew it into Grud's clothes,' suggested Pompio. 'He's the only one who'd be strong enough to carry all those coins and nobody would be daft enough to try and take it from *him*.'

Lexi shook her head. 'That's too much responsibility for anyone,' she said. 'Can you imagine how much his clothes would weigh after the Moon of Elnis?' She shook her head. 'No, I think there's a better answer. I talked to Dad about it last night. I told him that when we reach Ravalan, we should put the money in a bank.'

Boy and Pompio looked at her blankly. 'What, you mean, like bury it somewhere?' muttered Pompio.

'No,' said Lexi, 'not *that* kind of bank. It's a new thing. Haven't you heard about it? It's a big building where everything is kept safely under lock and key. The idea is, we give the people at the bank our money—'

'I'm not liking this idea so far,' said Pompio.

'They keep it safe for us. Then, whenever we need some, we ask for it and they hand it over.'

'That's very big of 'em,' said Pompio. 'Hang on a minute, let me get this straight. We have to go to them and ask if we can have some of our own money?' he snorted. 'I've never heard such nonsense!' He thought for a moment. 'What happens if they say "no"?'

'Oh, they can't do that,' said Lexi. 'It never stops being our money. The bank are sort of borrowing it, so they can use it for other things – you know, investments and so forth.'

'What are investments?' asked Boy.

'Well, for instance, the bank might decide to lend our money to somebody else who needs it.'

'You cannot be serious!' protested Pompio.

'They charge those people a fee for lending it to them.'

'But it's not even theirs to lend in the first place!'

'It kind of is, because we've given our permission and the bank guarantee that the money will be there if we ever need it.'

Pompio scratched his head. 'How can they give us the same money back if they've already lent it to somebody else?'

'It's not the same money,' reasoned Lexi, 'just the same value.'

Boy was still completely baffled. 'What's in it for them?' he asked.

'They charge us a little bit for looking after the money.'

'Ah right,' said Pompio. 'I thought there'd be a catch.'

'It's not a catch, so much as a *fee*. We only pay them a few gelts a month.'

'For doing what?' asked Pompio.

'For keeping our money safe.'

'People will actually pay you to do that?' he scowled. 'I'm clearly in the wrong line of work here,' he said. 'Maybe I should set up a – what's it called? A bank?' He lifted his hands as though picturing it. 'The Bank of Pompio,' he said.

'I'm not sure you'd be cut out for it,' Lexi told him. 'It's quite complicated. You see, the money will also have interest.'

'That's exactly the problem,' snarled Pompio. 'There's too many people interested in our money.'

'No, what I mean is, the money *makes* interest, which means it's worth a little bit more as time goes on.'

'How does that work?' asked Boy.

'It's kind of complicated.'

'I don't like the sound of it,' said Pompio, crossing his arms.

'You don't have to,' Lexi assured him, 'but let me tell you,

I'd feel a lot safer if we weren't carrying all of our earnings around in the back of a caravan.' She lifted the fingers of one hand to trace the dark bruise on her jaw. 'I'd rather not go through this again, if it's all the same to you.'

'What did you do in the old days?' Boy asked her. 'You know, when your mother was a big star and everything? There must have been a lot of money changing hands back then.'

'Oh yes, there was, but we employed a team of people. Four armed bruisers they were, Dad used to call them "the heavies".' She smiled fondly as though picturing them. 'Ex-sailors that were tough as old boots and armed to the teeth. They had their own caravan and they accompanied the money chest everywhere it went. They had one job and that was to look after the takings. '

'Well, couldn't we go back to that system?' suggested Boy.

Lexi scowled and shook her head. 'I don't think so,' she said.

'Why not?'

'The four of them ran out on us one night and took the money for an entire season. Of course, since they were so fearsome, nobody dared to go up against them – including us. We never saw hide nor hair of them or the money again.'

'Oh.' Boy raised his eyebrows. 'On the other hand, maybe this bank idea is the way to go,' he said.

'Don't let her talk you round,' Pompio advised him. 'I still think it sounds stupid.'

Lexi pointed ahead to where the trail ran alongside the banks of a wide, slow-moving river. 'Well, there's the Geela,' she said. 'Right on cue. That looks like a decent enough place to make camp for the night,' she added, pointing to an area of flat land, sheltered by thick screens of bushes and ferns. She steered the caravan towards it. 'The buffalo can skip their mulch for tonight and dine on some fresh greens. Pompio, maybe you and Grud might care to have a wander along the river and see if you can scare up a bit of fresh meat for our supper?'

'No problem!' Pompio ducked back into the caravan and emerged a few moments later, fully equipped for the hunt with his bow and a quiver full of arrows. He jumped down from the buckboard and ran back to the others, shouting for Grud. 'Hey, big feller! Wait till I tell you about Lexi's latest mad scheme. You won't believe what she wants to do with our money!'

Boy leaned over and gazed after him thoughtfully. 'He's a character, isn't he?' he observed. 'Does he ever shut up?'

'No, he doesn't. It's all part of his charm.' Lexi pulled the buffalo to a halt beside a screen of bushes. She climbed down and began to unhitch them.

'What are our plans for after Ravalan?' asked Boy.

'I think we'll maybe head out towards Gullamir,' she said. 'There's a big festival coming up there in a moon's time and some of the towns on the route have worked well for us before. Plus, they haven't seen *Young Adamis* yet.' She flicked Boy a sly glance. 'That's if you're not living in some luxury villa by then, spending your newfound fortune.'

He laughed. 'I'm not holding my breath for that,' he said. He studied her for a moment. 'What about you, Lexi?'

She looked back at him. 'What about me?'

'Well, what are your long-term plans? I mean, you're not going to carry on living this wandering life forever, are you?'

'Hadn't really thought about it,' she told him. 'As long as Dad is up for carrying on, I reckon I should be there to help him out. I have to say, things are looking more promising than they have in a long time.'

'Have you never thought about settling down somewhere?'

'I'd soon get bored with that,' she told him. 'The travelling life is all I've ever known. My parents took me on the road when I was just a babe in arms. I can still remember listening to them argue every night. They used to have the most terrible rows.'

'What's that dear?' asked Orson, stepping unexpectedly from the back of the caravan.

'Oh.' Lexi gave him a sheepish grin. 'I was just telling Boy about you and Mum – how you always got along so well.'

Orson chuckled. 'Hmm. I doubt that very much.' He looked at Boy. 'I think we had what is called a "volatile relationship",' he said. 'You must understand, my wife was a very vivacious woman. Wherever we went, she tended to attract admirers. I'm afraid, I could sometimes be a tiny bit jealous about that.'

Lexi sniggered. 'A tiny bit!' she repeated. 'That's the understatement of the century. You two were always falling out with each other. Sometimes I felt less like a daughter and more like a referee. You remember that time in Tanamacoola?'

Orson looked puzzled. 'I'm not sure I do,' he admitted.

'*I* certainly remember it,' said Mo, wandering over to join the conversation. 'There was this troubadour who had fallen madly in love with Velina. What was his name? Artimus? Bartimus? Something like that. He started following her everywhere. He had this annoying habit of standing under the window of whichever inn we were staying at.'

'We could afford to stay in such places at that time,' interjected Lexi. 'No kipping in the caravans in those days!'

'Exactly. It would be in the early hours of the morning, when everyone was trying to sleep. This lovelorn troubadour would come along after fortifying himself with a few goblets of ale at the local tavern—'

'More than a few,' said Lexi.

'A skinful,' said Orson.

'He would sing his latest, soppy ballad for her whilst playing an out-of-tune mandolin.'

Boy winced. 'Sounds embarrassing,' he said.

'You've no idea,' said Mo. 'It was "oh my love" this and "oh my heart is breaking" that – all kinds of sentimental tripe. One night—' She broke off and looked at Orson accusingly.

'Well, in my defence,' said Orson, affecting an innocent look, 'I had absolutely no idea he was standing under the window when I emptied that pot.'

Boy frowned. 'What was in the pot?' he asked. He studied the three faces around him for a moment and then grimaced. 'Oh no,' he said. 'It wasn't a chamber pot, was it?'

'Alas,' said Orson, 'I'm afraid it was. Well, I'd had a few goblets of wine myself that night!' Everybody burst out laughing.

'We never heard from him again after that,' shrieked Mo, tears in her eyes. 'I often think of him, wandering home that night, heartbroken and covered in . . .' She started laughing again and the others joined in with her.

Boy studied them fondly for a moment, thinking to himself that he couldn't remember when he had last felt so at ease with other people. For the first time since he had been robbed, it came to him that maybe he should just forget all about his stolen invention; maybe he was better off walking away from it and sticking with his new family. That was exactly how he was beginning to think of them: family.

Just then, the bushes parted and Pompio's face appeared in the opening, looking very pleased with himself. 'Who's the best hunter in the known world?' he cried proudly.

Lexi pretended to look puzzled. 'Umm . . . ooh, that's a tough one,' she said. 'Let me think now. Best hunter?'

'Me!' hissed Pompio. 'It's me. Say me!'

'Probably that fellow we used to know in Gullamir,' suggested Orson. 'What was his name? Hahn the Hunter?'

'Hengist the Hunter,' suggested Mo. 'Or was it Harle the Hunter?'

'It's me, you idiots!' cried Pompio. 'Obviously!'

'You?' Orson looked puzzled.

'Well, of course. I only went off two moments ago and look what I already have for you. Tonight, we shall dine like kings!' His arm came through the screen of bushes, holding a bird by its neck. 'It's a jub-jub bird,' he exclaimed proudly. 'They're supposed to be delicious these – a proper delicacy.'

Boy's eyes widened in surprise. The main problem was, the brightly coloured bird was tiny – no bigger than Pompio's fist.

Lexi leaned closer to inspect the bird. 'Well, let me see,' she murmured. 'Boy and I will have a wing. Grud and Mo can have a leg. That leaves the breast for Orson. You can pick the carcass. That's going to be a feast to remember!'

Just then, Grud came struggling along the riverbank, with something huge and glistening braced across his broad shoulders. It was a great, silvery fish with the dimensions of a tree trunk.

'I got this,' he said. 'Do you think there'll be enough to go around?'

Everyone laughed and this time, Boy couldn't help joining in.

Chapter Fifteen

RAVALAN

THE FOLLOWING morning, the caravan crested a rise and there, perched on the peak of an even bigger hill, lay the mighty, walled city of Ravalan. Boy couldn't help but catch his breath. Of course, over the years, he had heard many stories of its splendour from travellers who had actually visited the place, but Boy's imagination had been no match for the city itself, which seemed to shimmer in the early morning sunlight like a great sculpture carved from the finest marble.

'Incredible,' murmured Boy. 'I've never seen anything like it.'

Lexi smiled. 'I felt the same way when I first laid eyes on it,' she assured him. 'Of course, I was only a kid.'

'I wish we'd known each other back then.' said Boy, wistfully. 'I imagine we'd have been great friends.'

'Could be,' said Lexi, 'but I don't know. I was a bit of a tomboy. I liked to fight. Who knows? We might have ended up as enemies.'

He looked at her in dismay. 'You really think so?'

'I doubt it,' she said and grinned. She slapped the reins against the buffalo's haunches and urged them up the gentle slope that led to the city gates. As they drew steadily closer, Boy was able to make out some more details. The walls were sheer and high and the blocks of stone were so perfectly assembled that you could barely see the joins. They headed through a huge archway. Looking up, Boy could see the spikes of a massive, wooden portcullis hanging high above them.

'That can be lowered in the event of an attack,' Lexi told him, 'but the proud claim here is that there has been no war in Ravalan since Queen Gertrude ascended the throne.' She looked at Boy. 'Some history for you,' she added. 'I know you're fond of that.'

'Thanks,' he said. 'It's like having my own tour guide.'

'I do my best,' she said.

They continued onwards until they reached the gigantic, wooden gates – three times the height of a man. A couple of formidable looking guards stood to either side, armed with swords. One of the soldiers stepped forward, his face impassive beneath his crested helmet.

'Woah!' he commanded. 'State your business.'

Lexi smiled down at him. 'Good morning. We're the Wandering Star Theatre Company and we're booked to do a show in the city square at midday?'

The second guard produced a rolled-up piece of parchment. He consulted it for a moment, laboriously reading through a list.

'Yep,' he said at last. 'That checks out. Just the two caravans, is it? Any passengers in this one?'

'Just me,' said Pompio, appearing at the opening. Boy saw that he had already dressed himself as Bartrum. He wasn't doing the red waistcoat and fez routine for this show. Lexi had explained that the security checks needed to get into Ravalan were far too complicated and anyway, there was always a big crowd for the Moon of Elnis. Pompio bowed politely to the guards. 'Allow me to introduce myself,' he said, doffing his feathered cap. 'Pompio, the world's most talented boobo, at your service!'

The second guard grinned delightedly. 'I remember him from last year!' he said. 'He's very funny, that one!'

Pompio grinned delightedly at the compliment but the first guard looked unconvinced. 'A talking boobo. Whatever next?' he muttered. He shook his head and returned his attention to Lexi. 'Do you have any weapons, explosives, poisons or alcohol on board?'

'I have a sword,' said Boy, indicating the weapon at his side.

'I have a bow,' said Pompio, 'but I only use it for hunting game. Actually, I bagged a jub-jub bird last night. It was delicious but there wasn't very much to go around.'

The first guard waved a hand as if to indicate that he wasn't interested in what Pompio chose to hunt. 'Do you have a permit for said bow?'

Pompio grimaced. 'I don't think I do,' he said. 'I've never been asked before.'

'It's a new requirement,' said the first guard. 'We've tightened up on security after the threats to her Majesty.'

'Threats?' whispered Lexi. 'What kind of threats?'

'Oh, from one idiotic political movement or another,' muttered the first guard. 'Seems to be what happens when you're a member of royalty. We're very particular about unlicensed weapons.'

'To be fair, he doesn't really need a permit,' said the second guard. 'I'm not sure if they'd issue one to a boobo, anyway.'

The first guard seemed to consider this and nodded.

'You can go through,' he said and waved them onwards. Pompio leaned out to the second guard as they went past. 'You should come and see our show,' he suggested. 'It starts at noon.'

The caravan trundled along the main street of the city which was lined with busy market stalls, selling richly embroidered fabrics, multi-coloured spices, elvish coffee and all manner of goods. They went past a huge, open barbecue where a whole tunnel-rat was roasting over an open fire and a man dressed in white apparel was gleefully carving off sizzling hunks of meat for an eager queue of customers. The smell made Boy's stomach gurgle, even though he'd breakfasted well enough before they'd left the campsite.

'That smells good,' he said.

'Yes, we'll get something after the show,' Lexi assured him. 'We always eat well in Ravalan and as I remember, we don't usually have to pay for it.' As they continued through the bustle, a familiar sound came to Boy's ears – the sound of a pleasant voice singing a jolly refrain.

'Hey, that sounds like Archimaldo!' shouted Boy. He stood up in his seat and craned his head around to look for the troubadour. He spotted him, standing on a small, raised stage, performing the Wandering Star's jingle to a bunch of enthusiastic onlookers. Boy waved an arm and Archimaldo quickly spotted him. Once he reached the end of his refrain, he jumped down from the stage and hurried through the crowd, grinning.

'Well, well!' he cried. 'If it isn't my good friends of the Wandering Star! How are you faring today?'

'We're very happy indeed,' Lexi assured him. 'We have to say that your jingles seem to be working a treat. We've never played to such crowds!'

'I told you it would work,' said Archimaldo. 'It pays to

advertise! Wait till you see how many have gathered in the city square. There must be thousands there already.'

'That's great news,' said Pompio. 'We're really looking forward to performing.'

Archimaldo stepped closer and lowered his voice. 'A little bird tells me that you have been invited to perform for her Majesty Queen Gertrude this evening,' he murmured.

'Yes, that's right,' said Lexi. 'Obviously, we're thrilled about it. We've not done a Royal Command Performance since my mother's time.'

Archimaldo nodded. 'Of course, I cannot claim any credit for that,' he said. 'As I understand it, you were spotted in Gallibab, just before we met. However, I do feel confident that my jingles have directed a lot more customers to your noon performance. Of course, I shall be seeing you this evening as I am also appearing at the palace.'

'You?' Boy was puzzled by this news. 'Don't tell me you're going to perform your jingles for the Queen?'

Archimaldo chortled at the very idea. 'Of course not!' he said. 'I'm not just a one trick pony, you know. When I'm not doing my promotional work, I am also part of a harmony act with the two other members of Troubadours Unlimited. We perform songs of love and sorrow under "The Three Nightingales".'

'That's got a real ring to it,' said Lexi. 'We'll look forward to hearing you.'

Archimaldo bowed graciously. 'Until this evening,' he said. 'I would of course wish you luck for your performance, but I'm told you theatrical types are superstitious about that kind of thing. I will merely say, "break an arm".'

'I hope not,' muttered Pompio. 'That would really put a crimp on our show!'

Lexi slapped the reins against the buffalo's haunches and Archimaldo made his way back to the little stage. Boy heard his voice rising above the hubbub of the crowd.

'And now, good citizens of Ravalan, a little ditty about the wonders of Mistress Twinkle's celebrated lamp oil!'

'If you've no oil to fuel your light,
To brighten up the darkest night,
Then choose the fuel that's always right –
Mistress Twinkle's lamp oil!
It never smokes or makes you croak;
I swear this really is no joke,
I'm simply not that kind of bloke –
Choose Mistress Twinkle's lamp oil!
Bright, clear, have no fear,
'T'will light your way throughout the year.
Two gelts a bottle – cheap as beer!
Mistress Twinkle's lamp oil.'

The rest of the song was lost to them as the caravan headed towards the city square. Boy saw the giant fountains of Ravalan – two huge, marble structures that pumped clear, foaming water into the air. The twin plumes powered upwards, flashing in the sunlight, and then cascaded down into round, circular pools where it glittered enticingly. Women were happily filling buckets from the pools and some were even doing their washing. Boy remembered that Gordimo had mentioned these structures, saying that Boy's invention would mean nothing to these people.

'Oh, my great giddy aunt!' said Pompio, interrupting his thoughts and Boy lifted his head. Ahead of them lay the city square and further on, Boy could see the huge wooden platform, on which their show was to be enacted. Between it and the caravan, a massive crowd of people waited for the show to commence. When the nearest of them saw the caravans approaching, a roar of approval went up from the nearest of them. It seemed to rise and swell like magic, travelling through the entire crowd, until the combined sound of their voices was almost deafening.

'How are we even going to get to the stage?' wondered Lexi. A line of soldiers appeared in front of them and began to push onlookers to either side with their metal shields, making a wide avenue through their midst. Boy swallowed. He had managed the last few shows without too much trouble, but appearing in front of an audience this huge was intimidating to say the very least. He reminded himself that later on today, he'd be enacting the role of Young Adamis for the entertainment of the Queen and her Royal household. Not for the first time, he asked himself what he was even doing there. How had he got mixed up in all this? He was no actor. He was an inventor, who really ought to be concentrating on recovering his stolen property, but he also knew that Lexi and the others were depending on him. He could hardly abandon them now.

'Are you all right?' asked Lexi, as though sensing his nervousness.

'I'm just asking myself how I got into this situation,' he muttered. 'There are thousands of people out there. How will they even be able to hear us?'

'Just speak from the diaphragm,' said Pompio, tapping his chest. 'Here, repeat after me. Fee-fi-fo-fum. Say it!'

'Knock it off,' said Lexi. 'You'll only make him worse.' She studied Boy for a moment and smiled warmly. 'Just speak as loudly and clearly as you can,' she told him. 'We've played here many times. The marble surfaces give your voice a natural echo. You'll be fine.'

She steered the caravan around to the rear of the stage. A cordon of guards waited to protect them.

'At least we won't have to worry about anybody trying to break into the caravans while we're here,' said Lexi. 'It'd be a brave thief who messed with this lot.' She looked at Pompio. 'All right,' she said, 'get up on that stage and warm them up for us! And for goodness sake, give us enough time to get into our costumes!'

'No worries! I'll tell 'em a few jokes.' Pompio scrambled out of the caravan and scampered towards the steps at the rear of the stage. He went up them at a run. Lexi studied Boy for a moment. 'I'll go and get into my costume,' she said. 'Are you going to be all right?'

He nodded. 'I think so,' he said.

'Good.' She leaned impulsively forward and kissed him on the lips. 'For luck,' she said and ran across to Orson's caravan. Boy sat there, slightly stunned. He was aware of a tingling sensation where her lips had touched his. She'd wished him luck! Hadn't Archimaldo said that you weren't supposed to do that? Boy turned to shout to Lexi but she was already scrambling into the back of the other caravan.

'It'll be all right,' Boy assured himself. 'Just speak clearly.' He remembered Pompio's advice. 'Fee-fi-fo-fum,' he intoned and felt vaguely foolish. He saw that Orson, Mo and Grud were already in their costumes and hurrying to take their places up in the wings. Boy parted the curtains of the caravan and clambered inside. He put on the unwieldy costume of Young Adamis. He picked up the breastplate and noted the puncture hole that the crossbow bolt had made, just above his heart. He swallowed, as he thought about how close he'd come to losing his life.

Even at this distance, he could hear Pompio's voice. 'Good citizens of Ravalan!' he shouted. 'I have a question for you. Are you ready to be entertained?'

A great, thunderous roar of approval went up, drowning out whatever the boobo said next.

Chapter Sixteen

BEST LAID PLANS

A N HOUR later, Boy staggered wearily down the steps at the back of the stage and made his way unsteadily over to the caravan. He was sweating profusely, covered in fresh bruises and couldn't remember when he had last felt quite so excited. He unstrapped his breastplate, opened the door of Lexi's caravan and flung it inside. Then, he sat on the back step and started to remove his shin and arm guards with trembling fingers. He felt strangely emotional, as though at any moment, he might burst into tears.

He looked up as Pompio scampered down from the stage, his expression one of annoyance. 'I thought you said you were coming out here to get a shovel?' he cried.

Boy shrugged. He found it difficult now to form words. He pointed a finger towards the stage and took a deep breath. 'What just happened up there?' he croaked.

Pompio ignored the question. He hurried past Boy into the caravan. Boy could hear him rummaging around the cluttered interior as he searched for what he wanted. 'I know there's a shovel somewhere,' he muttered. 'I saw it just the other day. I reckon there's a basket too.'

Boy still couldn't seem to find the right words to form a coherent sentence. He knew only one thing. From the moment he'd made his entrance in the play, hurtling face down onto the wooden boards, he'd felt as though his life was somehow charmed. The last two performances had been pretty good – he knew that, but this one? This one had been perfect.

Every line had been as slick and polished as a gold doorknob. Every joke had hit its target square on the nose. Everybody's timing – even Grud's – had displayed the perfect precision of a military exercise. That massive crowd hadn't just laughed in all the right places – oh no! They'd roared. They'd screamed. They'd reacted as though they were witnessing comedy genius.

Then came the master stroke! Archimaldo's stooge had turned out to be the best one yet; a skinny old man with a doleful expression, who fed them a succession of grumpy lines that were just crying out for witty replies. When Grud had hung him on a peg at the end, he'd dangled there, his legs kicking helplessly while he studied the crowd with an expression of sheer misery. It was inspired. The audience had laughed and laughed until they could barely stand up.

When the players had taken their bows, the applause had been thunderous and they'd been obliged to do encore after encore, trooping gleefully off stage, only to return again and again, lured back by the seemingly endless clapping. Boy couldn't remember a time when he had felt happier. He was now an integral part of Wandering Star and what's more, he was *funny*. It was weird, because he'd never thought before that he was capable of such a thing. He'd never had any ambitions to be a comedian and yet, somehow, it had happened.

Somewhere around the eighth or ninth curtain call, the crowd had started to throw money at the stage and it quickly turned into a barrage of coins. The noise of metal bouncing off wood was almost deafening – and it went on for a very long time. When it had finally subsided and the crowds had begun to move away, the actors dared to peek out from cover, only to see that the wooden boards of the stage were piled high with metal disks of various shades and sizes. Orson stared out at it and once again, his eyes filled with tears. 'If only Velina could be here to see this,' he murmured. 'It's like the good old days.'

'She'd have been so proud,' agreed Mo.

Orson waved a hand at his cast. 'Well, I suppose we'd better start gathering it,' he said. 'It could take a while.'

'I'll go and find a shovel,' offered Boy, and that had been his excuse to leave the stage. Now, here he sat, completely overwhelmed by the experience and struggling to understand it.

Pompio emerged from the caravan, carrying a battered looking spade and dragging a large wicker basket behind him. 'No, no, don't shift yourself,' he said sarcastically. 'I'll sort it.'

'I'm sorry,' said Boy. 'I'm a little emotional right now.'

'Emotional?' Pompio looked disgusted. 'We're *actors*, we've no time for anything like that. We need to gather up all that lovely cash before somebody else gets their grubby hands on it.'

Boy pointed at the armed soldiers standing guard behind them.

'I don't think there's any need to worry,' he said. '*They* won't let anybody in. Look, Pompio, hang on for a minute. I need to talk to you.'

'Can't you see I'm busy?'

'Just give me a moment.' Boy pointed towards the stage. 'I need to talk about what just happened up there. It was pretty special, right?'

Pompio shrugged matter-of-factly. 'It was decent.'

'Oh, come on, it was more than just "decent". They loved us! It felt to me like. . . magic. For that hour, I was absolutely transported. I felt like I was flying. It was as though I could do anything I set my mind to.'

Pompio rolled his eyes. 'We all go through that,' he said.

'The first show where everything is just right. It *does* feel pretty special but savour it, mate, because trust me, it doesn't happen very often. Of course, it was so long ago for me I can hardly remember it. Let me tell you, the longer you're in this business, the more critical you'll become. Oh yes, you'll only have to say one word wrong in the whole script and you'll spend days fretting about it.' He chuckled. 'Don't worry, it's all part of the wonderful world we call show business.'

Lexi's voice shouted down from the back of the stage. 'Hey! Is somebody coming with that blinking shovel or what?'

'I'll be right there!' yelled Pompio. He gave Boy a quick look. 'Get over yourself, Sonny Jim,' he advised. 'It'll be better for you in the long run.' He was about to head towards the stage, but he hesitated for a moment, as though he'd just remembered something. 'Oh yes, there's one other thing that doesn't happen very often in this business. You'll be experiencing it for yourself in a short while.'

'Oh yes?' Boy was interested. 'What's that then?' he asked.

Pompio grinned delightedly. 'Payday!' he said and scampered off, dragging the wicker basket behind him.

★ ★ ★

They had their lunch in a local tavern that afternoon and, once again, the meal was on the house. A big table had been reserved for them at the Drunken Buffalo and Boy was quite excited when the landlady – a cheerful, elvish woman who called herself

Mistress Megan – informed them that today was Pie Day and that all the pies listed on the menu had been supplied by none other than Elgin's. She handed out some neatly written menus for them to look at.

'Elgin's wonderful pies!' cried Boy. 'This should be good.' He promptly ordered something called "spicy tunnel-rat bake". The others made their selection. Grud couldn't read so Mo helped him to choose something. Tankards of ale were brought to the table and Orson raised his drink in a toast to celebrate the company's unexpected, good fortune. They'd spent the last couple of hours counting and loading the massive collection of coins into the padlocked chest. It could barely be closed and Grud had trouble lifting it.

'That settles it,' Lexi had told her father, when the task was finished. 'Straight after lunch, we're taking this lot over to the bank, otherwise I won't be able to sleep at night.'

Typically, Pompio was the only one who opposed the idea. It was agreed that after they had eaten, some of the company would make the trip to The Bank of Ravalan. First, Orson handed a little cloth bag to each person at the table. Intrigued, Boy opened his bag to find that it contained five gold crowns. 'What's this for?' he asked.

'It's your wages, of course,' said Orson. 'You didn't think we were expecting you to work for nothing, did you?'

'Well, nobody mentioned money before,' said Boy, 'so I

suppose I just assumed acting was something you did for the love of it.'

'It quite often comes to that,' muttered Pompio, grimly. 'I don't mind telling you that it's been quite a while since anybody actually handed out some proper dosh.' He inspected his own payment critically. 'Five gold crowns,' he muttered. 'How come Boy gets the same as me? I mean, I don't like to complain—'

'Oh yes you do,' murmured Lexi.

'I'm a seasoned professional with years of touring behind me. He's only been with us for ten flipping minutes.'

'Oh, come on, Pompio,' said Lexi. 'You know perfectly well that all the actors get the same money.'

'No, they don't,' said Pompio, looking at her accusingly. 'How much did you get?'

'Well, I–I've got eight gold crowns,' admitted Lexi, 'but that's five for acting and three for actually writing the play.' She looked thoughtfully at Boy. 'Come to think of it, perhaps I should give you some of that,' she said. 'After all, you did help to change the direction of the show.'

'Oh no, I only made a comment,' said Boy. 'That's not worth much.'

'Yes, but if you hadn't said it, we'd still be doing the original script,' reasoned Lexi. 'Not that there was anything wrong with it, but this new direction does seem to have boosted our results.'

'Well, I wrote my own lines!' Pompio reminded her. 'So perhaps I should have a bit more for doing that?'

'We *all* wrote our own lines,' Mo reminded him, 'but they were based on Lexi's original script; so technically, she still wrote them.'

'That hardly seems fair!'

'Pompio,' said Orson. 'You know I always try to be fair.'

'Hmm.' Pompio looked accusingly at Mo. 'How much did you get?' he asked.

'Well, I got six crowns,' admitted Mo, 'but that includes an extra crown for doing the costumes.' She looked around the table defensively. 'Of course, if you'd all like to do your own alterations from now on . . .'

'Oh no,' said Lexi, 'No, I'm sure everybody is perfectly happy with the arrangement!' She looked around at the others. 'Aren't we?' she prompted them and everyone except Pompio nodded.

'Five gold crowns,' murmured Grud and all eyes turned to him. He was sitting there looking at the coins nestled in the palm of one of his huge hands. 'Look at them,' he said, enthusiastically. 'Aren't they the prettiest things you've ever seen?'

'I don't know why they bother giving you money,' sneered Pompio. 'You never spend any of it. Why don't you treat yourself occasionally?'

'To what?' asked Grud, looking puzzled.

'Well, there must be *something* you need.'

'Don't think so,' said Grud. He thought for a moment. 'Maybe a hat,' he said.

'Where would we find one big enough?' muttered Pompio.

'Can I just point out,' said Orson, 'that I don't actually pay myself *anything* for running the company?' He gazed slowly around the table as though expecting somebody to contradict him. 'Not a gelt,' he added. 'If at any point, anyone needs extra money, you only have to come and ask me and unless it's for something ridiculous . . .' He threw an accusing look at Pompio.

'I needed a better seat!' protested Pompio.

'A throne?' murmured Orson.

'It was half price and it did look great.'

'As I said, I'm open to sensible suggestions. I know we're flush, and it would be so easy to go mad and give ourselves a huge payout—'

'Keep talking,' said Pompio, enthusiastically.

'We need to think about the future of the company.'

'Oh, right,' muttered Pompio. 'That old speech.'

'There are debts to be paid off and running repairs to be made to the caravans—'

'Here we go,' murmured Pompio.

'Most of you will know that I have long nurtured a dream that one day, the Wandering Star Theatre Company shall wander no more – that we might have a permanent home.'

Boy was surprised to hear this. 'What, you mean, rather than taking shows to your audiences—'

'They would come to us instead!' finished Orson. 'Yes, that's it in a nutshell, Boy. Think of it! Velina and I often used to discuss the idea back in the day. We had the money to do it back then but ironically, we couldn't seem to find the right venue.'

Boy looked at Lexi. 'Could it work?' he asked her.

'Well, it's never really been put to the test,' she told him, 'but in theory, if you had a theatre located in a major city . . .'

'Somewhere like Ravalan?' suggested Boy.

'Yes, it would need to be a big place, with a cultured population, where people are prepared to go out for entertainment on a regular basis. Of course, you'd have to change your shows more than once a year; you'd put on what you might call a season of them. I suppose the place could also act as a hub for other travelling players visiting the city.'

'I see,' said Boy. 'Interesting idea.'

'You wouldn't just depend on people throwing money at the stage when the show finished,' added Orson.

'No?' said Boy.

'Oh, no. People would pay for a seat beforehand. You'd have a piece of paper to prove that it was paid for.'

'How would you know which seat was yours?' asked Boy.

'You'd number them,' said Mo, 'so there could be no arguments.' She smiled. 'Don't worry, we've thought it through.'

'The worst part of the theatrical life is the travelling,' said Orson, 'especially when you get to my time of life. Imagine, sleeping each night in a proper bed.'

'I hate proper beds,' said Grud. 'My feet stick out.'

'Obviously we'd have one specially made for you,' said Orson.

'Would we?' Grud smiled. 'Ooh, that'd be nice.'

'Let's not get ahead of ourselves,' Lexi warned them. 'I know we're doing very well at the moment but it would cost an absolute fortune to buy a theatre.'

'We're opening a bank account,' Mo reminded her, 'and if we could keep adding to the money in there, bit by bit, perhaps in a few years' time, we'd have enough to actually make it happen.'

'It's a pipe dream,' said Pompio and everyone glared at him. 'Look, I'm not trying to be Mr Wet Blanket—'

'Not much,' muttered Lexi.

'Theatre is a travelling concept; always has been, always will be.'

'Things can change,' Boy told him. 'A little while ago, I was a simple stable boy. Now, I'm a gifted comedian.'

'Let's not get carried away.'

'You heard those people earlier! They were laughing their heads off.'

'They *were!*' said Grud. 'They thought we were funny. I *like* making people happy. It's my favourite thing.'

'Yes,' admitted Pompio. 'They were all laughing like lunatics but this is the Moon of Elnis. People are in high spirits. They're in the mood to celebrate. You think respectable folk are going to pay for tickets every week so they can have a laugh?'

'We wouldn't just concentrate on comedy,' Lexi told him. 'We'd do serious drama, love stories, adventure and tales of mystery. I've even had this idea for something I'm going to call "a musical".'

'What's that?' asked Pompio suspiciously.

'Well, it was Archimaldo who gave me the idea, really. I'm thinking it would be a play with a story, but instead of speaking the lines, the actors would actually sing them, accompanied by musical instruments. They would dance around while they were doing it.'

There was a long, uncomfortable silence at the table while everybody looked at her.

'Ah, here come the pies!' said Orson, a little too loudly.

A plate was set down in front of Boy bearing a big, round meat pie with a golden pastry top. 'Ooh, this looks good,' he enthused.

'Do I take it that people don't care for my idea?' asked Lexi, sounding annoyed. 'The musical one.'

'It's certainly . . . an interesting concept,' said Orson, watching as his own pie was placed in front of him.

'What you might call *challenging*,' added Mo, helpfully.

'Yes,' said Orson, 'what Mo said.'

'I like a nice sing-song,' said Grud helpfully.

Pompio looked around the table in evident disgust. 'I'll reserve judgement until I know more,' he said, 'but I have to say, it sounds like something I'd pay to avoid.'

Boy glanced quickly at the others to make sure that everybody had been served. He picked the pie up from his plate, lifted it to his mouth and took a massive bite. He began to chew, but found that the chunks of meat were tough and gristly and rather difficult to swallow. Then, the flavour hit him – a concentrated rush of fiery spices that seemed to ignite in his mouth like a flaming torch. He grabbed his tankard and gulped down a mouthful of ale. Lexi looked at him, enquiringly.

'What do you think?' she asked him.

'I think,' croaked Boy, 'that you shouldn't believe every jingle you hear.'

She cut a small wedge from her own pie, something called a Savoury Jub-Jub Delight and tried a cautious mouthful. Her face contorted into a look of revulsion. 'Eww!' she said and pushed her plate away. 'That's awful.'

'That's not what Archimaldo's jingle said,' argued Boy. 'Elgin's wonderful pies, that's how it goes.'

Lexi smiled. 'True, but I don't think the bakers would have been too happy with a song that celebrated Elgin's horrible pies, would they?'

'It'd be more accurate though,' said Boy. He pushed his own

plate away and grabbed a hunk of bread instead. He took a bite and chewed more enthusiastically.

'I was thinking,' said Lexi.

'Oh yes? Don't overdo it, you might cause some damage!'

'Very droll. Well, as you know, some of us are going up to the bank after this, but we don't all need to go. This is your first time in Ravalan, so why don't you stay here and do a bit of sightseeing?'

Boy thought about if for a moment. 'I don't mind,' he said.

'Pompio knows the city. He can be your guide.' She lowered her voice. 'If he comes to the bank, he'll only ask a lot of stupid questions.'

'What about the caravans? Couldn't he stay with them to keep an eye on things?"

Lexi shook her head. 'The soldiers have agreed to guard them until we head to the palace. Pompio knows where that is. The two of you just need to bring my caravan there for the sixth hour and we'll be fine.'

'Yes,' said Pompio, leaning closer. 'Don't you worry, Boy. I know this city like the back of my paw. I'll show you some sights you'll never forget.'

'No drinking,' Lexi warned them both. 'Don't forget we've an evening performance and the Queen will be watching. We'll need to be on top form.'

'Oh, don't worry about us,' said Pompio. 'We'll be fine.' He lifted his own choice of pie – the Creamy Vegetable Surprise – and bit into it. His little face contorted into a mask of pure horror and he spat the contents of his mouth across the table in disgust. They hit Grud's chest with a dull splat and he sat there, looking down at them in dismay.

'Wait till I see that Archimaldo!' spluttered Pompio. 'What a flipping liar!'

Mistress Megan hurried over with a look of concern on her face. 'Is everything all right?' she asked them. 'How's the food?'

There was a short silence while everyone looked at each other.

'Lovely!' said Lexi.

'Brilliant!' said Boy.

'Perfect!' said Pompio.

They went on with their meal.

Chapter Seventeen

ON THE TOWN

BOY FOLLOWED Pompio through the crowded marketplace. He felt quite overwhelmed by the hustle and bustle of it – so different from the more modest markets of his hometown. Every way he looked, his eye was assailed by loud-mouthed merchants, waving their goods in his face and urging him to buy from them because they offered "the very best value in Ravalan"!

What an infinite variety of goods there was to choose from! Over there, a stall was heaped with colourful, aromatic platters of steaming rice and couscous. The smells of the food made Boy's stomach rumble after the disappointing lunch he'd been given. Opposite this, there was a stall hung with the finest rugs and tapestries; the brilliantly dyed fabrics teemed with eye-catching designs that would surely enrich any room. Next to this, there was a plump gentleman whose stall seemed to feature every kind of baked product you could imagine – flatbreads, wholemeal loaves, fruit breads, rolls, scones, pies, cakes and much more. Another man was selling knives of every shape and size. He demonstrated them to a bunch of onlookers, using them to slice up all kinds of vegetables and meats. The blades glided through them as if by magic. Everywhere Boy looked, his vision was dazzled by colour, light and movement, and he could feel the five gold crowns beginning to burn a hole in his purse. What should he spend his money on?

Pompio just couldn't stop talking. 'Oh, look Boy, over here! Did you ever see such fine clothes? Can't you just picture me in that golden cloak?' he shouted. 'Boy, Boy! Look at the size of those red apples, they'd feed you for a month . . . Boy, you need to try one of these candied fruits. You've never tasted anything so sweet in your entire life!' Pompio bustled from one vendor to the next, calling out to Boy and pointing to his favourite stalls. He dived in and out of the crowds, jabbering excitedly. Boy was having trouble keeping up with him. Now, the boobo had stopped at one particular stall and was clambering up its wooden framework. The elderly stallholder wore a bright, orange turban and sported a snow-white beard that tapered to a sharp point.

'Master Tragion!' cried Pompio. 'It's me. I'm back!'

'Aha!' cried the stallholder, looking genuinely delighted. 'If it isn't my old friend, Master Pompio! I was wondering when you would turn up. Can it really be a whole year since we last saw each other? Who is this with you?'

Boy had just managed to catch up.

'This is the newest member of Wandering Star,' announced Pompio. 'Allow me to introduce Boy!'

'Boy?' Master Tragion looked amused.

'That's what he calls himself.' Pompio leaned closer. 'Between you and me, he's a bit of a clown.'

'Is that right?' Master Tragion eyed Boy uncertainly.

'I think the word he's looking for is comedian,' said Boy helpfully. He reached out a hand and Master Tragion shook it enthusiastically. 'I'm helping the company move in a more light-hearted direction.'

'Is that so?' Master Tragion looked impressed. 'Well, I dare say we can all use a good laugh in these troubled times. Welcome to Ravalan,' he added. 'Your first visit?'

Boy nodded and smiled ruefully. 'Is it that obvious?' he asked.

'You have a slightly overwhelmed look about you. I've seen it before.' The old man gestured at his surroundings. 'There's a lot to take in,' he said. 'This event seems to get bigger every year. Why, I can remember when it was just a half dozen stalls and a troupe of dancing dogs.'

'That's hard to believe.' Boy studied the contents of Master Tragion's stall curiously. It consisted of a variety of straw baskets, all different sizes and each with a tightly fitting lid.

'I bet you can't guess what Master Tragion sells!' challenged Pompio.

Boy frowned. 'I really couldn't say.'

'Guess!' suggested Pompio. 'Go on, guess!'

'Erm . . .' Boy shrugged. 'Sweets?' he suggested but Pompio shook his head. 'Ornaments of some kind? Tools? Spices?'

'Why don't you have a look?' suggested Master Tragion. He considered the contents of the stall for a moment and reached out a bejewelled finger to tap the lid of one of the smaller baskets. 'Try that one. Lift the lid.'

Boy frowned, but reached out and did as he was told. Something long and colourful was coiled around the bottom of the basket. At first, Boy took it to be an elaborately patterned necklace, marked with blue and vermilion stripes, but then it moved slightly and Boy jumped back from the pot with a gasp of dread.

'It's a serpent!' he cried.

Pompio and Master Tragion laughed delightedly. 'Relax,' the stallholder told him. 'That one is just a rindasnake. It's completely harmless.' He reached into the pot and took out the serpent so that Boy could get a better look. It coiled and twisted around Master Tragion's wrist. 'These fellows inhabit the jungles down to the South,' he said. 'Would you like to hold it?'

Boy smiled and shook his head. 'No thank you,' he said and Master Tragion dropped it back into the pot and carefully replaced the lid. 'I have all kinds of serpents here,' he said. 'There are venomous species also.' He pointed to one of the larger baskets. 'That one contains a krelf. It's one of the most poisonous serpents in the known world. One bite from that and you'd be dead in moments.'

'Master Tragion is the foremost serpent trader in Ravalan,' said Pompio. 'People come from all over the known world to buy from him. Some of these creatures are worth hundreds of gold crowns, isn't that right?'

'That is correct,' agreed Master Tragion.

'Who would buy such things?' cried Boy, appalled. Remembering his manners, he looked apologetically at the stallholder. 'Excuse me,' he said. 'I mean no offence, but those things give me the creeps!'

Master Tragion laughed. 'No offence taken. I can assure you, you're not alone. People are, after all, born with a natural fear of serpents, but these are very sought-after creatures. Some of the harmless varieties make excellent pets for children and there are many householders who think of them as good luck charms. As for the venomous kind, their poison is often used in medicines. You simply have to learn how to milk them.'

'Milk them?' Boy was astonished. 'What, like you'd milk a buffalo?'

Pompio laughed at the idea. 'I'd love to see you try that on a krelf!' he sniggered.

'You use one of these,' said Master Tragion, and he showed Boy a little glass flask with a muslin cover stretched across the top of it. 'You merely get them to bite into this material and the poison drips through into the flask.' He thought for a moment and smiled mischievously. 'Perhaps you'd like to give it a try?' he suggested.

Boy was about to refuse when he froze, his mouth open to speak. He caught sight of somebody standing on the far side of the rectangular stall – a short, wiry fellow wearing a wide-brimmed hat. The man was examining the pots arranged on the other side of the display with interest. He seemed to suddenly become aware of Boy's gaze upon him and lifted his head to look across the intervening space, his thin lips arranging into a quizzical smile. His dark eyes widened in recognition and the smile vanished.

It was Gordimo.

There was a long moment where the hubbub of the marketplace seemed to fade to absolute silence. The two of them studied each other like a pair of old friends who had suddenly met in an unfamiliar location. Everything came rushing back to Boy as he remembered who this man was and what he had done.

'You!' he snarled and his hand moved instinctively to the sword at his waist.

Gordimo reacted. He grabbed one of the larger straw baskets from the stall, picked it up and threw it at Boy. The basket hit him square in the chest and the lid flew off. Boy was momentarily aware of something long and olive green bursting out from its confinement and lunging towards his face. He brought his hands up instinctively to fend the serpent off, caught hold of its thick body and flung it frantically aside. It squirmed into the crowd behind Boy. There were screams of terror as people scrambled frantically away from it, but Boy couldn't stop to consider them now. He recovered and looked across the stall to see that Gordimo had taken to his heels. He was running away along the crowded street, shoving his way through the crowd.

'Boy, what are you doing?' shrieked Pompio, but Boy ignored him. Knowing he didn't have time to go around the stall, he vaulted up onto it, scattering more baskets in all directions. Master Tragion let out a yell of anger but Boy didn't wait around to listen. He leapt from one side of the stall to the other, managing to tip over the far table in the process. Then, he was crashing down onto the cobbled surface of the street as various multi-coloured serpents wriggled and squirmed around his feet. He jumped clear of them and headed off in hot pursuit of Gordimo.

'Where are you going?' Pompio yelled, but Boy didn't have time to stop and explain. He powered through the crowd, yelling at people to get out of the way. 'Stop thief!' he cried, hoping that somebody might just grab Gordimo and hold onto him until he got there. Everyone seemed too dazed to take any notice.

Boy increased his efforts, his long legs eating up the distance between him and Gordimo. Then, he caught a glimpse of the man himself. His hat had fallen off, revealing his bald head. His long cloak was flapping behind him as he ran. Seeming to realise that he was losing ground, he veered abruptly to his left and disappeared through the open doorway of a tenement building. Boy went in after him, just in time to see Gordimo pounding up a steep, narrow staircase.

'Stop!' yelled Boy, his voice echoing in the gloomy interior but Gordimo took no notice. Boy started up the stairs after him. Gordimo reached a small landing where an old wooden chair stood. He took a moment to grab it. He whirled around and flung it down the stairs. Boy saw the chair coming and tried to duck beneath it, but it caught him a clout on the side of his head. He reeled backwards and would have fallen, but for his outstretched hand that managed to fasten onto the stair rail. He hung there for a moment, horribly aware that Gordimo was taking the opportunity to lengthen his lead.

Boy shook his head to clear the dizziness and started up the stairs again. Gordimo made it to the next landing. A doorway opened and an elderly woman stepped out of her apartment. Gordimo didn't hesitate. He grabbed her, swung her forcibly around and threw her back down the steps towards Boy. Boy heard the woman's shriek and saw her flailing towards him. He thrust up his arms and caught her around the waist. He held her for a moment and squandered valuable seconds as he set her down gently on the steps.

'Are you all right?' he asked her.

She nodded. 'Yes, thank you,' she said, 'but who was that?'

Boy was already taking the steps three at a time in his eagerness to catch up.

Above him, he heard the crash of another door and bright sunlight illuminated the floor above. Rounding the next corner, he saw that Gordimo had pushed his way outside onto the flat roof. Boy followed and emerged into dazzling sunshine. He blinked, trying to get his bearings. The roof was crisscrossed with lines of washing that flapped in the breeze and for a moment, Boy was unsure of which way to go. He noticed a white sheet being torn to one side as somebody ducked past it.

He inhaled a deep breath and pursued, determined not to let his quarry escape. He ducked under lines of washing and saw that Gordimo had reached the edge of the roof. He gingerly crossed a long, wooden trestle that bridged a wide gap between this building and the next. Gordimo jumped down. He saw Boy coming and a wicked grin crossed his face. He reached down to the wooden trestle and began to pull it away.

'NO!' Boy redoubled his efforts, determined to get there before the bridge was gone but it dropped into the alley, where it smashed on the cobbles far below. Boy stood there, panting for breath and glaring across the gap at Gordimo.

'Nice try, kid,' sneered Gordimo.

Boy didn't bother to reply. He retraced his steps for a short distance and stood for a moment, studying the gap between the two buildings. Gordimo shook his head. 'Don't be an idiot,' he said. 'You'll never make it.'

Boy ignored the remark. He put his head down and ran, knowing he would have to get up as much speed as possible if he had any hope of clearing the distance. He reached the parapet, slammed one foot onto it and thrust himself forwards. He hung in the air, his legs pedalling as he zoomed towards the other building. He saw Gordimo's triumphant grin fade quickly to a look of anxiety and then relief. Boy realised with a thrill of terror that he wasn't going to make it. His feet missed the other side by inches and he started to fall. His fingers closed on the edge of the parapet. He hung there, trying to summon the energy to pull himself up. Gordimo approached and smiled vindictively down at Boy.

'I have to give it to you,' he said, 'you're a real trier.' He clambered up onto the parapet and moved closer. Lifting his foot, he said, 'Sorry, kid, I thought you'd have died in the desert, but I suppose this place is a good as any.' Boy cringed and glanced down at the cobbles far below him, trying to judge whether or not he might survive such a fall.

Suddenly, a shrieking, furry shape came hurtling across the gap between the buildings and struck Gordimo in the chest. Gordimo fell backwards off the parapet and onto the flat roof. Boy hung there, not quite understanding what had happened. Then, he heard a familiar voice.

'Leave my friend alone!' yelled Pompio. There were the sounds of a frantic struggle. Pompio cried out as a fist hit him. Boy struggled to pull himself up onto the parapet. Gordimo was already back on his feet, wrestling with Pompio. With a strenuous effort, Boy managed to get one knee up onto the parapet. He started to lever himself upwards. Pompio gave a yelp. Gordimo had the boobo in both arms and was pushing him backwards over the edge.

'No,' shouted Boy, 'leave him alone!'

Gordimo gave a final push and Pompio fell. Boy closed his eyes, not wanting to see the impact. He was dimly aware of the sound of Gordimo's boots thudding across the roof as he fled the scene.

'Pompio, I'm sorry!' yelled Boy.

'Not as sorry as I am!'

Boy opened his eyes and stared down in disbelief. Pompio was clinging to an inn sign some ten feet off the ground. He hung there, staring up at Boy resentfully.

'Will you please tell me what's happening here?' he said.

'I thought you were done for!' yelled Boy.

'Never mind that,' retorted Pompio. 'Who is that man?'

'He's the one that robbed me.'

'Well don't just lie there. Go after him!'

'Yes, right!' Boy nodded and rolled onto the roof. He looked quickly around and saw the open doorway. Boy ran towards it. Below him, Boy could hear the sound of Gordimo's boots thudding on wood. Boy raced down with as much speed as he could muster. He was halfway to ground level when he heard an outside door being flung open.

When he finally made it outside, he found himself in an alleyway. At the top was what looked like a stable building, with rows of horses tethered outside. Gordimo was climbing astride one of the horses and there was something very familiar about the saddle he was settling himself into. Boy took one look at the weathered red star that was embossed onto the ancient brown leather and knew instantly that it was Belle's saddle.

Gordimo was already easing the horse away from the hitching post. Boy judged the distance and noticed a stack of barrels along the side of the alleyway. If he timed it right, he might just be able to get to Gordimo before he could ride away. He powered along, putting everything he had into his run. At the last moment, he sprang onto the nearest barrel, hopping from one to the next. As he neared the mouth of the alley, he flung himself headlong through the air.

His timing was perfect. He struck Gordimo side on, knocking him clean out of the saddle. The little man hit the ground and rolled over onto his front. He lay there, seemingly unconscious but the horse, panicked by the impact, reared up and tipped Boy backwards onto the cobbles. For a moment, he was in danger of being trampled by the horse's prancing hooves, but he managed to scramble quickly out of harm's way. He grabbed the bay's trailing reins.

'Woah girl,' he soothed her. 'Easy now. Easy!'

The horse stood, stamping her feet and tossing her head. Boy reached up and patted her neck. 'Good girl,' he said, and she quietened down.

'Boy! Boy!' He turned his head and saw Pompio scampering towards him, a look of concern on his grizzled face. 'Are you all right?'

'I'm fine, thanks.'

Pompio looked puzzled. 'Where did he go?' he asked.

'Huh?' Boy looked quickly around. He had fully expected to see Gordimo lying on the cobbles where he had fallen, but there was no sign of him. Boy noticed the open door of the stables a short distance away and he led the horse over to it. Looking inside, he saw Gordimo, mounted on a horse, that galloped out of an open doorway at the far end of the building. Boy considered jumping onto the bay and giving pursuit but told himself that by the time he got to the far end of the building, Gordimo would be well and truly gone. He gave a grunt of disgust and turned back to Pompio.

'He got away,' he said. 'There's no point in going after him now.' He shook his head and looked down at the boobo. 'Thanks for saving my neck back there.'

'Oh, that's all right. It took me a little while to find you, that's all.' He grimaced. 'I don't think Master Tragion is too happy with us. When I left, he was trying to recapture half of his stock.' He grimaced. 'Hopefully nobody has been bitten.'

'It all happened so quickly,' said Boy. 'There wasn't time to think.' He remembered something and turned back to inspect the horse. 'This is my saddle,' he said. 'I'd recognise it anywhere.'

'Well, that's something, I suppose,' said Pompio. 'I'm told that a comfortable saddle is a hard thing to find.'

'Ah, but this one is more than just comfortable,' said Boy. 'This one has a secret.' He slipped his hand under the smooth worn leather and felt around until his fingers located the hidden compartment. 'This one is . . .' His voice trailed away in surprise.

The compartment was empty.

Chapter Eighteen

COMMAND PERFORMANCE

BOY AND Pompio reached the entrance to the royal palace right on time. They drove Lexi's caravan up to the gates where a couple of armed guards were waiting for them.

'Ah, we were expecting you,' one of the guards said. 'Your troupe arrived just a little while ago. They're setting up for tonight's performance. Head on through and you'll see a loading bay on your right. That'll give you access to the Queen's Theatre.' He stepped closer. 'I heard you were a riot earlier today,' he said.

'We didn't start it!' said Pompio, misunderstanding. 'Somebody else threw those snakes. It wasn't our fault.'

'I think he's talking about the midday show,' murmured Boy, soothingly.

'Of course he is!' said Pompio. 'I knew that!'

'What was all that about snakes?' asked the guard, puzzled.

'Snakes?' echoed Pompio. 'Dunno what you're on about!'

Boy slapped the reins and urged the buffalo onwards through the gates. 'That was tricky,' he said.

'I don't think he noticed anything odd,' said Pompio.

Boy gave him a look of sheer disbelief. 'Is that right?' he muttered. 'Here's an idea for you: try thinking before you open your big mouth!'

Boy spotted Orson's caravan – standing outside a large pair of open doors – and pulled in alongside it. He and Pompio jumped down from the buckboard and went inside. They soon found the rest of the cast, setting up their equipment on a massive stage. Beyond it, rows of velvet seats were arranged on a gentle slope. Above them, the roof featured large skylights to make the most of the daylight. There was a multitude of huge oil lamps which could be lit for evening performances.

'Look at this place!' said Lexi enthusiastically, as Boy approached her. 'This is exactly the kind of thing we were talking about before. A permanent theatre! Don't you just love what they've done with the seating?' Then, she caught sight of Boy's grim expression. 'Are you all right?' she asked him.

'No, he's not,' said Pompio. 'We saw the man who robbed him earlier and gave chase, but in the end, the rascal got away'

'Oh, no,' said Lexi. 'That's terrible news.'

'We *did* get his saddle back though,' added Pompio. He strolled off to see what the others were doing.

'The saddle?' murmured Lexi, realising the significance of this. 'And the *Book of Secrets*?'

'It wasn't there,' muttered Boy, grimly, 'which means, I suppose, that Gordimo found it and now knows how to turn sand into water.' He sighed. 'In which case, he's won.'

'Not necessarily,' Lexi told him, 'and if he turns up here, we'll be ready to challenge him.'

Boy scowled. 'I'm not sure it will do any good,' he told her. 'It's starting to feel like a lost cause. Maybe I'd do better to concentrate on my new career.' He looked slowly around the stage and made a conscious effort to change the subject. 'So,' he said. 'I can't enter from the back like I usually do. I suppose I'll come in from behind those curtains at the side?' He remembered something. 'Oh, how did it go at the bank?'

'All right, I think. The money is now safely locked up in their vault. It's a relief not to have it in the back of the caravan but of course, Dad is convinced that the people at the bank are villains who will trick him out of it.'

'I can understand that,' said Boy, gloomily. 'I've learned the hard way there are plenty of crooks out there waiting to take advantage of honest folk.'

'Don't give up hope,' she told him.

He sighed, walked to the edge of the stage and gazed down at the plush, red seats before them. 'So, that's where all the lords and ladies will be sitting,' he murmured, trying not to sound apprehensive.

Lexi nodded and indicated an ornate gold throne in the front row. 'That's where Queen Gertrude will be,' she said. She looked at him doubtfully. 'I've never performed for royalty before. I'm wondering if we need to change anything for tonight.'.

'Like what?' he asked her.

'Well, it's all quite bawdy, isn't it? I was thinking, perhaps Her Majesty will have more refined tastes.'

Boy shrugged. 'She booked us because she heard we were funny,' he reasoned. 'I think it would be crazy to go making changes.'

'Changes?' asked Orson, wandering over. 'What was that about changes?'

Boy shook his head. 'No, I'm saying I don't think we *should* change anything.'

Orson frowned. 'I don't know,' he murmured. 'I was wondering about that bit where Pompio shows his bottom to the crowd. I know it always gets a big laugh but that might be considered an insult to Her Majesty. Perhaps we should cut that?'

Pompio scampered over. 'What's all this about cutting things?' he asked. 'I don't think it's a good idea to be making changes this late in the day.'

'Nobody said anything about changes,' Lexi assured him. 'Dad was just wondering about your bottom?'

'What about it?' cried Pompio.

'Well,' said Orson, 'we wouldn't want to insult the Queen, would we?'

Pompio glared at him. 'What's insulting about my bottom?' he cried.

'Pompio insulted the Queen with his bottom?' asked Mo, walking over to them. 'When did that happen?'

'He hasn't insulted her *yet*,' said Orson. 'I was just thinking that he *might* – you know – when he shows it to her.'

'Oh, we'll surely have to cut that bit,' said Mo.

'No, don't do that,' insisted Grud, shambling over. 'That's the funniest part!'

'We're not cutting anything,' protested Lexi. 'Dad was only saying—'

'I suppose I could do it the other way around,' suggested Pompio. 'Then, she'd only be looking at my—'

'Face!' said Mo, hastily.

'I was going to say face,' insisted Pompio.

'I'd rather be looking at your bottom,' said Grud.

'Wait a flipping minute!' snapped Pompio. 'What are you implying? What's wrong with my face?'

'Nothing,' insisted Orson. 'It's a perfectly decent face. Grud just thinks your bottom looks better.'

'My bottom looks better than my face? Well, what about *his* face? He's no oil painting.'

'They're doing an oil painting of my face?' asked Grud. 'Who's idea was that?'

'No, of course they aren't!' insisted Pompio. 'Who'd want a painting of that? Unless they wanted to scare some birds away!'

'Well, it'd still be better than a painting of your bottom,' insisted Grud.

'Look,' said Boy, holding up his hands. 'Nobody is painting anybody's face . . . or bottom, for that matter. I don't know where any of this came from. You've all got the wrong end of the stick. Lexi was simply wondering if the Queen might be insulted when she saw it.'

'When she saw what?' asked Mo.

'His face?' murmured Grud.

'No, his bottom!'

'When's he going to show her that?' asked Mo, bewildered.

'You know, the bit when he jumps up on me and his pants come down,' explained Boy, 'but I really don't think we should worry about that. We can only hope the show goes down well. If we start changing stuff at such short notice, it's only going to ensure that things go wrong.'

'But that's how we started down this path,' Orson reminded him.

'I know that, but . . . look, we've all worked really hard to make it as professional as we can, haven't we?' Let's not spoil it.'

There was silence. Orson nodded. 'You're right,' he said. 'Pompio's bottom stays in.'

'What about my face?' asked Grud, looking worried.

'That stays in too,' Orson assured him. 'Boy is right. It would be senseless to try and mess with the formula this late in the day.'

'Let's not forget,' added Pompio, 'this one is a set fee. We get paid even if they don't like it!'

Orson clapped his hands together. 'Right,' he said, 'let's get our props out of the caravans. It won't be long before the audience arrives.'

★ ★ ★

Orson was right. They had only just finished their preparations when the rear doors of the theatre swung open and a crowd of well-to-do people filed in to take their seats. The cast had pulled the big curtains across the front of the stage and were peeping anxiously out, watching intently. Boy – who was now dressed in his costume as Young Adamis – saw that there were gentlemen in finely decorated jackets and colourful tights. The ladies wore vibrant, silk gowns and elaborate bonnets. Soldiers wore chainmail singlets and leather breeches.

Boy noticed a very special guest. It was the old man who he'd heckled at the midday performance. He had been paid handsomely to make another appearance with them tonight and, as Boy watched, he was escorted to a prominent seat near the front. He sat there, looking around in evident awe, and Boy hoped he wouldn't be too bashful to stand up and shout the odds when it came time for his appearance.

It took a while but soon, most of the audience were in position. Tristan strode imperiously into the room, looking this way and that, as if to assure himself that everything was exactly as he wanted it to be. He hurried down the central aisle and climbed the steps to the stage, popping his head in through the gap in the curtains. 'Is everything in readiness?' he enquired. 'Her Majesty will be arriving at any moment and I don't want any delays.'

Orson stepped forward and bowed. 'We are all fully prepared for the show,' he said.

'Excellent,' said Tristan. 'As you already know, the competition shall take place directly after the play. You will need to vacate the stage promptly so that the three finalists can make their presentations.'

'Only three?' said Boy.

'You were expecting more?' asked Tristan. 'As I told you earlier, there weren't an awful lot of applicants to choose from.'

'I see. I, er, don't suppose you can tell me their names?'

'Certainly not,' said Tristan, irritably, 'and why are you so interested?'

'Oh, just curiosity,' Boy assured him.

'Never mind that. Just make sure you concentrate on your performance. Her Majesty has just ended a long period of mourning. She will doubtless be in dire need of some humour and I'm counting on you to cheer her up. I will go now to supervise her arrival.' He pulled his head back through the gap and the cast all looked at each other.

'What if she's a grumpy old mare?' asked Pompio. Everyone glared at him.

'You mustn't speak like that about the Queen,' said Mo primly. 'That's probably treason!'

'Well, I'm only asking the question!' argued Pompio. 'That'll be great, won't it, if we're working our socks off up here and she's down there with a face like a wet Wednesday in the rainy season.'

'Shush!' hissed Orson. 'Somebody in the audience might hear you criticising the Queen!'

'I'm only saying. If she doesn't laugh, I guarantee none of those other stuck-up people will bother. We'll look a right bunch of Charlies!'

'It'll be fine,' Lexi assured him. 'Just keep your mind on your lines. Oh, and don't forget to acknowledge the presence of the Queen in your introduction!'

'What do you mean?' asked Pompio. 'Nobody mentioned that before! We haven't rehearsed it.'

'I only just thought of it. You'll need to—'

Just then, a fanfare of trumpets rang out at a volume that made them all jump. Boy stepped forward to peer through the curtains and saw that, sure enough, all the guests were now down on one knee. Queen Gertrude entered the room; a frail, grey-haired woman, dressed in a shimmering turquoise gown that spread out around her like a wave. Boy studied her face for a moment. Though it was lined by the years and wore a grave expression, he still thought that it looked like a kind face. He noticed that her blue eyes glittered with intelligence. She walked to the front of the room – leaning on Tristan's arm as she did so – and then settled onto the huge, golden throne. Tristan perched on a more modest seat beside her. Boy let the curtains swing closed and motioned for Pompio to prepare. He and the others moved as quietly as they could to their prearranged places in the wings and Grud – who was standing by the ropes – reached up and pulled the curtains open.

The hubbub of the audience quickly subsided as Pompio strode out onto the stage and stood for a moment, looking out across the rows of seats

'Good citizens of Ravalan!' he began. 'I mean, my lords, ladies and general men – er, g–g–gentlemen! Oh, and of course, not forgetting your Moyal Rajesty!' There was a stunned silence but Pompio was clearly determined to bluster on. 'I stand behind you today – I mean, I stand *before* you today, to ask a very quimple sestion! Er, a simple question! Are you . . . Are you ready to be entertained?' He pumped a tiny fist into the air.

This was usually the point where a great cheer would go up from the crowd, but it was greeted today by complete silence. Pompio stared helplessly out into the audience. From his hiding place in the wings, Boy could sense the boobo's mounting panic.

'Quieten down, quieten down! Let me be heard.' Pompio realised he was telling a silent crowd to make less noise, which was ridiculous, but somehow managed to keep going. 'Please allow me to introduce myself,' he said. 'I am Bartrum – the closest friend of Young Adamis – the one with whom he shares all his greatest secrets! He bid me meet him here today at cloo o'tock – I mean, at two o'clock! Where the . . . where the flipping . . . I mean, where exactly *is* he?' He turned to look over his shoulder. 'Ah, wait, here he comes now!'

Boy took a deep breath and propelled himself out from behind the curtains. He came down with a crash that was all the more startling in the utter silence.

'Ah, look how trippingly he enters!'

Pompio delivered the tried and trusted line, waiting hopefully. For a moment, it seemed that it was doomed to the same response as the earlier jokes. Boy felt his heart sinking but a deep, throaty chuckle came from the crowd. Boy lifted his head to peer through his visor and saw – to his delight – that the sound had issued from none other than Queen Gertrude herself! Other voices joined in and he realised now what had happened. Everybody else in the room had been waiting for royal approval. Now it had been granted, people felt free to react accordingly.

As Boy lurched to his feet, his visor swung down with a clang. He was rewarded with more laughter. By the time Pompio was up on his shoulders – proudly displaying his bare bottom to the audience – the hilarity was widespread. From that point, everybody's nerves dissipated and they were able to give the performance their very best efforts. It was nowhere near the laugh riot of their earlier performance but it was, nonetheless, a creditable hit with the assembled crowd. When the old man got to his feet and started heckling, general merriment was evident and the company finally took their bows to genuine applause.

Tristan stood up and raised his hands to quieten things down. 'Her Majesty Queen Gertrude tells me that she would like to say a few words!' he announced. Silence fell. The Queen got to her feet and studied the troop of players on the stage, before speaking in a clear, warm voice.

'I should like to express my gratitude to our guest performers tonight and to thank them for travelling so many miles to bring us the gift of laughter – something that has been in very short supply here lately. Who is in charge of the troupe?'

'That would be me, Your Majesty,' said Orson, taking a step forward.

'That was a most agreeable performance,' said Queen Gertrude. 'May I ask who wrote the play?'

'That is the work of my daughter, Lexi, who also played the role of Neve,' said Orson, smiling proudly.

Queen Gertrude studied Lexi in surprise. 'A very accomplished script for one so young,' she said, 'and you are a delightful actress.'

'Thank you, Your Majesty,' said Lexi demurely.

'I see, my dear, that you are of the elvish race.' Queen Gertrude smiled wistfully. 'Many years ago, I had a very close friend who was elvish. I am sorry to tell you that I lost touch with him and that is a sad state of affairs.' She turned her gaze to Pompio. 'As for you, Master Boobo, I cannot recall ever encountering a creature quite as talented. Your capers made me smile exceedingly.'

Pompio performed a bow. 'My pleasure, your Moyal Rajesty – er, I mean–'

The Queen laughed delightedly, thinking no doubt, that he had made the error for comic effect.

'What of our giant?' continued the Queen, pointing to Grud. 'Was he not a most wonderful villain?'

There were general sounds of approval.

'It's only an act, Your Majesty,' insisted Grud. 'I'm quite nice when you get to know me.'

'I'm sure you are! Well, I'm afraid I must now ask you all to vacate the stage, so that our three inventors may take your place and unveil their wonders. You are, of course, most welcome to watch.'

Boy and Lexi glanced at each other and nodded.

The Queen settled back onto the throne and the actors moved obligingly into the wings, taking their various props with them. Lexi made sure she was close to Boy. 'Wait for the right opportunity,' she whispered to him. The two of them settled down to observe. Tristan got up from his seat and walked slowly towards the stage. He climbed the steps and, turning to face the audience, he cleared his throat.

'Her Majesty has kindly asked me to be Master of Ceremonies for this event,' he said. 'While I am sure my poor efforts will not compare with what we have just seen . . .' He looked into the wings and smiled. '. . . I shall endeavour to do my very best.' Again, he cleared his throat. 'As everybody here knows, Her Majesty, Queen Gertrude, recently announced a very special competition. She will pay the handsome sum of ten thousand gold crowns to the individual who has come up with the best invention. Her only stipulation was that the chosen invention must be one that would in some way benefit mankind. Over the past months, I have met with the people who entered the competition and from *several* entries, I have selected a shortlist of three contenders – one of whom will take the grand prize. Who shall it be, ladies and gentlemen? Who has the best idea? Who has come up with something that will truly make the world a better place? It's time to find out.' He took a roll of parchment from his pocket and consulted it for a moment. 'Our first contender is Danius of Spottiswood. Danius is a keen amateur carpenter and part-time inventor. He has come here tonight to tell us all about his invention: the Chable! Danius? The stage is yours!'

Tristan returned to his seat. Then a door at the back of the room opened and a thin, pale-faced man ambled in. He carried an oddly shaped, wooden contraption, which was fitted with what looked like a set of shoulder straps. He walked slowly along the central aisle, climbed the steps up to the stage and turned to face the crowd. He took a breath and cleared his throat.

The competition began.

Chapter Eighteen

THE CHABLE

DANIUS BEGAN to speak in a thin, wheedling kind of voice. He held the wooden contraption proudly out in front of him like an offering.

'Ladies and Gentlemen – Your Royal Majesty – I'd like to begin by talking about a very familiar problem. It is one that I'm sure you have all experienced.' He looked around as though expecting somebody to disagree with him. When nobody did, he continued. 'Let us say that you are at some palace function where food and wine is being served. You are hungry and thirsty, and at the same time, rather tired after a long day. Oh dear! You appear to have only one pair of hands and there is not a vacant seat to be seen!' He made a show of looking hopefully around the room and affected a disappointed expression.

'What do you do in such circumstances? How can you ensure that you will be able to eat and drink your fill?' He looked intently at the audience as if seeking an answer, but when he didn't get one, he lifted the wooden contraption. He opened it out and raising it above his head, he lowered the straps onto his shoulders. Boy saw that this left him with a flat, shelf-like arrangement sticking out from his chest and a curious stick-like thing dangling down below his buttocks. 'That's when you need one of these,' he said brightly. 'Ladies and Gentlemen, I give you, the chable! It's a chair and a table – all in one.'

He relaxed backwards with an exaggerated sigh. The long stick created an uncomfortable-looking seat. 'I can now sit here and eat and drink away to my heart's content,' he said. 'Waiter!'

The door at the back of the room opened again and a young woman stepped into the room. She carried a goblet of wine and a plate of food. She prowled along the aisle, and climbed the steps to the stage, placing the food and drink on the shelf in front of Danius. She turned, performing a bizarre pirouette as she grinned inanely at the audience. Then, she retraced her steps and strode happily out of the room, closing the door behind her. 'Thank you to my glamorous assistant and fiancé, Letitia,' said Danius. He raised his goblet of wine to the audience. 'Cheers!'

he said and took a gulp from its contents. He picked up a raw carrot from the plate and bit off the end of it. 'Mmm,' he said, 'delicious!'

He looked out at the audience again, as though he had expected more of a reaction from them, but they stared silently back at him. 'So . . . of course, when I have eaten and drunk my fill . . .' he continued. '. . . I simply . . . stand up.' He did so and the plate and goblet dropped onto the stage with a loud clatter. Danius looked down at them in dismay. Clearly, this wasn't supposed to happen. Just then, the door at the back opened again and Letitia stepped brightly into the room. She hesitated as she saw the goblet and plate at Danius's feet, and her confident grin faded abruptly. She turned quickly around and went out again, slamming the door shut. Danius smiled feebly at the audience. 'That went better in rehearsal,' he muttered. He lifted the chable off his shoulders, folded it shut and placed it beside him. Then, he took a bow.

There was a puzzled silence before a feeble smattering of applause came from the audience. Danius straightened up and looked eagerly around the room. 'If anybody has any questions regarding the chable, I'd be more than happy to answer them,' he said.

There was another long silence before one of the merchants finally raised a hand and asked, 'how much do you envisage this thing selling for?'

Danius smiled. 'Provided we can make them in sufficient quantities, I would think one gold crown per unit would be about right.'

The merchant took in a sharp breath of air as though indicating he thought this was way too much.

'Possibly even fifty gelts,' added Danius, hastily. Then, seemingly as an afterthought, he said, 'thank you for your interest, sir. Anyone else?'

A woman put up her hand. 'If you are lucky enough to win the competition, what would you do with the money?'

'Excellent question,' said Danius. 'Well, I envisage opening a large warehouse on the city square and selling more of my inventions. I'd call it Danius's Doo Dahs. I've got plenty of other ideas. For instance, there's an eating implement, which is a cross between a spoon and a fork. I call it a spork . . .'

'That'll never catch on,' Boy whispered to Lexi.

'. . . There's a bookcase crossed with an armchair which I call a book chair . . .'

'Or an arm case!' whispered Lexi, trying not to giggle.

'I have a question,' said Queen Gertrude unexpectedly. Danius bowed respectfully from the waist.

'Your Majesty honours me,' he replied.

Queen Gertrude gave him a stern look. 'This benefits mankind . . . *how*, exactly?'

'Well, Your Majesty, it . . . solves an age-old problem, doesn't it? Let's face it, none of us want to be standing there with food in one hand and a drink in the other, do we? I mean, how is anybody expected to cope with that?'

Queen Gertrude sighed. 'When I devised this competition,' she said, 'I must admit that I didn't expect that an aid for mankind's general gluttony would be one of the shortlisted inventions.' She looked at Tristan. 'Really?' she murmured.

'Your Majesty, I could only choose those ideas that had some merit,' reasoned Tristan, in a quiet voice. 'Trust me when I tell you, this really was one of the better ones. Some of them . . .' He shook his head and held his hands out to each side.

Queen Gertrude frowned and turned back to look at Danius. 'Thank you for coming all the way from Spottiswood to show us your invention,' she said. 'It is . . . an interesting concept. You may now leave the stage.'

Danius frowned. 'Your Majesty, as I said, there are so many other ideas I could offer in place of the chable. For instance, I also have something called a bedrobe. That's a—'

'A bed and a wardrobe,' said Queen Gertrude. 'Yes, I get the general idea. No doubt that one is aimed at people who can't decide whether they want to get dressed or go to sleep.'

Danius stared at her. 'That's incredible, Your Majesty,' he said. 'How on earth did you—'

'Call it intuition,' said Queen Gertrude. 'Next!'

Tristan got up from his seat and approached the stage.

'Thank you for your presentation,' he said. He pointed to one of three empty chairs at the foot to the stage. 'If you would collect the chable and wait over there.' Tristan climbed the steps to the stage and once again, turned to face the crowd.

'Well, I think we can all agree, that has got things off to an exciting start,' he said. He looked hopefully around but if anybody agreed with him, they were keeping it to themselves.

From his hiding place in the wings, Boy studied the Queen's face. Her sour expression suggested that she really hadn't been impressed by the chable. Boy agreed with her.

'What have we next?' asked Tristan. He consulted his piece of parchment. 'Ah yes, the next of our three inventors is a full-time milkmaid from the Rancoom Marshes. She claims that her idea came to her in a flash of inspiration, early one morning, when she was hard at work. Please allow me to introduce, Mistress Clarabel and Bessie!'

The door at the back of the room opened and a woman plodded into the room. She was dressed in a plain hessian robe and had a huge pack on her back. She was leading a buffalo on a length of rope and the huge creature clumped obediently along behind her. The two of them came slowly down the central aisle and reached the stairs, where Mistress Clarabel was obliged to try and get the buffalo up onto the stage. This proved to be no easy matter as its hooves were simply not designed for such tricky, polished surfaces. Boy and Lexi hurried out from the wings to lend a hand. After much energetic pushing and shoving, they managed to get Bessie into position on the stage. Mistress Clarabel looked shyly out at the audience and cleared her throat.

Then, she began her presentation.

Chapter Nineteen

MISTRESS CLARABEL'S CREATION

'**M**OST HONOURED to meet you all,' she said in a quiet voice. 'I hope you will forgive my rough ways. Out in the marshes, we lead a hardy old life. We don't go in for very much in the way of airs and graces. Now, this is my prize buffalo, Bessie, who I don't mind telling you, has won many a competition for being the finest milker in the land. My invention is an aid to milking a buffalo.' She looked around at the faces of the audiences, most of which were arranged into looks of blank incomprehension. 'I'm sure you fine city folk are not aware of this but first thing every morning, the milk maids of the marshes spend hours milking buffalo, so you fine city folk can enjoy bottles of fresh milk with your breakfast.'

She paused to look around, as though expecting somebody to contradict her, but nobody did. 'Now, I'm sure you will have no idea of what is involved in the milking of a buffalo. That is all well and good considering that you are royalty. You should not have to concern yourself with such matters, but it is hard and backbreaking work that can go on for hours without a break. My invention is intended to put a stop to all that.'

She unslung the pack from her back and lowered it to the ground. She opened it, revealing a large glass bottle, a long hose – that looked like it was made of some kind of waxy material – and what appeared to be a pair of bellows. She set the various items carefully down on the stage. 'Now,' said Mistress Clarabel, 'to demonstrate my invention, I must first fasten this contraption to the buffalo's udders. Those amongst you with a delicate constitution may wish to avert your gaze.'

Boy looked out into the audience and was astonished to see that several people had actually followed her advice. Some of the ladies-in-waiting lifted their hands to cover their eyes, as though it was too horrific an act to behold.

'Now that the contraption is in place,' continued Mistress

Clarabel, 'I need to attach the end of the tube to the milk-collecting device, like so. I shall attach *this* tube to my bellows, here and now, I am ready to begin.'

Boy found himself holding his breath. He could see exactly what Mistress Clarabel had come up with and, what's more, he was pretty sure that it would work. As he watched, the woman lifted one sandal-clad foot and placed it on the bellows, which were now lying flat on the stage. She began to move her foot vigorously up and down. Almost immediately, a rich spurt of milk started to pump into the jar.

There was a gasp of astonishment from the audience.

'As you can see,' said Mistress Clarabel, still pumping as she spoke, 'the milk arrives, ready to be decanted into smaller bottles. Furthermore, this means that I can milk five buffalo in the time it would normally take me to milk just one. I should also like to add that if I was lucky enough to win this competition, I would spend the prize money on making more of these devices and distributing them free of charge to milkers around the known world.'

'That's amazing,' whispered Lexi into Boy's ear. 'That's certainly a whole lot better than a chable!'

'I agree,' said Boy. 'Hopefully, the Queen will think so too!'

'Any questions?' asked Mistress Clarabel.

'A merchant put his hand up. 'What's your invention called?' he asked.

Mistress Clarabel looked baffled. 'I haven't given it a name,' she admitted.

'Well, you should certainly think about it,' said the man.

'Thank you, sir, I shall do that.'

Oddly, it was Danius who raised his hand next. 'I was just thinking,' he said, 'wouldn't it be better if you could sit down while you're doing the pumping? I could easily make a device called a chump.'

'A chump?' muttered Mistress Clarabel.

'Yes. A chair and a pump – all in one. What do you think?'

Mistress Clarabel just shrugged. 'Well, I dunno. If I feel like sitting down, I generally just use a stool,' she said.

'Oh,' said Danius, looking dejected. 'A stump? Doesn't quite work, does it?'

'No, but thank you for the thought.'

'Mistress Clarabel,' said the Queen. The milkmaid stopped pumping and bowed her head respectfully.

'I am honoured that Your Majesty would speak to one such as me,' she said.

Queen Gertrude waved a hand to dismiss the notion. 'Please don't think so little of yourself! You clearly have a brilliant mind. I must tell you that I heartily approve of this clever device.'

'You do?' Mistress Clarabel's ruddy features broke into a grin of sheer delight. 'That's wonderful news!'

'I can easily see how your invention will better the lot of all kinds of people at a stroke. Indeed, I would like to invest in this idea. So, let me assure you that in the unlikely event that your device does not win this competition, I will ensure that those machines are made and distributed – exactly as you suggested – to every milk farm in the Kingdom of Ravalan. You will receive full credit for it.'

Mistress Clarabel beamed delightedly. 'Oh, thank you, Your Majesty! Thank you so much! On behalf of the Milkmaids of the Marshes, I give you our gratitude.'

The audience broke into enthusiastic applause. This startled Bessie who immediately pooped on the stage and stood there, looking vaguely embarrassed.

'Naughty buffalo!' said Mistress Clarabel, wagging a finger at her. 'Look at the mess you've made!'

Tristan got up and waved her down from her position. 'Congratulations, Mistress Clarabel! It would seem you are a winner whatever happens. How exciting! Now, bring your apparatus down with you – if you would be so kind – and sit over there next to Master Danius,' he suggested. 'Could somebody please get this buffalo into the wings?' he asked hopefully. Lexi jumped up and hurried over to lead the creature away, taking great care not to stand in the mess Bessie had deposited on the stage. Mistress Clarabel grabbed her equipment and hurried down the steps to her seat, beaming happily at everyone around her. They were ready to proceed. Tristan climbed the steps and turned to face the audience. He reached into his pocket for the parchment.

'The competition is certainly heating up!' he announced dramatically. 'It would seem that our latest entry has already found favour with Her Majesty, which is what I believe is known as a win-win situation.' He smiled in Miss Clarabel's direction and turned back to the crowd. 'So, ladies and gentlemen of the royal court, we have just one more invention for your consideration; one more creation that – I feel quite confident in saying – is something that is sure to amaze you. I saw it for the first time only a couple of days ago and it certainly amazed me!' He glanced awkwardly at the Queen. 'Not that I'm trying to influence anyone here,' he added hastily. 'I wouldn't want to give that impression. Our next contestant describes himself as a soldier of fortune, a seeker of wisdom and a keen traveller. He is also, of course, a gifted inventor. Will you please give a warm welcome to our final contestant: Gordimo of Ackitara!'

The door at the back of the room opened once more and Gordimo came in carrying a hessian sack.

Chapter Twenty

SAND INTO WATER

GORDIMO STROLLED slowly down the central aisle, a confident grin on his face. Boy felt his hands bunching into fists and he started to get to his feet, but Lexi placed a restraining hand on his shoulder. 'Wait!' she whispered. 'We need to choose our moment.'

Gordimo was swaggering up the steps to the stage. He lowered the hessian sack and untied it. He carefully removed the gourd, the three bottles of liquid and a small pot of what could only be yaricoola seeds. He set each of them down and lifted his head to gaze challengingly into the crowd, giving them an oily smile.

'I can guess what you're thinking,' he said. 'That doesn't look like very much. A pot, three bottles and a bowl? What does he hope to achieve with that?' He paused for a moment to let the remark sink in. 'But, Ladies and Gentlemen, your Royal Highness, what if I told you that with this simple equipment, I can do something that will change the world forever? Something that will rock the very foundations of your belief? Something that sounds absolutely impossible?' He paused for dramatic effect. 'What if I told you that I can use this device to turn sand into water?'

There was a gasp of disbelief from the audience.

'Ridiculous!' shouted one man.

Gordimo smiled, nodded. 'Oh, don't worry, I know it sounds like the ramblings of a madman. Please believe me, if I hadn't invented this myself, I'd have to agree with you.'

Again, Boy felt impelled to get to his feet and walk out onto the stage, but once more, Lexi held him in place. 'Not yet,' she hissed. 'Let's hear what he has to say for himself.'

Gordimo bent down and picked up the gourd. He removed the lid and carried it down the steps to the front row of the audience. 'I would like you to examine what is in the gourd,' he said. 'It is simply filled with desert sand which I collected on my way here. Of course, sand is in short supply in this fabulous city but let me tell you, I travelled many miles to get here and – for a great distance – it was the only thing I could see for miles in every direction. Ravalan is famed for its wonderful fountains and its great dam in the mountains. There is no shortage of water here but there are other countries in the known world where the landscape is perpetual desert; where families have to travel miles in search of life-giving water.' He handed the gourd to a man in the front row. 'Now, sir, I would ask you to examine the contents of the gourd and tell me what it contains.'

The man stared into it. 'It's sand,' he said.

'You are sure? Have a proper look. Dig around. Assure yourself there is no hidden compartment, no other substance mixed in with the sand, no way I can be pulling a trick.'

'No, it's just sand,' said the man.

'Pass it along the row, if you will. Let's make sure that others have a chance to examine it. After all, no offence, sir, but you could easily be a stooge.'

'Master Gordimo,' said Queen Gertrude, impatiently. 'This is beginning to feel suspiciously like the preamble to a magic trick.'

Gordimo bowed. 'I appreciate your concerns, Your Majesty, and let me tell you that what I am about to demonstrate will certainly seem like magic, but it is science! You see, Your Majesty, I am a scientist. That's a man who knows how the world works; a man who tries to uncover its mysteries and finds ways of helping other people.'

Boy felt his blood heating up as he heard his own words uttered, as though they belonged to the speaker himself. He gritted his teeth and watched in silent anger.

Gordimo took back the gourd and retraced his steps up to the stage. 'Now, ladies and gentlemen, I must apply the science. A little drop of this liquid, another drop of this one and a third drop, like so! Finally, one of my very special seeds – which I will bury in the sand – and it's done!' He replaced the lid and set the gourd down on the stage. 'Now, we must wait.' He smiled down at the crowd. 'Does anybody have any questions while the time passes?' he asked.

Queen Gertrude did. 'Are you honestly expecting us to believe that the sand in the gourd will turn into water?' she asked.

'Your Majesty, I expect you only to believe the evidence of your own eyes. In a moment, you will see that I have not exaggerated my claims, but while we wait, let me explain that this little gourd is only for demonstration purposes. If we were to make huge tanks from the same mysterious substance – well, I have no doubt that the rulers of the known world's desert cities would have no hesitation in paying you handsomely for the details of the process.'

'Paying?' Queen Gertrude's eyes narrowed. 'Mistress Clarabel just spoke about distributing *her* invention to people for free but you would require payment?'

Gordimo looked benignly down at the milkmaid. 'No offence,'

he said, 'but I am a businessman. It took me years of hard work to perfect this formula and when it wins the prize, I shall—'

'When?' echoed the Queen. 'That's a little presumptuous. Don't you mean, if?'

Gordimo shook his head. 'That must have sounded arrogant,' he admitted, 'but trust me, Your Majesty. When you see the process completed, I believe you will want to appoint me as your winner. That is no idle boast – just my due – and of course, I shall in return give you the page from this.' He reached into his pocket and withdrew the familiar, leather-bound book that had belonged to Boy's father. 'Here is my *Book of Secrets*, Your Majesty. In it, I have recorded details of all my inventions; some of them finished, some still in progress. You will of course be free to do with this invention what you wish, but it would seem to me to be a foolish thing indeed to simply give the idea away when there will be people across the known world who will pay handsomely for it.'

Queen Gertrude gave Gordimo a cold look. 'I am already rich beyond the wildest dreams of most people,' she said. 'Why would I seek to make even more profit?'

'Because that, I'm afraid, is the way of the world,' said Gordimo. 'Who among us can truthfully say they are content with what they already have?' He looked challengingly around the audience, but nobody seemed inclined to give an answer. 'Enough of this idle talk!' he concluded. 'I believe the transformation is complete. Ladies and gentlemen, prepare to be astonished.' He picked up the gourd, carefully removed the top and took out a clear glass. He tilted the gourd and poured the fresh water into the glass.

At first, there was complete silence as the audience's mouths fell open in amazement. Gordimo lifted the glass to his lips and drank deeply, giving a contented sigh. 'Delicious,' he said.

Suddenly, everybody was talking at once, turning to their neighbour to discuss what they had just witnessed. Tristan raised his arms to quieten them down. 'Silence, please!' he cried. The hubbub gradually faded away.

'Are there any more questions?' asked Gordimo, smiling confidently.

Boy was about to shout something, but before he could, Lexi had jumped to her feet and strode out onto the stage, her hands on her hips.

'I have one!' she cried. 'Are you not ashamed of yourself, sir?'

Gordimo looked at her in surprise.

'Who the hell are you,' he asked her, 'and why would I feel ashamed?'

'Because you are an imposter and a thief!' said Lexi. She turned to look at Queen Gertrude. 'Your Majesty, I pray you will forgive my rude interruption, but this man . . .' She pointed a finger at Gordimo. '. . . this man – only a week ago – stole that apparatus from its true inventor and left him to die in the desert.

It was only fate that brought me and my fellow travelling actors along in time to save his life.'

The Queen stared at her in astonishment. 'Who is this true inventor?' she asked

'You have already seen him earlier, Your Majesty.' She turned and motioned to Boy to step forward. 'The very actor who played Young Adamis.'

Boy got hastily to his feet but though he had already dispensed with Young Adamis's helmet, he was still wearing the armoured breastplate, and the arm and leg guards, which obliged him to clatter awkwardly onstage. In his haste, he inadvertently stepped in the pile of poop that Bessie had left on the wooden boards. He skidded in it and came flailing down onto his back with an ear-splitting crash. Lexi hurried forward to help him up but the damage was already done, and the former silence was rudely shattered by the sound of the audience subsiding into helpless laughter. Lexi got her hands under Boy's arms and managed to get him upright again. She waved her hands to quieten people down but she could see that even Queen Gertrude was struggling to contain her mirth.

'This is all part of your act?' she chuckled.

'No, Your Majesty,' insisted Boy. 'Lexi told the truth. That invention is mine.'

Queen Gertrude stopped laughing. 'Yours?' she asked incredulously. 'I must say, that seems very unlikely. Tell me more.'

'Your Majesty, I was on my way to Ravalan to take part in your competition when I fell in with this man and his friend, Kaleb, in the great desert. The villains plied me with drink and I made the mistake of demonstrating my invention to them. When they had seen it, they set upon me. They knocked me unconscious, stole the invention and left me for dead.'

Queen Gertrude stared at Boy in evident disbelief. 'You are asking me to believe that a young man of – what? – sixteen summers has created something as incredible as this? I'm sorry, young man, but that sounds very farfetched.'

'It's not my invention, Your Majesty, but my father's. At least, it's something he started, which I perfected. The details were left to me in the *Book of Secrets* – the same book that Gordimo is now claiming as his own.'

Queen Gertrude transferred her attention to Gordimo. 'What do you say to this extraordinary accusation?' she asked him.

Gordimo smirked unpleasantly. 'I know this youth,' he said. 'He's a fantasist. I'm not surprised he's turned up here today. He's been following me for ages.'

'How do you come to know him?'

Gordimo sighed wearily and spread his hands in a show of helplessness. 'You want to know the truth, Your Majesty? Then I shall tell you. On the way to Ravalan, I stopped in the small desert town of Sorth and while I was there, I performed an act of mercy for an old woman I encountered. She was –

quite literally – dying of thirst. I used my apparatus to save her. What else could I have done in such circumstances? This boy witnessed the act and has been following me ever since, in the hope of getting his hands on the formula. He clearly thinks he can make his fortune off the back of it.'

'That's a lie!' cried Boy. 'He is trying to paint me as the villain when *he* is the guilty party!'

Gordimo sneered. 'Yes, well you w*ould* say that, wouldn't you?' He turned back to look at the Queen. 'Let me tell you about this delinquent,' he said. 'It's not my first run-in with him today – oh, no. He accosted me in the market square earlier; started throwing live serpents at me! I was terrified! It was only my fleetness of foot that allowed me to escape.'

A man in the crowd – wearing the uniform of a city sheriff – got to his feet. 'Your Majesty, please forgive my interruption,' he said.

'Sheriff Toomes?' said Queen Gertrude. 'You have something to add to this account?'

'I do, Your Majesty. There *was* an incident in the marketplace today. Witnesses to the event spoke of somebody hurling venomous serpents into the crowd. One of them said that the perpetrator was a teenage boy. It's a mercy nobody was bitten.'

'Thank you, Sheriff,' said Queen Gertrude. 'You may sit down.' She turned to look at Boy, a stern expression on her face. 'It sounds very much as though you were the one at fault,' she said. 'Flinging snakes at people? Why would anybody do such a dangerous thing?'

'Your Majesty, that's not what happened,' Lexi insisted. 'Boy told me all about it afterwards. It was the other way around. Gordimo threw those snakes in order to cause a diversion, so he could escape.'

'You were there?' asked the Queen.

'Well, no, but Pompio was! I'm sure he can tell you better than I can.' Lexi looked around and waved her hand towards the boobo. He came cautiously out onto the stage, an apprehensive look on his face. The Queen studied him for a moment.

'You saw what happened?' she asked him.

'Well, your Moyal Rajesty . . . your Royal Majesty . . . I *was* there. That much is true. Unfortunately, it all happened very quickly. Boy saw Gordimo by the stall and gave chase, but he managed to get away.'

'So, the young man *was* the aggressor?'

'He was chasing Gordimo, yes, but only because Gordimo stole his . . . thingummy . . . his apparel.'

'Apparatus!' Boy corrected him.

'Yes, that! Gordimo robbed him.'

'You actually saw that happen?'

'No, that was before we found Boy. We happened upon him wandering barefoot in the desert. He told us then what Gordimo had done to him.'

'I see. So, you only have the youth's word on it?'

'Well, yes, but I *do* trust him.'

'You saw Gordimo throwing serpents?'

'Well, no, not really. I was talking to the stallholder at the time and it all happened when my head was turned, but Gordimo *did* run away.'

'Well, I'm not surprised he ran if he was being threatened.'

'He acted like he was guilty.' Pompio thought for a moment and then seemed to remember something else. 'Oh, yes! He tried to push me off a roof!'

Gordimo sighed. 'With respect, Your Majesty, the boobo attacked me without the slightest provocation; he went for my eyes like the wild beast he undoubtedly is.'

'Wild beast!' cried Pompio. 'Well, that's charming. *You* were the wild beast, trying to stamp on Boy's fingers! Of course I went for you!'

'Who was trying to stamp on Boy's fingers?' boomed a voice and Grud strode out onto the stage, looking very angry 'This worm?' he cried. He took hold of Gordimo by the collar of his cloak and lifted him bodily off the stage. 'Boy is my friend!' he roared. 'I won't let anyone hurt him.'

Orson and Mo ran on to the stage to try and restrain Grud from doing any damage.

'Let him down!' cried Mo. 'Please Grud, you'll only make things worse!'

'But he tried to hurt Boy!' protested Grud.

'He was attacking *me*!' yelled Gordimo, wriggling helplessly in Grud's grasp, arms clasped protectively around the gourd. 'He and the boobo chased me up onto a roof. I only did what any man would do in self-defence. Tell this brute to put me down immediately!'

'Yes, let go of him,' snapped Orson. Grud reluctantly released his hold. Gordimo came down onto his backside with a thud.

'Oww!' he roared. 'That hurt!'

'Good!' said Grud. 'That'll teach you to attack my friend.'

'You should fling the whole bunch of them in jail,' Gordimo told the Queen, scrambling to his feet. 'They're evidently all in this together. You know the sort of reputation these theatrical types have – lying, thieving layabouts. Never done an honest day's work in their lives!' He seemed to remember something else. 'Oh, by the way, Your Majesty, during the pursuit today, the youth stole my horse and my saddle. I'm sure I don't need to remind you that's a hanging offence in many cities.'

'I need no reminding,' Queen Gertrude assured him. 'Indeed, that used to be the case in Ravalan in less enlightened times but happily, things have changed.' She seemed to ponder for a moment then turned her gaze back to Boy. 'It would appear that you are a thorough villain,' she said, 'a thug, a liar and a scoundrel.'

'I shall tell the jailor to prepare a cell for him,' suggested Tristan but the Queen waved him to silence. She studied

Boy intently for a moment.

'Can you think of one good reason why I should not charge you?' she asked.

Boy swallowed. 'Your Majesty, I know it looks bad,' he admitted, 'but I'm begging you to believe me! Everything I have heard about you tells me that you are a wise and noble Queen; that you are not the sort to be taken in by a trickster like him.' He pointed a finger at Gordimo. '*He's* the villain. He knew I was coming here to take part in the competition. He wormed the details of the invention out of me. Oh, Your Majesty, if you'd seen how he left me with no horse or water. He even stole my boots.' He waved a hand around the stage. 'If it hadn't been for these good people, I'd have died, and there would be nobody to tell the world what a deceitful, venomous, little toad this man is!'

Gordimo shook his head. 'Listen to the brat!' he snarled. 'Daring to tell a Queen what she should think! The impudence!'

Queen Gertrude looked at Gordimo. 'That's funny,' she said. 'Weren't you doing the same thing a little while ago?'

Gordimo looked at her in surprise. 'I – Your Majesty?'

'Yes, indeed. You said that I would be a fool to give away the secret of turning sand into water, that I should make other people *pay* for the information.'

Gordimo bowed his head. 'Please forgive me, Your Majesty. I had no intention of offending you,' he assured her. 'I was only speaking business sense.'

The Queen sighed, shook her head. 'It seems to me, Master Gordimo, that the competition has been well and truly won. As much as I admire what Mistress Clarabel has achieved, it cannot compare to the device you have just demonstrated. It's truly amazing and something that will benefit mankind. I rather think that the prize money is destined to go to its inventor.'

Gordimo's grin spread across his face. 'I am honoured,' he said, 'and, of course, delighted.'

'Now, you both mentioned a book, did you not?'

Gordimo frowned. 'The . . . *Book of Secrets*?' he murmured.

'Yes, bring it to me, would you?'

'Of course, Your Majesty.' Gordimo put down the gourd, descended the steps of the stage and made his way over to the throne. He took the book from his pocket as he did so. When he reached the Queen, he opened it, found the relevant pages and prepared to tear them out. The Queen put out a hand to stop him. 'What are you doing?' she asked him.

'I'm going to tear out the pages that pertain to the sand-into-water formula,' he said. 'I'm sure Your Majesty would not require me to give up the secrets of my other inventions unless, of course, you were thinking of buying them also?'

'*Buying* them? Is that what I'm doing with sand-into-water?' asked the Queen. 'I thought I was simply awarding it a prize.'

'Well, yes, but the prize is money – so it is a sort of purchase, don't you think? Surely if one idea is worth ten thousand gold crowns, the other ideas must be worth just as much?'

'Let me see the book as it is,' suggested the Queen, 'before you start ripping out pages.'

'Oh well, if you insist, Your Majesty.' Gordimo handed it over with visible reluctance and she waved him away.

'Go back to the stage,' she suggested. 'Prepare yourself. The presentation of the prize will follow shortly.'

Gordimo retraced his steps. 'What of this rascal?' he asked, indicating Boy. 'I trust Your Majesty has a suitable dungeon where he can await his punishment? I would think he deserves at least a good whipping for his lies.'

Queen Gertrude lifted her head from the book. 'Do you really think his crime deserves such a fate?'

'At least that,' said Gordimo, scowling at Boy. 'If I cannot persuade you to hang him.'

'Well, we'll see.' The Queen browsed through the book and a tense silence descended on the room. Gordimo paced around the stage nervously, aware – no doubt – of the baleful looks he was receiving from the cast of Wandering Star.

'Oh, Master Gordimo?'

'Yes, Your Majesty?' Gordimo stopped pacing.

'Now, here's a thing. I wonder if you can help? Perhaps you'd be good enough to explain something to me. After all, you are the scientist and I am just a lay-person.'

'Of course, Your Majesty. What's on your mind?'

'Well, I cannot help but notice that the opening page of this book has a whole series of random numbers written on it.' She held it up to show him. 'These ones.'

'Yes . . . of course . . .' Gordimo looked suddenly evasive.

'Would you care to tell me what they mean?'

There was a long silence as Gordimo stared at her. 'They are . . . well, they . . .'

'I'm waiting, Master Gordimo.'

'Well, Your Majesty, they are . . . actually scientific formulas. Very complicated stuff. I really wouldn't expect you to understand them.'

'No, but luckily, as you are the person that claims to have written them, I'm sure you can share their meaning with me. Just tell me in simple terms.'

'Well, they . . .' Gordimo waved his hands. 'They pertain to the . . . stars and the . . . tides and . . . things like that.' Boy snorted at this and Gordimo glared at him. 'To be honest, Your Majesty, I wrote them a very long time ago, I would need to . . . sit a while and figure them out thoroughly before I could give you an accurate explanation.'

'I see.' Queen Gertrude's gaze moved across the stage to Boy. 'I don't suppose you could enlighten me, could you?'

Boy smiled confidently. 'I can tell you exactly what they mean,' he said. 'It's something my father wrote to me before he disappeared. He transcribed it into a fairly simple code and he deliberately left no key to it. I think he wanted me to work it out for myself.'

'Pah!' said Gordimo. 'What utter nonsense!'

The Queen ignored him. 'Did you ever manage to understand it?'

'Yes, Your Majesty. It's really quite straightforward. Each number represents a letter in the alphabet. So, for instance, if you take the first two numbers . . .'

'Twenty and fifteen?' said the Queen.

He nodded. 'That becomes 'T' and 'O' and we have the first word.'

'To,' she said.

'Correct. The next number – if I remember correctly – is the number 10, which of course stands for J, the first letter of my childhood name, Jeremiah. Shall I tell you what the letter says? I know it by heart. I read it over and over after my father's disappearance. It helped to ease my grief at his absence.'

'Please do,' said Queen Gertrude.

Boy began to recite the letter he had read so many times.

'To Jeremiah.

If you are reading this and can understand it, it probably means that I am no longer in this world. I have confidence however, that you will quickly

*decipher the simple code I have used here. This book –
the Book of Secrets – contains information regarding
my work as an inventor. All my inventions are listed
here. Some are complete, others have only just been
started. It is my fervent hope that you will continue
working on them after I am gone.*

*These inventions have but one thing in common:
they are all designed to enrich the lives of those around
you. Please pay special attention to the sand-into-
water formula. I feel I am so close to a breakthrough
with this and yet, some little detail still eludes me.
I hope, one day, that you will be able to bring it to a
satisfactory conclusion.*

*Jeremiah, there is a lot more I could tell you here,
but the most important thing is that I love you and
you have always made me so very proud to be your
father. Please take care of this book. Make sure it
never falls into the hands of anybody who is not
worthy of carrying it. Everything in here is important
to me, but nothing as important as you, my son.*

Your loving father
Quinlan'

By the time Boy had finished talking, he had tears in his
eyes. Queen Gertrude smiled at him. 'Well-remembered,' she

said, 'and what a beautiful letter.' She got up from her throne and pointed at Gordimo. 'Guards! Take this man and throw him into the dungeons!'

Soldiers rushed to obey her but Gordimo acted quickly. He stepped sideways, flung his left arm around Lexi's throat and pulled her tight against him. His right hand emerged from his cloak holding a knife.

'Nobody move,' he said quietly, 'or our little actress here takes her final—'

His voice trailed away into a squawk of alarm as he was jerked unceremoniously into the air. Grud – who had been awaiting his opportunity – stepped smartly forward and grabbed Gordimo by the back of his cloak. He was now holding him out at arm's length. Gordimo hung there for a moment, kicking and struggling frantically. He made desperate attempts to reach Grud with the knife. 'Put me down, you animal!' he screamed. 'Put me down!'

Grud looked hopefully at Boy, who had run forward to check that Lexi was unharmed. 'Can I?' asked Grud.

'Yes,' said Boy, without hesitation and added hastily, 'not into the crowd.'

Grud nodded. He turned and looked towards the back of the stage, where a fancy, painted backdrop depicted a pleasant mountain scene. Grud pulled back his arm and swung Gordimo over his head, as though he weighed no more than a bundle of washing. He threw him hard. The little man went flailing across the stage. He hit the backdrop with a loud thud, revealing that it had been painted directly onto a solid wall. He seemed to stick there for a moment before gravity claimed him, and he slid to the ground with a thud. Several guards raced up onto the stage to arrest him.

Tristan got up from his seat and shouted to the audience. He pointed at Boy.

'My lords, ladies and gentlemen: I give you the winner of our competition!'

There was a moment of intense silence and the room erupted into thunderous applause.

Chapter Twenty-One

AFTERMATH

BOY WOKE with a pounding head. He lay for a moment, waiting for his vision to swim back into focus. Eventually, it did. He found that he was lying, fully clothed, on an unfamiliar, four-poster bed in a luxurious and equally unfamiliar room. Things started to come back to him. It was hard to believe that it had already been three days since he won the competition.

When the result had been announced, everything had been frantic. The audience had swarmed up onto the stage, shouting and cheering. He had been hugged and his hand had been shaken. He had been kissed and yelled at, and after rushing to the caravan to hastily change out of his poop-smeared costume, he had been brought back to the stage and officially presented with his prize money – a huge bag of gold crowns, so heavy he could barely lift it. He had no idea where that money was now, which was vaguely alarming.

Directly after receiving the prize, Tristan had escorted him to Queen Gertrude's quarters, where she had eagerly discussed her plans for distributing the sand-into-water equipment to various points around the known world. She did not want to waste any time on it.

After that, she had invited a whole bunch of people in to talk to him – politicians, builders, explorers, writers and philosophers. He had lost track of how many people he had spoken to; all of them wanting to wish him well and to insist that if there was anything he needed – anything at all – he had only to snap his fingers. Then, Queen Gertrude had appeared again and spoken to him in private, telling him that she had decided to offer him the position of Chief Scientific Officer of Ravalan; a new and prestigious post that came with a huge salary and a luxurious villa.

He'd said yes, which seemed to delight her, and she had then appointed Tristan to take him directly to the villa and show him around. He had wandered through its white marble interiors open-mouthed. He had truly seen nothing like it in his entire life and he couldn't quite believe that it now belonged to him.

He had fully intended to go and find Lexi and the others from Wandering Star, to tell him of his good fortune, but found himself swept up by a whole cohort of Lords and Ladies from the Royal Estate who had insisted on taking him out on the town to celebrate. They weren't prepared to take 'no' for an answer. He'd gone with them and of course, there had been food and drink, and every time he tried to make an excuse to get away, he was pulled back again. Everybody in Ravalan wanted to meet this bright new star who had captivated the Queen and earned himself a dazzling future. He dimly remembered meeting Archimaldo in one of the taverns he visited, who told him he was already working on a ballad about a young actor who had bested an evil rival; the man who had sought to steal a brilliant invention from him.

There had been more drinks and Boy had ended up singing while Archimaldo accompanied him on the lute, even though Boy had a voice like a crow. It didn't matter because he was celebrating his success. He was the luckiest fellow in the world and quite suddenly, he had everything he'd ever wanted.

He had staggered back to his villa in the early hours of the morning, telling himself that he would find Lexi the following day, but when he rose the next morning, he found Tristan waiting impatiently to escort him to the coach. He was to embark on a tour of the major towns around Ravalan, where he would be introduced to the local bigwigs and be called upon to demonstrate his wonderful invention. The tour had taken him from town to town and in each place he had visited, he was once again whisked away by the locals and treated to good hospitality. Then, he had wandered back to an inn, where he slept like the dead, only to be woken by the impatient sounds of a coachman, banging on his door and ready to take him on to his next appointment. He had been gone three nights and arrived back at his new home in the early hours of the morning.

Now, he lay in the main bedroom of his luxury villa; a place that stood in the grounds of the Royal Palace beside the workshop where he would be based. There, he would command a whole team of scientists and they would work on the ideas in the *Book of Secrets* and bring them to fruition. Boy struggled off the bed and got unsteadily to his feet. He looked around at the unfamiliar furnishings, the tapestries, the oil paintings on the walls and once again, thought how he couldn't wait to show all this to Lexi and the others.

There came a tapping at his chamber door and he grunted. 'Come in?'

The door swung open and Tristan stepped into the room, looking bright-eyed and as always, impeccably turned out.

'Are you ready to go?' he asked.

'Go?' muttered Boy. 'Where to now? I thought we'd finished with the tour?'

'Oh dear.' Tristan gave him a wry look. 'I rather think

somebody might have overdone it while he was away. Local hospitality a bit overwhelming, was it?'

Boy nodded. 'They were very generous,' he muttered. 'Too generous.'

'Well, I suppose you did have good cause to celebrate. It's not every day you win a competition like that.'

'What happened to the prize money?' wondered Boy.

'Oh, don't worry. It's all safely deposited in the Bank of Ravalan.' Tristan pointed to a fancy writing bureau. 'You'll find a cheque book in the drawer.'

'What's a cheque book?' muttered Boy.

'Never mind, I'll explain it all to you later. Quickly, go and wash your face. The Queen is waiting!" Tristan ushered Boy through an adjoining doorway and into an equally luxurious bathroom. Boy poured water from a jug and splashed it on his face. The cold water revived his dulled senses. 'So, what's happening this morning?' he asked feebly.

'A working breakfast!' Tristan assured him. 'Don't you remember? Queen Gertrude arranged it with you before you went away on tour.'

Boy shook his head. 'Remind me,' he pleaded, 'my head's a blank.'

'She wanted to discuss a timetable for taking the sand-into-water policy forward. She's already drawn up a list of potential sites. Of course, we'll need to organise an expedition to Samilan to mine the substance we need to make larger tanks. It's quite an undertaking.' He smiled. 'I can't remember when I last saw her so fired up by a project. It's wonderful to behold.' He handed Boy a fluffy towel. 'There now, that will have to do,' he said. 'Follow me.'

Boy trudged blearily behind Tristan. They went down an ornate, marble staircase and through a series of opulently furnished, ground floor rooms. 'It's hard to believe that this place is really mine,' he murmured, gazing around. 'It all happened so fast, I can't quite—'

'Believe it,' Tristan advised him. 'Goes with the job, doesn't it? I can understand your amazement. I hope I don't need to remind you that such a prestigious position has never before been offered to somebody of your age. You've put a lot of noses out of joint.'

'Have I?' Boy stared at him. 'How have I done that?'

'Well, there were naturally much older and more established people who had their eyes on the job. You'll have to work very hard to get them to accept you.'

'I see. Well, I'll do my best.' He thought for a moment. 'Maybe the Queen has something more modest I could live in – a shed or a barn?'

'Don't be ridiculous!' Tristan looked outraged at the suggestion. 'You need to have something worthy of your position. A barn? The very idea!' He waved a hand at his surroundings. Of course, I still need to sort out some servants and so forth, but the Queen thought it was important to get you installed. I trust it meets with your expectations?'

'It's incredible,' said Boy. 'Really, I don't know how to thank Her Majesty.' He shook his head, trying to rid his mind of the last traces of sleep. They reached a huge doorway. Tristan opened it and led Boy out into the morning sunshine. 'The Queen is waiting for you in her orchid garden,' he said. 'She thought the two of you could eat breakfast as you went through the details of the new initiative.'

'Yes . . . but can I have a few minutes first? It's just that I need to—'

'Use the facilities? I wish you'd said while we were still up in your chambers. There's a built-in commode up there!'

'Oh no, not that! I just wanted to grab a quick word with Lexi.'

Tristan gave him an odd look. 'Lexi?' he murmured.

'Yes and the others from Wandering Star. I'm afraid I didn't get a chance to speak to them after the competition. Goodness knows what they must think of me! Before I knew what was happening, I was in a coach galloping around the countryside. I kept trying to find an excuse to get away but people just wouldn't let me leave. I don't suppose you know where they parked their caravans?'

Tristan frowned. 'I'm afraid they've gone,' he said.

Boy stopped in his tracks. 'Gone?' he gasped.

'Yes, they've camped out by the city gates the last couple of nights, but finally set off this morning at dawn. They seemed to be in a tearing hurry; said they were going to Gullamir for a festival. I couldn't even persuade them to grab breakfast before they left. Very odd behaviour.'

'Didn't they leave me a note or a message or something?'

'I'm afraid not. The girl – what was her name? Alexa?'

'Lexi.'

'She did call around to your villa a couple of days ago. I was there getting a few things sorted on your behalf. I explained that you had gone off on the Queen's business and that you were very busy. She seemed to understand.' Tristan gave him a wry smile. 'You know these theatrical types,' he said, 'fly by nights, the lot of them! She probably realised you were out of her league now.' He chuckled. 'Well, come along, we can't keep Her Majesty waiting, can we? Busy, busy, busy!'

He led the way onwards and Boy staggered after him, wondering why he felt as though something had just sucked the insides right out of him.

★ ★ ★

The Queen was already seated at a table in the sunshine. Brilliant flowers bloomed all around her in vivid explosions of colour. She beamed at Boy as he approached. 'Ah, here's our new star!' she exclaimed. 'Good morning, Jeremiah. I trust you don't mind me calling you that? I don't feel that Boy is the right name for our Chief Scientific Officer, do you? Oh, but what's the matter? You look deathly pale. Did you overdo the celebrations while you were away?'

'I think perhaps I did,' mumbled Boy and he slumped into the seat beside her.

'I'm sure you'll feel better once you've got some food inside you.' She gestured to Tristan. 'Tell them they can serve breakfast whenever they are ready,' she said. Tristan headed off in the direction of the kitchen. 'I'm actually feeling hungry for once,' enthused the Queen, rubbing her hands together. 'All this thinking has given me an appetite. By the way, I think you should know that Gordimo is now residing in our deepest, darkest dungeon while we decide his fate. I thought you might have an idea about that.'

Boy looked at her. 'Please don't have him executed,' he said. 'I don't much care for that kind of thing.'

'Oh, me neither,' said Queen Gertrude. 'Don't worry on that score; we abolished the death penalty in Ravalan three years ago. No, I just thought you might have an idea of how long he should remain a prisoner.'

'Until he's learned his lesson,' said Boy. 'That'll do for me.'

'For me also.' Queen Gertrude indicated the small, black, leather-bound book that lay on the table beside her. 'Thank you, by the way, for leaving this in my safekeeping while you were on tour. I've been reading through it and there truly are some fascinating ideas in here.' She leaned a little closer. 'The one about harnessing the power of the sun to provide energy – could such a thing be possible?'

'My father certainly thought so,' admitted Boy, 'but there's still a lot of work to do on it.'

'Well, you just let me know what you need and I'll make sure the money is made available. I feel like I want to do as much as I can while I still have the ability. I feel as though I'm making up for lost time.' She studied him for a moment. 'I thought you'd be more pleased about all this,' she said.

'I am,' he said. 'Really but . . .' He looked at her warily. 'Your Majesty, may I speak frankly?' he asked her.

'Of course.'

'I feel I've done something unbelievably stupid.'

'Oh dear. What's that?'

'The Wandering Star Theatre Company? I just found out that they left this morning without even saying goodbye. In all the excitement and commotion of the last few days, I failed to contact them and I feel terrible about it. Those people saved my life. If it wasn't for them, I wouldn't be here now to enjoy my success. More than anything else, I really wanted to say something to Lexi.'

'The elvish girl?' The Queen smiled. 'She is rather extraordinary, isn't she?'

'Yes, she is. I think I'm only just realising that. I've acted like a complete idiot. I can't let her go without speaking to her. I just can't.'

'No, I quite understand.' She looked thoughtful. 'You know, Jeremiah, back when I was around your age, I made a decision. I had just become Queen of Ravalan and I had a choice to make. I went with my head instead of my heart. I don't mind telling you that I have regretted that decision just about every day of my life. Doing what your heart bids you do is important. I imagine this meeting can wait for a while if you need to see her.'

'Thank you, Your Majesty.'

She slid the book across the table to him. 'You'd better take this,' she said.

'No.' He pushed it back to her. 'You hang onto that. That's the proof that I will return once I've sorted things out. It's the most precious thing I own and I trust you with it.' He smiled at her. 'The job you've offered me . . . I'm really honoured and I want to do it. I'd be mad not to. It's what I've always dreamed of. It will allow me to complete my father's work and to take his ideas out across the known world, where they can help so many people. Here's the thing though, I really don't know if I can do the job if it means not seeing Lexi and the others again. They mean a great deal to me. They are like family. So, there's something I need to discuss with you before I go after them. Something really important.'

The Queen smiled. 'Go on,' she said. 'I'm listening.'

Chapter Twenty-Two

JOURNEY'S END

BOY URGED Belle up the ridge and reined her to a halt. He sat looking down into the green valley below him and after a few moments, spotted what he'd been looking for. The two caravans were moving slowly along the road to Gullamir. He thought about the first time he'd seen them. He'd been standing alone, barefoot in the desert – the closest to dying he'd ever been in his life. The people in those caravans had saved him from certain death and though that was a debt he could never fully repay, still he thought he could at least try and make a decent start.

He clicked his tongue and guided Belle down the green

hillside. He reached the road and she broke into a canter, shortening the distance between him and the caravans. It was Mo who saw him first. She was sitting on the back step of Orson's caravan, peeling vegetables into a metal bucket. Her eyes appraised him as he drew nearer and he thought he saw the ghost of a smile on her lips, but it was only there for an instant.

'Well, well,' she murmured, 'look what the wind's blown in.'

'Hello,' he said, cautiously. 'So, I got back from my tour and they told me that Wandering Star had left. Imagine my surprise.'

'Wasn't my idea,' said Mo. 'Lexi seemed to think we suddenly had an urgent appointment in Gullamir, which is odd, because the festival doesn't start for weeks.'

Boy nodded. 'That's what I thought. I'll talk to her,' he said.

She dropped a vegetable into the bucket with an audible plop. 'Good luck with that,' she said.

He kicked his heels into Belle's flanks and overtook the caravan. As he came abreast of the buckboard, Orson and Grud turned in surprise. 'Fancy meeting you out here,' said Orson.

Grud just beamed delightedly. 'Boy!' he cried. 'I'm so glad to see you again. I told the others we shouldn't leave without saying goodbye, but nobody ever listens to me.'

'It really wasn't our idea to go,' reasoned Orson. 'Lexi insisted.'

'Yes,' said Boy. 'Mo already told me.' He looked cautiously at Orson. 'Do you think Lexi will even talk to me?'

'That's hard to say,' admitted Orson. 'She can be stubborn when she puts her mind to it. Takes after her mother in that respect. I'll certainly keep my fingers crossed for you.'

'Why are we crossing our fingers?' asked Grud, bewildered.

'Never mind,' said Orson. He looked at Boy. 'Give it your best shot.'

'Who's he going to shoot?'

'Nobody, Grud. It's just a figure of speech.'

Boy smiled and urged Belle onward. As he drew closer to Lexi's caravan, he could hear a familiar voice asking a question.

'So what exactly do we do when we get to Gullamir? I mean, the festival is more than three weeks away. What are we going to do about work? We had a nice cushy number in Ravalan. They were feeding us, inviting us to things—'

'That's not the point, Pompio!' Lexi sounded irritated. 'We were getting soft. I was starting to feel suffocated.'

'Suffocated? How exactly?'

'Too much luxury. I need to start writing our next production and for that, I have to have some space.'

'And regular bouts of starvation?'

'We won't starve! We've got a decent amount of savings in the bank.'

'Yes, provided that bunch of thieves haven't lent it to somebody else! How long do you think that will last if we haven't got any work lined up? Let's not forget, we're supposed to be saving for our future.'

'We'll pick up some bookings along the way. We just have to . . .' She broke off as Boy rode into view and slowed Belle's pace to walk alongside the buffalo.

'Hello, hello, hello!' exclaimed Pompio. 'If it isn't the flipping Boy Wonder! Don't tell me they've thrown you out of Ravalan already?'

Boy grinned. 'Not exactly,' he said, 'but after chatting with all those bigwigs, I was starting to crave a little creative conversation.'

'Well, you've certainly come to the right place,' said Pompio. 'Did I ever tell you about the time I was stranded on a raft in the middle of an ocean? I was obliged to exist on a diet of seaweed and jellyfish for a whole month.'

'You *did* tell me that,' said Boy. 'Several times. Listen, Pompio, I wonder if you wouldn't mind taking Belle for me and hitching her to the back of Orson's caravan? I need to talk to Lexi.'

'Oh, I get the picture!' Pompio looked from Boy to Lexi and back again. 'Don't worry, Sonny Jim, I know when I'm not wanted.' He got to his feet and leapt nimbly from the buckboard onto Boy's shoulder. Boy swung himself down from the saddle and Pompio jumped into his place and picked up the reins. 'Look at me,' he said, 'like a proper flipping gentleman!' He winked at Boy and turned Belle back along the road. Pompio looked decidedly odd riding a horse, Boy thought, but he turned back and matched his pace to Lexi's caravan. He walked alongside it, looking up at Lexi as he did so. Her gaze was fixed on the way ahead, her expression arranged into a permanent scowl.

'Mind if I climb up beside you?' asked Boy.

She shrugged. 'Suit yourself,' she said.

He clambered up and slid onto the buckboard. They rode in silence for a while, looking at the straight road winding onwards across miles of countryside.

'I was hurt when they said you'd left,' said Boy.

She snorted. 'Hurt? I'm surprised you even *noticed*.'

He sighed. 'I guess I deserve that.'

'I kept thinking to myself, "he'll get in touch soon. He'll find the time to pop over and tell me what stardom is like." The days came and went and there wasn't so much as a word from you.'

'I suppose I just got caught up in the rush of it. It was kind of crazy there for a while. I didn't know whether I was coming or going.'

'Going, mostly,' she said. She glanced at him accusingly for a moment and then looked away again. 'I saw your villa,' she added. 'It's very spacious. Looks like you're all set up now. I expect it beats sleeping in a caravan, eh?'

'It's pretty good,' he admitted. 'Comfortable.'

She snorted. 'So, what brings you all the way out here?' she asked him. 'Finally come to say goodbye, have you?'

'Only if that's what you want me to say.'

She shook her head. 'I don't know what I want any more,' she told him. 'I used to know, but lately I've been confused.'

'Me too,' he assured her. 'Terrible, isn't it? Listen, I need to tell you that I had breakfast with Queen Gertrude this morning.'

'Ooh, get you!' she said. 'Breakfast with the Queen! It's a wonder you can even bear to put your clean backside on this dirty, old caravan!'

'Stop that,' he said. 'You know you don't mean it.'

'I don't know what I mean.' She turned to look at him again and he was shocked to see that her green eyes had filled with tears. 'You're the reason I'm confused, Boy. I thought . . . I thought you wouldn't even *want* to talk to me anymore, what with you being so successful and everything. What did Tristan say your job was now? Chief Science Person or something. He said you were very, *very* busy. He took great delight in telling me that.'

'He shouldn't have said it to you,' Boy told her, putting an arm on her shoulder. 'I didn't ask him to but in a way, it was true. I *was* busy. I was dragged halfway around the country to meet people I'd never even heard of; people who were all dying to meet me. I really wanted to get away but couldn't . . .' He shook his head. 'Listen, like I was saying, I spoke to the Queen this morning and I pitched her an idea. She seemed to like it.'

Lexi looked puzzled now. 'What idea?' she muttered.

'Well, you know that great big theatre we did our show in? The one with the raised seats you liked so much?'

She nodded. 'Of course I know it. It was only a few days ago. I'm not simple!'

'I know that. Anyway, that theatre is not used much. Just the occasional royal function, the odd visiting company – small time stuff. I was talking to the Queen and I suddenly had this great idea. I'm not sure where it came from. It just hit me out of the blue. It felt right, so I pitched it to her and she went for it.'

'What idea?' cried Lexi, impatiently.

'Picture this,' he said. He raised his hands in front of him. 'The National Theatre of Ravalan,' he said.

She looked at him. 'What's that?' she asked him.

'It's nothing yet. It's just an idea but Her Majesty told me she'd love it to be a thing. She has the money to make it happen. She asked me if I know of a theatre company with a really great writer who might be prepared to take it on? I told her I'd see what I could do.'

She stared at him. 'No way,' she whispered.

'Way. Oh, she also said that if the brilliant writer doubled as a brilliant actor, that would be even better.'

'Boy . . .'

'Then, she added that if it had a resident giant and a talking boobo, that would be the clincher.'

'You . . . you're saying we'd get to use that theatre?'

'More than just *use* it, Lexi. You'd kind of get to *own* it. You'd be putting on productions that would bring in people from all over the known world. You'd be hosting visiting companies from just about everywhere and you'd have the budget to make the shows exactly as you—' He broke off as she threw her arms around him and pulled him into a fierce hug. 'Of course,' he continued, whispering into her ear, 'I did tell Her Majesty how important the festival in Gullamir was to you and that she might have to look elsewhere.'

'You'd better not have!' she told him. 'Oh.'

'What's wrong?' he asked her.

'What about a leading man? We haven't got one anymore.'

'Well,' he said, 'I do know this young scientist who likes to dabble in acting. I'm sure he'd be able to spare the time to put in the occasional appearance, if you think he fits the bill.'

She smiled. 'I think he's exactly what I've been looking for.'

She released him suddenly and pulled hard on the reins to bring the buffalo to a halt. Behind them, there was a curse from Orson as he was obliged to swerve his caravan and bring it up alongside Lexi's.

'What the hell's going on?' he demanded. 'I nearly ran into the back of—'

He broke off as he saw that Boy and Lexi were kissing, their arms wrapped tightly around each other.

'Look at those two!' exclaimed Grud disapprovingly. 'They're being all sloppy!'

Mo and Pompio's faces appeared in the opening of the caravan behind him. 'Blimey,' said Pompio. 'Whatever he said to her, it seems to have worked a treat.'

'I don't approve of sloppy stuff,' said Grud, crossing his arms.

'Leave them alone,' said Mo. 'They're just saying hello.'

'The way they're going on, you'd think they hadn't seen each other for months,' muttered Pompio.

Lexi disengaged herself from the hug and looked at her father. 'Don't just sit there gawping,' she told him. 'Turn your caravan around.'

Orson looked at her. 'What about Gullamir?' he asked her.

'Never mind that dump. We're going back to Ravalan to set up a national theatre!'

'As you do,' said Mo, with a chuckle.

'How does that work?' asked Orson.

'Not really sure,' admitted Lexi. She looked at Boy as if seeking his advice.

He smiled. 'I guess we'll just have to make it up as we go along,' he said.

THE END

ACKNOWLEDGEMENTS

As ever, there are a few people (and places) to thank for helping me in the creation of this book.

The National Library of Scotland and its fabulous reading rooms have given me a warm, quiet space where I can allow my imagination to run free. All a writer needs to access and utilise this fantastic space is a library card. How good is that?

I would also like to extend my thanks to the Scottish Book Trust, a wonderful organisation that has enabled me to visit schools the length and breadth of Scotland to share my work with young readers. Long may they continue.

I am indebted to the Edinburgh Writers' Salon, whose monthly meetings at The Wash Bar offer an opportunity for writers – and would-be writers – to meet up and exchange ideas and opportunities.

ACKNOWLEDGEMENTS

Finally, I guess I should also thank Danny Weston, who was kind enough to dedicate his last novel to me. Danny is a promising writer who – if he can just learn to lighten up a little – clearly has a bright future ahead of him.

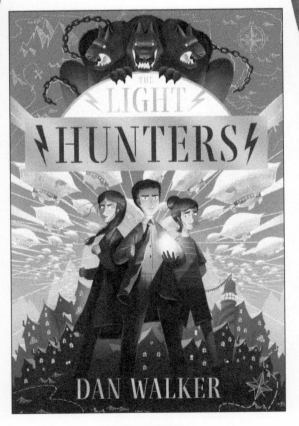

9781912979103

Dare you travel to Inchtinn –
where sinister beings stir and
tormented souls seek revenge?
What if survival relies on facing
your greatest fears?

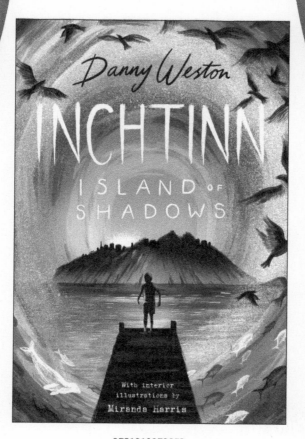

Danny Weston

INCHTINN

ISLAND OF SHADOWS

With interior
illustrations by
Miranda Harris

9781912979059

The first book in a gripping new
fantasy adventure series from new
york times bestselling author
A. J. Hartley.

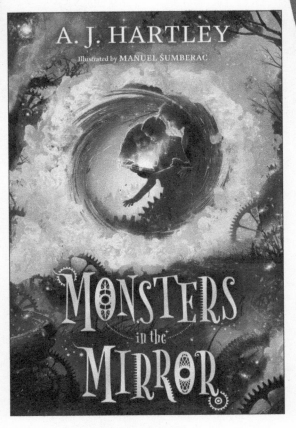

9780995515598